For Cerys

Hidden Secrets

with best wishes

[signature]

2QT
PUBLISHING

First Edition published 2021 by

2QT Limited (Publishing)

Settle, North Yorkshire BD24 9RH United Kingdom

Copyright © Frank English 2021

The right of Frank English to be identified as the author of this work has been asserted by him in accordance with the Copyright, Designs and Patents Act 1988

All rights reserved. This book is sold subject to the condition that no part of this book is to be reproduced, in any shape or form. Or by way of trade, stored in a retrieval system or transmitted in any form or by any means, electronic, mechanical, photocopying, recording, be lent, re-sold, hired out or otherwise circulated in any form of binding or cover other than that in which it is published and without a similar condition, including this condition being imposed on the subsequent purchaser, without prior permission of the copyright holder.

Printed in Great Britain by IngramSpark

A CIP catalogue record for this book is available from the British Library

ISBN 978-1-914083-17-4

Hidden Secrets

FRANK ENGLISH

Chapter 1

The dark grey mist swirled and eddied like a living being around the gaunt bare trees as the icy darkness closed in on the forest, stalking like the beast it hid. The occasional harsh screech of peacocks on the nearby Tors Manor estate punctuated the gloom like the fog beacons they so closely resembled, sending convulsions of chilling fear down the spine.

A sudden crashing in the dense bushes cut through the eerie silence over towards the Black Lake, as of some panic-stricken creature at bay, desperately, frantically trying to escape the tearing claws of its closely pursuing enemy. The threshing of undergrowth became more frantic and violent as it drew nearer. The mists and gloom were torn apart with desperate urgency to reveal the limping, blood-stained form of a young girl, hair matted with sweat and gore, eyes rolling in abject terror, and clothes in shreds from the struggle with the close, tearing thorns and thickets she had battled in her desperate haste to escape.

A further snorting and crashing a way behind made her catch at her breath, already laboured, hoarse and rasping from her exertions. Her face contorted into a grimace of blank terror as she recognised the relentlessness of her pursuer. This added renewed vigour to her already failing strength as she again hurled herself onwards, ever seeking sanctuary from her tormentor.

She forced her battered body through a dense copse of saplings to be brought up abruptly by a muscular, hairy arm around her chest. Cold panic invaded her senses, and as she felt the strength of the grip, a shriek of impotent horror and a shudder of nauseous revulsion convulsed her already battered and violated body. She turned sharply to see the face of her captor, and the scream died in her throat as she passed out.

The weak watery rays of the early morning sun struggled through the upper branches of the surrounding trees, dispersing the last vestiges of darkness and mist. Their feeble attempts to reawaken and re-enliven a sleeping world were split by the urgency of a hard male voice which rattled from tree to tree.

"Jamie! Quick! Over here, by the byre!"

The voice belonged to Joseph McIntyre, son of Joss and heir to the prosperous Boulders Wood Farm in Yorkshire's heartland, which he worked with his father and two brothers, Jamie and Ross.

"What is it? What have you found now?" came Jamie's irritable reply, annoyed he had been disturbed from his milling. His enormous frame covered the distance to where his brother was kneeling quickly, and even he gasped as he beheld the face now cradled in his brother's arms.

"It's our Annie!" he spat out. "How has she—?"

"Shut up!" came Joseph's brusque answer, cutting off his inane question. "Quick, damn you, get in and rouse the house. I'll bring our Annie along."

Jamie careered off, clattering across the pebbled driveway,

rattling the shutters and door as he squeezed his huge frame between the protesting jambs. Joseph picked up the body in his considerable hands with incongruous gentleness, as if she were no more than an ill-used, crumpled rag doll, and headed towards the waiting house.

Joss, little shorter than his two sons but much wider, stood, back to the crackling log fire in the kitchen, thumbs under thick, wide trouser bracers, and with his face impassive. Master in his own domain, he surveyed the devastated body of the young woman pitifully draped over Joseph's arms as *he* awaited orders from the older man.

"Mother!" Joss growled to his wife, who was standing close by, without taking his eyes from the form before him. "Go with thy daughter and tend to her. We will see later why she was out against my order."

Nell, his wife, little more than a dwarf in a house of giants, obediently led her son with his burden up the balustraded and carpetless stairway to some unseen sanctuary to try to repair the ravages wrought on her daughter.

Downstairs, the Master still warmed his backside, imperturbable in the extreme, he excited both fear and curiosity in his people; fear for his awesome physical presence, and curiosity to discover his driving forces and passions. At his 'Go about thy business, then!' the room emptied. Servants and hired hands hurried about their chores.

Emptied, that is, save for the youngest of the three brothers. Ross was large by anybody's standards, but slightly smaller than the other males in the family. Yet, he was the one that stood up to his father's intractability, despite earning many a cuff for his temerity. He was also the intelligent and sensitive one, and he loved his sister, Annie, dearly. They had often found a mutual comfort in the face of their father's hardness on them. He was the one she always ran to when she was hurt, and he was the one who always dried her tears and brought laughter back into her eyes.

"Get out to thy work Ross," the old man growled. "Slackin's not about to bring in t'bread."

"I will wait to see how little Annie is," came his quietly defiant reply.

"Ye'll do as I say," Joss glowered, his tone threatening.

"No, I'll –" Ross started.

"Stop arguing, you two," came a softer voice from the stairs. It was Ross's mother. Always placatory, always the intermediary, Nell McIntyre took her job as smoother of troubled waters very seriously. "I'll have no more arguing," she went on. "Go about your business, Ross, my dear. Annie's going to be fine. She's delirious but fine."

Satisfied, Ross shot a last disdainful look at his father, and, turning on heavy-booted feet, he strode out of the house towards the barn, and his day's labour.

The house was a paradox of styles; a comedy of errors to the trained eye but conveyed only awe and beauty to the ignorant. The façade was imposing in the extreme. Porticoed and pillared ostentatiously, it imposed its will on the beholder. It had been started more than fifty years before, simply, almost humbly, when the family fortunes were in embryo, and had been nurtured, growing and spreading from the simple farmhouse in pace with the family's finances.

The outside promised an internal splendour that did not live up to its fanfare. The portico was reached by a long sweeping driveway of deep, noisy gravel which jumped out of the surrounding forest and hurried across an attempted lawn of untended and unkempt grass. The inside was unimaginative, uninspired and utilitarian as befitted a working farm – wholly out of keeping with the outside but reflecting exactly the character of its occupants.

Joss McIntyre's family had farmed Boulders Wood for six generations, but only the last fifty years has seen a steadily increasing prosperity. Owd Tom, Joss's grandfather, had been the originator of their upturn. A hard, gutsy Scot, he had farmed wisely and improved the animal stock cannily, and with more than a hint of shadiness. It was under his hand that the building had begun to take shape.

Joss and Nell McIntyre were opposites, not complementary opposites, but glaringly, incongruously, jarringly so. He was large, bullish, dominant, powerful, she the dominated, powerless mouse. He had plucked her from the obscurity of a poor apothecary's family where she had been cherished, and introduced her to the hard unrewarding and unremitting grind set down by this prospering, ambitious, ignorant, lowland farmer.

Why had she married him? Simple economics. Her maternal home ties were strong in emotion but weak in finance. Marrying into the McIntyre family would provide security. Girls of her station had to marry to achieve any sort of social acceptance and financial comfort for the future. Mating with a man who was neither physically nor spiritually attractive to her was a small price to pay for that comfort.

Their love making had never been any more than an act of copulation; a mating where the dominant male exercised his physical right whilst she, the servant, gave all, laying in quiet subservient oblivion, waiting, hoping for the usual violent climactic thrust to release her quickly from further conjugal humiliation. Immediately the climax had subsided, the change from sexual beast satiating its primeval urges to mountainous, snoring animal was swift and total. He lay, dead in sleep, satisfied, while she endured that cold spreading discomfort which was the product of their mating.

Now as the years of plenty had long passed and the fruits of her once firm body were no longer palatable to his animal tastes, he had forsaken her; she who had borne him four children and given satisfaction to his eager, rapacious appetite. At least for that one she was grateful. Her nights could now be devoted to the rest her tired body needed yet was so often denied during her years of service.

"Mother!" his harsh voice grated, destroying the tranquillity of the sick room into which Annie had been brought. "Has the lass said anything yet?"

"No, Father," was her gentle reply. "She's resting; asleep."

His hob-nailed boots echoed along the bare, pine-clad floor as he paced irritably and impatiently in the doorway of the room, not daring to enter too far, lest his fear of illness catch him unawares at last. As he turned, ready to clatter his way sullenly downstairs again, an almost inaudible sigh escaped Annie's lips, mingled with a few indistinct words.

"What was that?" he half shouted, spinning on his heels on the threshold. "What did she say?"

Again, as if obeying the master, she gasped, and clearly audible were her words – almost a profanation to his ears. "My baby! My baby!"

He turned, tight lipped, eyes fixed in a malevolent stare, and left the upper floor, stairs protesting at his passing. Flinging the outer door wide on its hinges, he disappeared into the strengthening morning sunlight.

The mid-autumn sun brought cheer and warmth to the

countryside, dispelling the dull mists by jumping out from behind their swirling being to surprise the unsuspecting world. By noon, the toilers in the fields were removing outer layers to conserve body fluid which wouldn't be replenished until dusk.

Deep within the forest, last bastion of a more ancient and greater order, the sun's stabbing rays rarely penetrated its virginal canopy. Here and there an ephemeral shaft of saffron light pierced the humid blanket, to be swallowed and extinguished by the forest's protective sheath. Few animals could survive its cloying, clinging airs for long, and so it was surprisingly free of the animal and bird noises so abundant in ordinary woods.

Free except for … one being.

That one being lived in suspicious and superstitious rumour and legend, and was spoken of in hushed, almost reverend tones. Did he really exist or was he a figment, a phantom fairy tale figure to frighten and subdue naughty children? Some had seen him and evidence of his insatiable appetite for young humankind, male and female. Bad harvests were often blamed on this apparition, and it had been suggested even, by the less god-fearing, that sacrifices should be made to appease. These were never made, of course … or were they?

Annie was delirious for two days, and during that time, Nell barely left her side and Joss never went near. He had decided that his purpose would be best served by biding his time. Throughout her delirium Nell had endured many dark hours of inward despair. Outwardly calm and in control, inwardly in turmoil. She watched over her daughter, a child barely halfway through her teens, yet in every sense a woman. Hardly out of puberty, here she lay, nurturing that insignificant scrap of innocence within her womb. Nell herself had started *her* producing at eighteen, but Annie was only sixteen, and with scant prospect now of marrying well. Who was the father? She would no doubt be able to tease answers from her daughter when *she* was physically and mentally able to provide them. She no doubt would make a doting grandparent, allowing her grandchild a better start in life than it had a right to expect or demand in its circumstance. Her husband would be a different matter, but she would cross that bridge when she reached it. Generally, in her sure, quiet almost self-effacing way, she was more than a match for his bullying and bombastic demeanour.

"There, my dear one," she started again in that quietly reassuring tone that she had often used repeatedly with all her children throughout their lives. "No need to worry. Mamma's here. We'll face the world together where no-one else matters."

Her daughter's face was peaceful, almost serene, and in that serenity Nell herself found an inner strength which would hopefully help her to steel her resolve against likely opinion about Annie's condition.

"Who can the father be?" she muttered quietly to herself, gazing this time through the half-shuttered window onto the forest wall beyond.

"I don't know, Mamma," came the hoarse reply from the bed.

Nell's head jerked around, surprised, to see her daughter's red-rimmed and sunken blue eyes peering back at her. Tired they were, but they contained also that inner defiance which had brought her into conflict with her stubborn father on many occasions.

"No need to talk about it now, my love," Nell reassured, smoothing back Annie's fine blond hair from her brow. "It wasn't a question, only—"

"But I *must* tell you," Annie butted in, half raising herself on an elbow, but sinking again into the covers, unable to maintain that exhausting position for long. The fear had returned to her eyes, conveying her inner terror that must have stalked her for days. "You've *got* to understand and believe me. *I ... don't ... know!*"

She lapsed again into dark mumblings, half sighs and groans, swimming in and out of consciousness.

Nell's instinct was to listen to what she had to say and to talk it through, but Dr Riggs had given precise instruction that she was to be given the sedatives that he had left. She needed untroubled sleep to sooth away gently and naturally the fears and hurts she had experienced. Nell reached for the little bottle of laudanum and was about to administer part of its contents when, suddenly, Annie sat bolt upright, eyes staring fixedly ahead, lips mouthing unheard words.

"What is it ... my dear...?" she started but stopped, and slowly turned her face towards the bedroom's doorway. There, to her consternation and annoyance, barring the way as effectively as any barrier, stood her husband, legs apart, immobile, planted in huge knee-high boots, thumbs beneath trouser bracers.

"Yes, Father?" Nell asked quietly, outwardly calm and measured, whilst inwardly her very core trembled with apprehension and loathing at the sight of his bulk.

"Whose bairn is thy carrying?" he asked his daughter roughly, ignoring Nell's question. That was his way; the only way he knew – head down, barge in and don't care who is trampled on the way.

"I *don't* know, Father," Annie replied submissively, none of the old defiance coming to her defence. She was spent, and he couldn't have come at a worse time for her. No fire, no spark, only embers remained, and they were all but extinguished.

"Tha doesn't *know*?" he went on, volume rising along with his ire and the pulsating vein in his temple which always was clearly visible when he was agitated. "How can this be? Who is it…? Is it yon Sam Spencer's lad? Him as walked thee 'om from t'dance last month? Tell me! If it is, I'll kill the bugger!"

Annie sank back into her pillow and rolled over slowly, deliberately, knowing the effect it would have on Joss. She had no wish, no strength for a fight, but her action was calculated to whip his anger to a fury. She knew how to wind him up, and then, with one almost casual act, put him down lower than he'd been before. Usually, he stamped out in impotent rage, but this time she'd gone too far. He clenched and unclenched his huge, knotted fists slowly, and took one step forward, threatening to throw her out for bringing dishonour and disgrace on his house. That was as far as he got. Nell, mother hen guarding her chick against this monster of horn and hide, calmly picked up her long-bladed material shears, and for the first time in her marriage to Joss, she stood her ground in a way that was to alter her life for ever.

"You lay one finger on my baby, Joss McIntyre, and I'll stick these shears between your ribs, so help me," she hissed.

Joss, seeing the determination in her face, and hearing the contempt for him in her voice, stopped in mid-step, dropping his hands to his sides, looks of amazement and confusion fighting for supremacy in his face. He hesitated, and after a few moments that seemed to occupy the rest of Nell's life, he, who could have crushed her with one blow, in the best tradition of all bullies, turned and strode out through the door. The last he heard was Nell's soothing voice telling Annie not to worry, and that she would go to Aunt Jessie's to have her baby.

"Annie! Annie!" shouted Ross playfully at the bottom of the stairs. "Come on, thou hussy, the wagon's been waiting for hours. Thy trunk's on, and if we don't get started soon, we'll not be there before Christmas!"

Three weeks had passed largely uneventfully, since Annie had been brought in, and in that time Nell's healing attention – and her cooking – had repaired most of the hurt done to her. Autumn was preparing to sneak out of the back door, allowing Winter to usurp her kingdom. Those early warm moisty days inimitably hers, had given way to progressively colder ones, with the first morning frosts of early winter the harbinger of worse to come. This was Annie's time of year. She had risen early for as many years as she could recall, to watch the birds scratching away the hoar frost in desperate attempts to uncover the grain she had put out for them the night before.

Today was no different, except that watching the chaffinches and sparrows hopping around on the gravel, pecking, she had a strange feeling of disquiet and growing unease. Ross's cheery voice soon dispelled that.

She looked steadfastly at her mother's eyes, and each held the other's gaze for a few moments. They understood each other perfectly; smiling and hugging but saying nothing. Brother Ross carried her baggage to the wagon, and helped her along, a comfortingly strong hand under her elbow.

"Take care now!" Nell shouted as the great wagon and pair ground their way along the protesting gravel of the driveway. Annie poked her well-wrapped head out at the side and shouted back to her mamma, as Ross steered his magnificent shires between the granite gate posts which marked the beginning of the outside world. The only part of Annie's hurled farewell was something about seeing them all next autumn.

Joss was not at the parting.

"Don't take on so," Joseph said trying to comfort his mother, whose shoulders were heaving as she sobbed. "She'll be all right. You'll see, and then we'll all have another little'un to dote on." He picked her up and planted a kiss on her forehead.

"Put me down, you big oaf," she smiled, the tears at last subsiding. "I can't help but feel that she should be here where she needs me."

"It's for the best, mother," Jamie joined in, unbuttoning his coat and warming his hands in front of the fire. "It's going to be a hard winter. Snow's started on yon fells already."

Beads of perspiration formed on her forehead and began to trickle down the sides of her face as she worked to push out of her body the struggling infant. Every inch a woman in her own world of pain and anguish bringing forward a new generation. Yet, that youthful face, contorted by the severity of each contraction, was still that of a girl. At sixteen, Annie was not a member of that band of happy first-time mothers. For her the preceding nine months had been a personal hell not again to be repeated; at best an interruption of her childhood, and at worst its termination. The baby's father unknown, she faced her uncertain future with a stoical composure out of keeping with her years.

The contractions, quickening in pace and duration, brought involuntary gasps of pain to her already bloodless lips. The chloroform or laudanum given to her to ease her suffering, brought her short periods of drowsy ease, when she allowed the dulled pain to carry her along through its various peaks and troughs before she was thrust through the barrier again.

Aunt Jessie had been a tower of strength, supporting her throughout a difficult and complicated pregnancy and confinement, but now she was alone. At the very source of life, she was utterly alone.

"Push now, my dear," came an insistent voice close by. "It's almost here. I can see the baby's head. Come along, push!"

"Ah! Ah!" she burst out through the intolerable pain, eyes rolling with fear of the unknown, and yet, even here amidst uncertainty and immaturity, instinct took over. She bore down and down, pushing, forcing that protesting, resisting bundle of blood and flesh into a hostile world.

"Doctor! Quickly!" the nurse urged. "The girl … she's stopped breathing…!"

Aunt Jessie and Uncle Jack were in the new waiting room, the smell of fresh paint vying with that of disinfectant, when the doctor came to them. Jessie knew immediately that something wasn't right.

"What is it, doctor?" hardly wishing to hear the reply. "Is there something the matter? The baby…?"

"The baby's fine. A healthy girl…" he announced quietly, eyes drifting towards his toe caps.

"Then, what is…?" she went on. "Annie? Oh no … not our Annie…!"

"I'm sorry," he went on. "There was nothing we could have done."

Jack put his arms around her as she buried her face in his chest and burst into uncontrollable, quiet sobs.

Nell's eyes were cold, indifferent, lifeless. The joy and laughter she once knew were there in that smooth unadorned casket. How the light from the surrounding candle flames flicked and danced along its silky sides! Appearing, playing, disappearing like the young life that had been taken.

Nell had wept bitter tears since the news had come to her, but now those ageing eyes would cry no more for her lost Annie. She would remain forever young in Nell's heart and mind.

Little Poppy needed her now, and *she* would fill her every waking hour, just like her Annie did before her...

Chapter 2

Watching that elfin face upturned towards her with its snub nose and freckles and that wavy hair the colour of ripening corn, it was difficult not to believe Annie had come back. For Nell the past five years had left her empty inside and yet strangely fulfilled; empty at the loss of her beloved Annie, fulfilled in that she had been offered a second chance.

Poppy was like Annie in so many ways, and yet she had that unique identity. That wilful indomitable defiance was there, indeed it was, but she seemed able to handle and temper it with that quiet serenity that made her appear much older than she was.

"Unca Ross?" that piping voice caressed the silence.

Ross looked up from the newspaper his father called 'idlers' broadsheet'. Yes, she was very like his Annie, but *she* had never been *this* deep, this quick or this in control.

"Yes, my poppet?" Ross replied, laying aside his paper. Talking to Poppy needed your full attention. "What is it?"

"Where is my mummy?" she asked quite simply. "And why isn't she here?"

It had to be only a matter of time before the little one became curious about her origin. Even at her tender age, she could see that Nell was too old to be her mother, even though she behaved as though she were.

"Come and sit here and I'll tell you," he said, indicating his lap. She bounded across the hearth rug in front of that perpetually roaring fire, a huge grin threatening to swallow half of that fine-featured face. Of all the places in the world, she loved best of all to be snuggled up on Ross's lap, with her head on his chest, being told one out of his endless store of stories.

His explanation for the most part was received in silence. He felt no need at this stage to tell her she died in childbirth. This would only have upset the sensitive part of her nature.

After a few moments in frowned thought, her next question caught Ross and everyone else present completely off-guard.

"I know when I've seen the ewes and rams mating, and the bull with his cows, that children have to have a mummy *and* a daddy," she went on, "but you haven't told me about *my* daddy."

"Well …" Ross went on, taken aback, shooting a glance across at his mother who had been listening intently to all this.

"Your daddy left your mummy a long time ago, my little one," Jamie interrupted. "In fact, before you were born, and…"

He was cut off by the crashing of the outside kitchen door and the heated exchanges of two human male voices.

"I don't care if the farm *is* yours, I'll have to farm it when you're dead and gone. I say your ideas on cropping that north field again are foolhardy and will kill the soil. It's been cropped now for the last six years and yields have steadily declined. It should be grassed and grazed for the next two."

It was Joseph, eldest son of Nell and Joss.

The two men, he and Joss, strode into the room, not

heeding anyone else, the anger and frustration standing on Joseph's face and showing in his white clenched fists.

"I say it will be cropped," snorted Joss. "And *I'm* the boss."

"OK," Joseph retorted, cool detachment reasserting itself at last. "You *are* the boss, but if you persist with this foolhardy plan, I'm warning you, I'm leaving."

With that stark warning, he turned deliberately on his heels and strode out of the room, leaving a stunned and speechless father in his wake.

Joss sat down in his armchair with a bounce, without either saying anything or looking at anyone. He took out his pipe pensively, filled it with that horrendous shag tobacco that had everyone lurching for the nearest window in anticipation, and, once lit, began sucking on it, much as a baby sucks a nipple, with the same absent-minded pleasure.

"Come on then, Poppy my dear, time for bed. It's gone seven," Nell said, knowing this would not be a popular move, but even so, she would accede, with only a look of 'Why must it be *that* time already?'

"Ready in five minutes and I'll tell you one of my stories," Ross offered.

He was a magician with children, was Ross. He knew always what they were wanting. This was pure magic to Poppy that he should know she would do anything for one of his stories. It was easy for Ross. He had entranced another five-year-old with all these stories, several years before when he was in his late teens. Why was it he had never had any of his own, never gotten married? He was handsome, tall, and very personable, yet…

"What are you thinking about?" Nell's quiet unassuming voice broke gently into his thoughts.

The room was empty but for mother and son. Jamie had

gone to bed already as it was his turn early morning with the milking and feeding. Joss had taken himself off into the night to ruminate sulkily on Joseph's ultimatum. That left the two of them.

"You were very far away," she added with a loving smile.

"Oh, nothing much really," came his slow, sighed response. He paused again, sliding his gaze from the licking red tongues in the hearth to the careworn lines on his mother's face. She must have been very pretty once. She was still a strikingly good-looking woman but worn now, and used.

"Just thinking on where my life has gone, and where it's going," he answered eventually. "Listening to the same old arguments, the same old jousts with the Old Man makes me think, well, surely there must be more to life than just … living, existing."

She smiled ruefully, not knowing really how to answer, but knowing within herself what he was feeling. She had felt that same frustration, degradation, hopelessness and futility during the time she had been married to his father, but it was different for a woman. Hers wasn't the lot of the earner, the provider. She had to hold things together, to provide a home, be a comfort in mind and with her body … and to serve. His following question caught her off guard.

"Why did you marry *him*, Mamma?" he asked, using the name for her he used only in private when they were together. "You must have had the pick when you were young."

She drew breath sharply. Why does one always have to have inquisitive and sometimes hurtful offspring? Her eyes filled with tears, and immediately he knew he shouldn't have asked; knew that that was the one question that should have remained unbroached. He arose quickly to comfort, but she waved him away. There was such a bond of feeling between mother and son, that there was no need for words.

"I'm sorry," he said softly. "I shouldn't have…"

"No," she waved weakly. "You have a right … and I will tell you because you are my … our … son." She broke off to wipe her nose, and laughed nervously.

"I had no choice," she started.

"Not…?" he said.

"God, no! Nothing like that," she said with a half-smile. "No. A matter merely of finance. I couldn't afford to turn down his offer. Neither could my father. You see, not only was I, fortunate girl of eighteen able to gain quite a wealthy secure future, but my father gained quite substantially as well."

"You mean," Ross went on, incredulous at what he was hearing, "your father all but sold you to Joss McIntyre?"

"I wouldn't put it quite like that," she replied, "but, I had no choice in the matter, and no other suitors had sought my hand, bearing in mind my father's straightened circumstance. I don't blame him, because that's the price you have to pay for being poor."

Silence covered them both for a while, until Nell again drew back the veil.

"I wouldn't say this to anyone but you, Ross," she went on sadly, staring into the dying fire. "I have never loved him, your father. I have accepted him over the years, out of duty, fulfilling my part of the contract. His ways are nor my ways. You and I are two of a kind – sensitive and intuitive – who are not really part of this scene at all." She paused to sweep the rest of the house with her outstretched arm in a mock theatrical gesture.

Ross nodded his agreement slowly and sadly, reflecting on what might have been.

Witness to this remarkable baring of the soul after years of pent-up frustration, was one little girl, kneeling behind the huge oak newell post at the top of the stairs. Tired of waiting for her promised story after keeping her part of the bargain, she had wandered out of her bedroom to find her favourite uncle. Although much of what she had heard she didn't understand, the overall impression of dislike for Joss, and her Nanny's obvious sadness in that marriage, impressed themselves on her immature but impressionable mind. Confused and cramped, she shifted her position enough to creak the floorboards.

The conversation stopped mid-word, and both mother and son looked at each other and, simultaneously, slowly, hardly daring to move too quickly, turned their gaze to the head of the stairs. Ross's countenance displayed a mixture of puzzlement, doubt and relief as he sprang to his feet and bounded up the stairs.

"My poppet," he cooed, "I'm sorry. Have I kept you waiting? Tell you what, to make up, how about one of my extra-special, extra-long stories?"

A grin split Poppy's face and dispelled any sign of confusion and doubt as he tossed her in the air and straddled her across his muscular neck. They went up, each taking joy in the physical contact with the other.

Nell slept fitfully that night. A moving picture roll of brief moments from her largely uneventful life invaded her subconscious. Her important events which to anyone else would have been staggering in their unimportance, passed before her fleetingly. Her episode with Ross the evening before took on a bizarre turn, as Poppy, at her appearance, changed suddenly into the forbidding form of Joss.

Her eyes jerked open to relieve her mind of its monstrous apparition, to find that waking reality was no relief at all. Joss was not there, but the soft grey dawn of late autumn had been blotted out by a screaming wind of unparalleled ferocity. Sheets of unremitting black rain drove horizontally against the window, through the veil of which nothing penetrated.

She threw on her dressing gown and shuffled, half dazed with fatigue, to the window sash to shut out the noise, to find it closed fast against the elements. She could just make out across the small lake that last evening had been the yard, several stooping figures battling against the wind. Wasn't that Joss ... and the boys? ... Why on earth...?

"My God!" she blurted out. "The stacks!"

The blast hit her like a wall as she opened the outside door, hurling her back into the room across the floor, as if she were a handful of chaff. Slowly, painfully, bleeding profusely from a nasty half-moon gash below the cheek bone, she struggled to a kneeling position. The elements that had picked her out, just as comprehensively slammed the door. It was here that Jamie found her some minutes later, dazed and not really knowing where she was.

"Mother!" he yelled above the banshee wail from which he had sought momentary respite a while before. He hurled himself across the void between them, and for only the second time in her life, she was plucked from the floor as if she were a waif. And was carried aloft to the great settee before the sputtering fire in the grate.

"What on earth...?" he gasped.

"Oh, I'll be all right," she muttered, head swimming.

He staunched the blood flow and yelled for Mary, their kitchen help who was in the kitchen by now, preparing food and drink for the men.

"What's happening?" Nell asked Mary slowly, as she tended her facial wound. "Is it...?"

"You steady on now, Missus," Mary soothed in the only way she knew how. "Mister rushed out, followed by Master Joseph and Master Jamie, well before first light. Master Ross had raised the alarm that the stacks were in danger of blowing away, and they should be capped as soon as possible. They've been at it ever since. I never seen men work so hard for so long. They must be done in, poor dears. The men from Ablesons have just arrived, so it should be done soon … I hope."

Nell closed her eyes and let the pain wash over her. Jamie had gone back as soon as Mary had come, but conditions he found no better. There were six stacks close by the outer fence and within the lea of the near edge of the forest, where usually they had a good deal of cover and rarely needed attention. This was one of those freak occasions when the wind had veered, attacking the stacks from the opposite direction.

The men were clearly on the point of exhaustion but would not, could not, stop for rest. If they did, their winter feed stuffs would follow the way of the autumn leaves. Three had been capped already with great heavy canvass sheets and were pegged down securely. The remaining three were proving to be more of a problem, partly because they were bigger and partly because they were furthest away from the forest's shelter.

"You Ableson men," Joss yelled, barely audible against the blast, even though he was scarcely a foot away from them. "Over there and help Joseph with yon stacks."

Even in need, when they were giving their all for his benefit, he couldn't hide his dislike of them. This didn't affect them at all. They were the sorts who would aid a dire enemy in need. Dutifully, they fought their way across to Joseph who was in immediate danger of being taken away with the great sail-like canvass.

"Jeb!" he yelled as loudly as his lungs would allow. "Ower

here! Tek this rope!"

The wind's twist of fate was as cruel as it was unexpected. A ferocious blast whipped around the fifth stack, taking its top clean off and with it two of the four ropes, one of which sliced through the dark with devilish speed guided by the hand of fate. When the scavenging trailer gust had cleared the straw into the next county, Jeb was nowhere to be found.

Joseph crawled back over the fence from where he had been deposited by the wind, to stumble over one of their helpers, prostrate nearby.

"Come on, Jeb," he shouted. "Let's give you … a—"

Joseph's voice was blown away almost before it fell from his lips. The words had been allowed to trickle out of his mouth for, bending over Jeb, he was able to recognise him only by his clothes. His head was missing, taken off cleanly by that murderous scythe of a stack rope. Joseph turned around quickly and vomited over the small fence.

"Well, that's a good job … Oh, my God!" Ross's voice gasped. "Is it—?"

"Jeb," Mr Ableson muttered uncomprehendingly.

"Tom," Joss offered. "My God, I'm sorry."

Tom Ableson bent over the maimed body of what was once his beloved son, as he reached to scoop up the lifeless form. His other sons tried to restrain him, but he would have none of it. He had given him life, and so he was going to bury him with his own hand.

"Is there anything we can do?" Joseph asked quietly once they had gained the outer shed where they wrapped the corpse in canvass.

"No," came Tom's stern reply. "I think enough's been done already. I'm tekin my boy 'om. His mam has to be told, though I don't know what I'm off to say."

They left in their wagon, grim-faced to a man, ruing the day they had ever heard the name McIntyre.

Joss led his sons wearily into the house while the storm's rage continued to release its pent-up fury against the world of man and his offspring. Tearing open the door, they flung themselves into the living room and barred the door against the elemental onslaught.

Barely able to lift arms and legs, they were almost spent from their battle with the storm. Nobody said anything. The slightest movement of an eyelid was torture of the most excruciating severity. The day was still black; black as the pits of hell that had so nearly claimed them all; black as the deepest depression that had assailed their mind through near-broken bodies. Each had known fear; fear according to his stature and character. It was this fear that had brought each close to his limit of physical endurance.

"Mary," Joss croaked. "Mary!" he yelled, more to his usual manner. "Where is that bloody slut of a girl?"

Girl? And she was no more than eighteen months his junior; such was the arrogance of the man.

The kitchen door swung slowly open on silent hinges, and into the room shuffled the lady in question, arms quivering under the weight of an enormous oak tray laden with food and drink, realising they would need refreshment after their ordeal.

She had been with the McIntyres almost all her adult life, put in service originally by her father who could see it as the only way to secure a future life for his daughter. Little did it matter that she would never share anyone else's bed; never enjoying that union to perpetuate her image throughout eternity; never having to worry when the next feed would be due or whence it would appear.

"Coming, Mister," she gasped as she clattered the tray onto

the great table nearby. "Thought you might need this. There be bread and cheese, ale, and steaming tea if that's to your liking."

"That's beautiful, Mary. Many thanks," Joseph said, always playing his father's part; always the gentleman.

"Where's mother?" Ross asked, puzzled that she wasn't there. Normally, she would have been the first down.

"She's resting, Master Ross," came Mary's deliberate reply.

"You mean she's still in bed?" Joss's question followed quickly, more than a little put out.

"In a manner of speaking," Mary replied. "You see, she was on her way out to you when the wind blew her back across the room and threw her into the hearth. She has a deep cut under her eye which doesn't seem much, but she's shaken up."

She shot a glance across at Jamie, expecting him to support what she had said, only to find that he was fast asleep, stretched out on the settee.

"I'll go up and see how she is," Ross said, pushing himself slowly to an upright position. He reached the top of the stairs, not with his customary two-at-a-time bound, but with considerable difficulty. He hadn't realised how sore his right side from buttock to armpit had become. He paused at the top, leaning heavily against the post and gasping for breath. He lifted his shirt gingerly to see a great wheal of red broken skin across the full side, which was rapidly turning to a deep purple. He winced as he tucked in his shirt again, not daring to explore the extent of his injury further.

Nell lay on her bed, face away from the door so that he couldn't see whether she was asleep or not. He crept around the door jamb gingerly, trying, craning to catch a glimpse of that precious, injured face, but to no avail. He was about to steal out again when he was stopped by her quiet tremulous voice, "Don't go, Ross. I'm awake."

29

He spun on his heels and was at her side in an instant. She turned her head slowly, painfully, until he could see for himself the damage the accursed storm had wrought on that poor, aged face. It had become considerably swollen, even taking into account the unusually enormous dressing for which Mary had achieved notoriety over the years.

"My poor Mamma," Ross soothed, slipping his arm around her shoulders and pulling her to his chest. He stroked her tortured face gently, as he used to stroke his sister Annie as a baby, kissing around the wound, willing it to heal. "You must be in great pain," he went on. "Why wasn't I told?"

Their relationship was close, almost sensual in its nature; so close they were more like lovers that mother and son. He was to her what Joss had never been, and would never understand; so undemanding, unselfish and pure. He would never hurt her, never leave her. In him she found total peace, rest and solace, and needed no other stimulus than his presence and love. He held her as a lover might, his protecting arm around her bent shoulders; her head resting peacefully, contentedly against his steadily undulating chest, a smile of happiness playing around her mouth corners.

She loved all her children, but Ross held a special place in her heart. It had always been so; secretly in her mind from his birth, she had known that he would be special to her.

"No, Ross," she objected finally. "I must get up. I have to—"

"You don't *have* to do *anything*," he insisted. "Everything is in order, so down you go and get some rest. How could I possibly manage without you if you made yourself worse? Now, please do as I ask."

She allowed herself to be 'bullied' into submission because her head did rather hurt and she felt surprisingly tired, even though it was still only very early morning.

The wind hadn't let up at all, but the interminable blanket of rain had begun to ease slowly, and daylight had begun to appear at last. How right they all were to fear the blasts. They had taken their toll in the forest with many venerable trees unable now to reach ruinous age; trees which had sprouted when Joss's father was a lad. The survivors – the oaks and beeches – had lost limbs that could not be replaced, but at least they were still standing.

"We must be out again very soon," Joss interrupted their rest. "T'animals need seeing to, wind or no wind—"

He wasn't allowed to finish his sentence as the door crashed back on its hinges, and Ted Gittins hurled himself across the room and almost into the fireplace.

"It's … it's …" he stammered, unable to wrap his tongue around what he wanted to say. It was difficult to tell whether it was from fear of the elements or of Joss that had surprisingly removed his power of speech.

"Well?" Joss glowered. "What is it? Out wi' it man!"

"It's … t'owd elm at t'other end o' t'yard," he blurted out finally in broad dialect.

"What about the elm?" Joss sighed, still waiting for a satisfactory conclusion to this conversation.

"It's off ower. Wind's tekin it," he added finally.

"Which way, man?" Joseph asked urgently. "Come on! Is it coming towards the house or towards the fields?"

"Towards t'ouse," Ted gasped.

"The stables are directly in line," Jamie muttered as he finally awoke, partially refreshed. "And so are all our breeding mares. I needn't tell you what will happen to our blood stock if that tree goes ower."

"You'd better get down there then!" Joss ordered. "I'll hold you responsible if anything happens to any of my stock."

Just such a look as Jamie gave his father now would have killed him several times over had it been within his power. He heaved himself slowly and very stiffly to his feet and headed towards the door, without either another word or a backward glance. Joseph followed him without speaking either. His hatred for his father was felt keenly by all in the family but never overtly expressed.

Joss didn't mourn the loss of his sons' love, because he hadn't sired them out of sentimental claptrap. He had had sons for two reasons; firstly, as a by-product of copulation – that primeval urge he *had* to satisfy; secondly, to work on the farm and to keep *him*, particularly in his declining years. Any other, more sentimental, feelings were utterly irrelevant.

Once outside in the still-raging storm, Jamie and Joseph spoke little, conserving their energy for their physical battle with the elements. What each was thinking, feeling at any moment was implicit between them. They were close, sharing a mutual respect born of a common hardship and proven skill in handling any task on the farm.

"I'll go in and bring out the horses," Jamie yelled. "You join the men and try to get a rope round yon elm to peg it down to the ground at the other side. By the look of it, she'll not be long as she's ower."

On Joseph's nod of assent, he forced his way through the gale towards his beloved stables and their precious occupants. When he had reached his beauties and had slammed the door fast against the wind, the scene greeting him was one of panic, fear and desperation to escape. Terrified neighs and clattering hooves all but blotted out the wind's wail. The wooden walls between the stalls had been shattered by almighty hooves trying vainly to beat their way out of a chamber which echoed with terrifyingly magnified sounds of the storm. Eyes rolled with fear and mouths foamed around champed bits.

He headed for the lead stallion who had wrought the greatest havoc in his attempt to create a passage to lead his herd to freedom and safety. This horse, Jamie's favourite, recognised his master immediately and began to quieten, nuzzling his hand which proffered his favourite apple. Once the stallion was quiet, almost all of the others followed suit.

Jamie gathered all the compliant ones together just outside the stables two at a time, ready to take them to safety. His problems started when the last mare backed into an empty stall and refused to move despite all his coaxing skills. She was terrified by the noise and was in a heated sweating state, foam and spittle dripping from her jaws, eyes wide with fear.

Jamie tried to approach her a second time, when a rolling crack of thunder shook the walls as if they had been kicked by a giant boot. The mare reared, eyes wide, front legs pawing the air like some grotesque, broken puppet, and in a flash her leading leg caught Jamie a glancing blow across the temple, sending him backwards into the stall. Stumbling over a bucket, he fell and, although he flung his arms wide to try to cushion the fall, he struck his head on the brick half-wall between the stalls, collapsing senseless in a growing pool of blood.

Joseph saw the last horse shoot out of the building to join its fellows in the open paddock nearby. Thinking it rather odd that Jamie hadn't come out with the mare, a thing he would never do normally, Joseph leaped forward towards the building, fighting off crowding feelings of impending catastrophe. He was halted yards from the side door by a frighteningly ominous series of staccato cracks from behind. He swung around on his heels as Ted yelled for all he was worth:

"Ger out o' t'road, Maister. She's gone!"

It was all Joseph could do to dive out of the way, and

yell a last despairing, desperate warning to his brother, as the two-hundred-year-old Old Man of the Forest toppled, splitting across the base as surely as axes had been set to its once sleek and beautiful skin. It came to rest amidst a great cloud of dust and leaves, and a murderous hail of blue slate splinters.

When, after a few brief, eternal minutes the commotion and blinding fog of bark and shredded heart wood had been taken away by the element responsible for its demise, all was finally settled. Joseph dragged himself out of the mud, head bleeding profusely from a scalp wound caused by a flailing branch. As his eyes focused through the mist of pain and filth, the starkness of what he saw sank him to his knees again.

The old elm lay like a dispossessed phallus across the shattered remains of the old stables. The only remaining relics to show this was a building were the opposite gables standing out against the dark forbidding forest beyond, like two giant decaying fangs.

Chapter 3

The front entrance's oak double doors swung wide on great brass hinges, like enormous ships' rudders in dry dock encrusted with brass barnacles. The doors themselves had belonged to Snettisham's only parish church which had been demolished in the great storm of fifty years before, and never rebuilt. A good part of the stonework, lintels, mullions, leaded windows, roof lead and grey slate had mysteriously disappeared, presumed blown away.

Boulders Wood Farm was renowned, famed for its huge brass-hinged oak doors, intricately carved stone mullions, leaded windows, and doubled leading under the only grey slate roof in the county.

Slowly, like a hearseless cortege, the sombre procession of brothers and farm workers carried in the inert scarcely breathing, barely alive body of Jamie McIntyre. They laid him down on the bare stone flags of the living room floor, on the splintered door from the stable, now only fit to be used as a makeshift stretcher.

Nell made her way downstairs on Ross's arm until she

had reached the bottom, when she took off towards the body, wailing, "My son! My son!"

Joseph stopped her from getting too close to Jamie's mangled remains, as they all stood there looking at the poor shattered body that was once a healthy young man. His genitalia and left leg had been exquisitely dismantled as though under the dispassionate knife of the surgeon. How cleverly and skilfully had the storm removed his manhood! It would have been kinder had it taken his future suffering with it.

Nell gently but firmly disengaged herself from her eldest son's hold, to take up her second son in a pitiful embrace, not knowing, really, where to hold him. She cradled him softly to her gently heaving bosom, remembering days of not so long ago when she suckled this new-born baby, now but an echo in her head. How could life have been so cruel to give him back to her so few years later, broken; better that he had never been given life at all!

Solid Yorkshire lass that she was, she would never have given up hope while ever life glimmered in her boy. She would care for him, nurse him back to health. But where, how, would she start?

The room was silent. Everyone stood around, immobile, heads bowed, deep in sorrow. Nell remained, cradling her son's battered head on her lap, her soft gentle tears gathering simply on her lashes and falling onto his ruined face. It was those same tears that awoke her suckling infant twenty-eight years before to his small world of wonder, but they were tears of joy then. Now, her tears of sadness awoke his crumpled form to a harsh world of anguish, pain and bitter fruitlessness.

His would never be an autumn of plenty following a spring of seed sown in the fulness of his manhood. He could never share that headlong chase to overtake the first flood of ecstasy.

He would never taste that sweetness of exhaustion after lovemaking, when the whole being had become suffused with that peculiar scent of sexual fulfilment. *His* life was shattered, left hanging by a thread. Here was an end to *his* line.

He groaned. His eyes opened a crack, and closed again, to try to shut out the interminable nightmare. Soon it would be over, and he would awake the next morning refreshed and ready to tend his mares. No! That pain wasn't going away. It *was* the next day, and that tree and the devastation it had wrought were not figments of his subconscious.

His eyes opened again upon the softly weeping visage of his mother. Why was she so upset? She didn't seem to see him. Perhaps he *was* dead, and it was his disembodied spirit—God! The pain! Disembodied spirits don't feel as if they have had their guts torn out! Only one answer. That tree ... must have damaged him somehow, and that look on mother's face ... Why is she looking at me so pityingly?

"What ... happened?" Jamie asked haltingly, head beginning to swim with the blood loss and pain. They had managed to staunch the flow of blood and bind the wounds while waiting for the medic.

Then, from his position, as Nell held him closer, he was able to survey the damage. A look of helpless horror engulfed his face, a glazed screen was drawn across his eyes as a convulsion of agony arched his once strong body. As he lapsed into oblivion, his body became limp in Nell's tightening grasp. She remained, unmoving, clasping to her what was left of this crumpled bundle, trying to shut out of her mind the inevitable, her complete loss of the life she sparked so many years before.

Throughout the whole scenario, Joss stood, back to the fire, immobile, impassive, face unchanging, making no move to help, showing no emotion. When the final act had drawn to its inevitable conclusion, he simply turned on his heels and walked into the slackening late autumn breeze.

Through their consuming grief, Joseph and Ross couldn't hide their revulsion for their father's lack of compassion and feelings for his son's wasted life, and his own wife's all-consuming sorrow.

During this whole time, the tiny figure of Poppy had crouched at the head of the stairs, eyes uncomprehending what she had seen. It wasn't until Jamie's last moments that she was noticed; an unlooked for witness to this bizarre scene. Ross caught her from his eye corner, an inconsequentiality drawn into this adult world of pain and sorrow. He reached the head of the stairs just as she was taking the first bold step, determined to see what the matter with Uncle Jamie was, and, sweeping her into his arms, he about-faced and hurried into her room.

"Unca Ross?" she asked when he had regained his breath. "What's the matter with Unca Jamie?"

"Well, my poppet," he answered deliberately slowly, choosing his words with care. "Do you remember what I said last month when you asked about Thumper, your rabbit? You see, Uncle Jamie was so very badly hurt in the storm that he has gone to join your Thumper with Jesus."

She thought for a moment, and then said, with great solemnity, "Will he feel any hurt now, Unca Ross?"

"Oh no, little one," Ross soothed, stroking her silky hair. "They'll both be at peace now and in no more pain."

"Then we don't need to cry anymore," she said, quite disarmingly.

"We need to cry a little longer, I think" he went on, "because we'll miss him, but he'll be happy now, and at rest."

This satisfied her, for she snuggled down against his chest, and would have settled there had they not been joined by Joseph and a softly weeping Nell. Poppy stiffened slightly at the sound of Nell's sorrow, and very quietly but very surely said, "Don't weep, Nanny. Unca Jamie is at peace now. He's with Jesus."

Nell, strengthened by the child's candid appraisal, swept her to her ample bosom, gently rocking her, both weeping for their lost relative, until dusk once again overtook them.

They buried Jamie the following week in the churchless graveyard at Snettisham in the family plot, which was the last earthly resting place of all McIntyres in recent memory, on a cold grey cheerless morning. The priest from a neighbouring parish conducted the ceremony, with no one to mourn save immediate family. The significance of the day was lost to all save Nell; that on such a day almost twenty-nine years before, the bundle being consigned to eternal ash was conceived under the straw and stench of that self-same stable that took him away from her. Fate had once again dealt her a fearful blow; fearful but not quite mortal. She would wail; she would weep; she would mourn. However, life would continue for her, gathering the remains of her brood, she would jealously guard them – until the next time…

Why oh why did this have to descend upon her? Though Nell had never been given much to philosophising on her situation, the inevitable questions recurred in her every waking moment. She had never before questioned her life's path, simply accepting the position she had had thrust upon her with resignation and equanimity. It was only in recent years, since the death of her daughter, that she had begun to rebel, inwardly and silently at first, but gathering momentum through her husband's infidelities and unreasonable and more unacceptable sexual demands. And now the death of her son.

And God? Where was he now in his infinite bounty? Could this be the God of Love so venerated by clergy and lay alike? Or was it a God of Hate that had taken firstly her daughter and now her beloved Jamie? How could she reconcile her unquenchable love for Him with what He had done to her for her loyalty and love? Would He soon decide to take her *remaining* bairns? What final punishment was He going to devise for her to deprive her of the remaining two reasons for her living?

Two? Did she say *two*?

Poppy! She had forgotten Poppy!

She had to have her chance at some sort of a life. If all else were lost, she must live on for her Poppy.

Had this *hell* of a life on Earth been worth just one scrap of humanity? Had all the degradation, depravity, and humiliation that had been heaped upon her in one short lifetime with a man she loathed, been for just one purpose? *Oh, my God! Why me?*

Why hast Thou chosen me among Thy handmaidens to bear these burdens? In expiation of the sins of this world? Leave me not these bitter dregs! Rather, let the cup pass from my hands to another more worthy. I am but a woman, and my mortality draws nigh. Wilt Thou be waiting to greet me beyond when I have served Thy will?

Nell's chin had sunk to her chest finally, from one soothing cleansing communion with her God. The fire in the hearth had retreated through its many levels, until it had reached its present dull, sullen glow only an echo of the roar at its birth some hours before. Only the slow, peaceful rise and fall of her bosom was testimony to her being alive at all. She was woken by a fierce warm ache in her neck and the insistent tugging of the sleeve round her numb right arm.

"Nanny! Nanny!" came a plaintive little voice. "Please don't be dead!"

It was Poppy; dear, sweet, innocent, mysterious little Poppy, the one real light left in her futile existence.

"You're not going to die, are you Nanny?" came her startled cry, a look of desperation on her tiny, crumpled features.

Despite the very real ache in her neck, a smile crept across her worn visage. "No, my angel," Nell answered. "I am not going away. I had nodded off, that's all. Don't be afeared."

A wave of ecstatic relief swept over the child as she flung her arms around her nanny's neck, tears flowing down Nell's aching shoulders, soothing them as they flowed.

The scene of pure domestic innocent bliss was not as secret or as pure as Nell would have wanted. The thick grey glass of one of the living room's small side windows, framed hideousness and malevolence in the extreme. Features pressed against the glass filled the entire frame like some living Pantagruel, drinking in the peace and tranquillity described beyond its glass, and yet rejecting its very essence.

The grizzly visage stopped moving suddenly as its eyes settled with longing and loathing on the little girl's supple and developing form. That silky hair, those rounded buttocks, those shapely legs, awoke and excited a desire in its being it had not experienced for twenty years or more.

A noise? What was that? A flick of his matted hair left an

ephemeral imprint of his face on the glass, and he was gone, the faint droplets from his foul reek rapidly disappearing from the pane. Nell turned slowly, disquieted by some cold hand on her heart, to hear her two remaining sons removing mud from their boots on the cast iron scraper by the front doors.

"Have you had a visitor, Mother?" Ross asked as he followed Joseph into the living room.

"No. Why?" was her puzzled reply. "Should I have? What—?"

"Joseph thought he saw some strange black creature by the front window," he replied.

"Aye," Joseph re-joined. "T'was no trick of the light or my imagination playing me up either. It was man high with a huge, matted mane of black and grey-steaked hair. It wasn't so much his appearance that disturbed me, but the speed and manner of his departure."

"I didn't so much 'see' it as feel its presence," Ross added. "A vital, evil power it had, and one that I feel about me still, though he is by now long gone. It reminds me of the legends of the herm—"

"Shut up," Joseph urged quietly, nodding towards Poppy. "That's enough fantasy for now. T'youngster doesn't need her head filling with fairy stories at this time of day, and what's more—"

He didn't finish his speech, as Poppy's small insistent voice cut through his deep rumble.

"Who was that man at the window?" she asked innocently.

The room slowed to a tangible silence, as though a volume knob had been turned down deliberately. For several seconds, the silence hissed around them as quizzical and surprised looks bounced from one to the others. Poppy's innocently open face overwhelmed them all, embarrassed and made them feel uncomfortable. All their careful subterfuge has been as nought in her openness. Her second, more decisive blow came only moments later.

"I've seen him before," she added. This time the effect upon Joseph was startling. He swept her into his arms and marched across to the settle in front of the fire, sat down and set her upon his lap.

"Now then, little one," he started softly, "tell me about it. When did you see him before?"

"I've seen him in the forest, and I've seen him here," she answered dutifully. "In this room."

Puzzled, Joseph was just about to ask her when she had seen him in this house, when her face broadened into a grin.

"Don't you recognise him?" she said. "He's just like Grandpa Joss – without the face hair of course."

Ross's thoughts raced. His mind flew back to the snatched conversation he had caught between his parents as he passed their open door some years before. What was it his mother had said? Something about his ancestry coming home to roost? He hadn't understood it at all ... until now. It was all beginning to fall into place.

He looked over at his mother, who was sitting immobile in the armchair opposite, tight-lipped and gazing straight ahead, almost unseeing but not uncomprehending. Finally, the stark realisation, the half thought she had hidden even from herself had been forced rudely to the forefront of her mind.

She was trapped - a prisoner. She had been a prisoner always in this god-forsaken building, never being free to follow her own desires. *That* she had accepted as the price for financial freedom. Her spirit had been imprisoned at the expense of her future physical life. Now she was a prisoner of her own thoughts, too. She knew but couldn't share, not even with

Ross, who was by now looking sideways at her. A tear gathered slowly in her duct, grew and welled at its source. Gathering pace, it sought the lowest point so that it could course its natural way. Slowly at first, but gaining speed, it careered down her cheek, its progress periodically halted momentarily as it negotiated the many lines and wrinkles. Before it reached its ultimate goal, she removed it as deftly as it had begun life, noticed by no-one ... save Ross.

Chapter 4

Christmases at Boulders Wood had always been jolly affairs. Even Joss entered into the merriment of the occasion, although the celebration was far removed from any religious significance for him. Heathen in the extreme, his interest solely was in serving Mammon, his one true god. Sensing for some years that his headlong chase towards eternal damnation was quickening in pace, he strove with every sinew to discover that elixir of youth which had eluded every dissolute throughout history.

He had lately taken again to the idea that such a quest would be fulfilled through his partiality for young virgins. This had been an open secret in many quarters for a long while and was shared in certain areas of society by those of a higher social standing than him. It had always been his curse that he had not been born into medieval aristocracy. Then, seigneurial practices could have been enjoyed as a right, not as the matter of negotiation he had to accept now. Deflowering the whole maiden population had always been his aim, but in such a society as this, the choicest blooms either had been plucked or were being nurtured away from the likes of his jaded yet insatiable appetite.

Christmas provided him with the opportunity to explore new pastures through the parties *they* threw, and *he* encouraged, although parents of most of the younger stock had become increasingly wary of the old bull. Old bull he may have been but lacking in patience he wasn't. It was that patience that had brought him many of his newer conquests.

Poppy had just passed her eighth birthday and daily she was turning into something of a beauty, a matter which had not escaped Joss's notice. She was developing a roundness and firmness to her body that excited every nerve with anticipation. The fact that she was his granddaughter had never entered his head, such was his overwhelming desire for young new flesh.

"Well, my darling," Nell had said one crisply cold early December morning in the kitchen, "it's time we introduced you to some other children of your age."

Poppy's head had lifted from her doll, Tossy, and had looked towards her Nanny in mild surprise. She had never met other children socially, except of course for those brief moments when family visited, or they saw acquaintances at market. Those brief moments were unreal, and she could get no proper understanding of how she was supposed to act or react in public in relation to others of her age. She possessed no inclination concerning the conventions normally employed. To her all was at face value, with no visible meaning. Now here she was in the middle of town waiting for Uncle Joseph with her grandpa, but *he* also seemed to have melted into the throng, leaving her to fend for herself.

To her, Maggie Jenkins' "Oh, what a quaint little dress! It

must surely be the only one of its kind still in existence" had been a pleasing compliment. She hadn't seen the patronising smirk on the ten-year-old's face, and the half-hidden but barely suppressed giggles of her circle of like-aged cronies by the Bull Ring that early December afternoon.

"Well," Maggie had said as she turned towards her circle, with that insolently arrogant half-smile which said 'Watch carefully. We'll have some fun at this sap's expense'. "If it isn't young Mistress McIntyre – if that's the name. What a thoroughly nice plain coat you're wearing my dear."

The other well-dressed urchins formed a semi-circle around the two girls, some sniggering behind their hands and others openly giggling at their leader's cleverness. Some even felt a short-lived sympathy for Poppy but would never have dared to show it. They didn't want to share her fate.

Poppy became a little confused, as she was unused to this sort of conversation, and so remained silent, not really knowing how to answer. Even though she hadn't encountered these sorts of conversations before, she detected a sharp undertone to Maggie's sugar-coated words.

"Lost our tongue, have we?" Maggie went on, relentlessly pressing what she assumed to be her advantage over a soft uncomprehending adversary. "And how is our mamma today?"

The last remark, uttered in complete and confident knowledge of Poppy's family background, was designed not to stab and taunt as usual, but to wound. Mature in her immaturity, Maggie, spiteful little horror that she was, had struck at the very heart of Poppy's existence. The reaction was at once predictable, but mostly what Maggie did *not* expect. Poppy felt the hot salty tears well up in her eye corners and threaten to cascade down her cheeks, heralding the direct hit that Maggie had sought. Poppy fought valiantly, but the damage was done.

With a whoop of triumph, Maggie's face split into a victorious grin while turning to her cronies in her moment of triumph.

Many feelings invaded Poppy's senses at the same instant. She felt humiliated that her tears had betrayed her innermost private feelings about her mother. She was angry with herself for allowing such a nothing as Maggie Jenkins to upset her. After the fleeting initial tears, her McIntyre stubbornness reasserted itself – that basic vital element that she had inherited from her mother. She was not going to be overwhelmed by her vindictive adversary without a fight. All those feelings crowded her already confused mind into a whirlwind of fury, with devastating results.

Her anger exploded from her like the eruption of a long-dormant volcano. She whirled her dolly, from below knee-height, with considerable force across the side of Maggie Jenkins' head. The resultant crack as solid wooden doll's head met flesh and bone, resounded around the market square. The noise, combined with flying pieces of skin and spurts of glistening, crimson blood, stunned the group of admirers and froze their grins into dithering grimaces, as they witnessed the unleashing of Poppy's pent-up fury.

Gasps and screams broke from those deathly grimaces almost immediately, as Maggie's unconscious and seemingly lifeless body crumpled in a gathering pool of darkening blood.

The battlefield with its disarray of uniformly crimson-striped and spattered dresses, was in a confusion of wailing, hysterical childish voices. Amid the chaos, Poppy had disappeared.

The thick blue smoke lay in heavy almost impenetrable blankets in the dimly lit room where neither daylight nor children nor women ever set foot. This was no place for either the faint-hearted or the weak-chested. Furnished, decorated and looking the same as it did fifty years before, The Black Swan Inn had changed little over the years since it had become one of the principal meeting, refreshing and resting places of local farmers and labourers after a morning's business at the twice-monthly cattle and horse market. This was often where the *real* bargains were struck, over a tankard or two of good strong ale.

The inn had been in Joshua Booth's family since before he was born, and certainly as long as many of his regulars had been farming *their* holdings. No market day could possibly have been the same without its uncomfortable, smoky, dim hospitality.

"I'm tellin' thee now," Tom Garside said, "these new gentleman farming Tom Noddies'll be t'death o' business in this area. Them as what knows nowt and ower-farm can onny do 'arm."

"Aye," Joseph replied pensively as he drained his tankard and peered through the murk at the bodies propping up the bar, while trying without success to recognise some of them. "I was only saying t'same to fatha t'other day."

His thoughts shot back to his largely heeded threat which seemed to have had at least some effect, however short-lived it might turn out to be, on his father's farming outlook. Old Joss wouldn't accede totally, but just enough to keep Joseph where he was.

"Tek young Toby Birkenshaw now," Tom went on. "'Is gaffer, Owd 'Arry, were a real farmer. Went to t'board school wi' me, he did. We weren't there long, mind, but we got *some* learnin'. Now, 'e knew more'n all t'others put together about farmin'."

"Aye, we all had a high regard for old Harry," Joseph added. "His passing was a downright pity."

"I tell thee," Tom confided almost in a whisper, bringing his large bluff face closer to Joseph's while looking around to make sure no-one else was sharing his confidence, "Young Toby's teken to wearin' ... a collar and neck tie. Does tha believe it? ... Two more on these, Joshua, ifn thou please," he called to the host loudly.

Joshua duly obliged while there was a lull in the conversation. The whole attraction and comfort of the Swan, although uncomfortable and spartan to the outsider, was the welcoming atmosphere created, particularly by its proprietor. A large round man, Joshua Booth made his customers feel as though the Swan had been conceived solely for each individual that drank there; a feeling he consciously perpetuated in his dealings with them.

He also kept an orderly house, one of the few in the town, where a man could be sure of peace and a good ale. The only time disorderliness of any sort occurred in the Swan was a few months before when Joey Walsh nearly knocked over Big John Tenby's ale. Big John's roar of disapproval silenced the crowded bar, and all but parted the haze. He turned slowly around, surveyed the gathering throng for the miscreant, selecting his foe by the froth from *his* tankard on the person's elbow. He stretched himself to his full six feet nine inches, took hold of Joey's waistcoat middle in one huge paw and lifted him a full foot from the sawdust. Now, Joey was no dwarf who took pride in being able to look after himself with the best of them.

His look of utter amazement that anyone should be able to treat his bulk like a bag of grass clippings, betrayed his feelings to the gathered tipplers. Big John put him down slowly, his great glowering eyebrows almost covering the upper part of his face.

Forever afterwards Joey was affectionately known as Little

Joey, and he swore with increasing regularity that Big John had more than a little gorilla blood coursing through his veins.

"Niver trust anybody that wears a neck tie," Tom went on unabashed. "Ifn 'e 'as to think too much abaht 'issen, 'e won't be payin' too much attention to owt as what matters."

"Are you satisfied with those two broodin' mares?" Joseph changed the subject after a respectful gap.

"Aye," Tom rejoined, "but tha strikes a 'ard bargain."

"Well, you can afford it, Tom," Joseph went on. "They are the only two of their kind in the county, so you should have the mekkings of a good stock, what with yon stallion of yours. You'll double your value in five years."

A short fat tousle-headed man joined them at the bar. What he lacked in stature, he more than made up for in girth. Almost as soon as he had set hand to bar, a tankard brimming with strong frothy ale had been placed within his grasp by an obliging landlord. The tankard had barely touched his lips than it was drained. Without a word being exchanged a replacement was readily to hand and despatched in the same way.

"I've known thee for countless years, now, John," Tom broke into the ritual, "but I've niver known thee so quick on thy ale before."

"Well, Tom lad, does tha know," John replied, taking breath after the fourth tankard had followed the previous three, "some weeks ago I had a fright. I were in t'King's 'Ead down Barmby way on. There were quite a crush on near to time, when this great lump of a lad were flailing his arms around at t'bar, and, does tha know, he nearly knocked mi ale ower! Since then it's bin straight down t'atch for me!"

Joseph supressed a rising guffaw and almost choked on the mouthful of ale he hadn't quite swallowed before John finished his tale. When he had eventually removed all the froth from his face which had given him the appearance of a barber's apprentice, the conversation had inevitably returned to Tom's pet hate – gentlemen farmers.

"Aye, and young Toby Birkenshaw, now, he's aspiring to the hoy poloy," Tom went on. "Likes to be called 'Squire', he does, and he's taken to watching the real workers in the fields with his missus. By all accounts," he went on, dropping to a whisper, "he has paintings on his walls and a carpet on t'floor!"

While Tom was describing the trappings of the social parvenue, Joshua had beckoned Joseph to the end of the bar and his whispered message had had a profound effect on him. Almost throwing down his half-filled tankard, he hurried around the end of the bar into the back room.

Seeing Poppy's blood-spattered form and tear-washed face huddling over a steaming cup of cocoa, his heart lurched. His gut reaction was to hurl himself forward, scoop her up into his arms and beat a retreat to the family strong-hold at Boulders Wood. Fortunately, dour pragmatic Yorkshiremen don't allow emotions to cloud judgements. Women become emotional and often worsen situations which might be resolved logically. His pragmatism in dire circumstances was legendary.

"Poppy, thou hussy," he chided mildly. "What has thy done with thy best clothes? Has thy hurt thyself?"

It was obvious by the way she burst into uncontrollable sobs with her face buried in her almost unrecognisable blood-matted doll, that this line of questioning was about to collapse in failure. He had to change tack quickly otherwise he would have a hysterical child on his hands, and that certainly would not please his mother.

He scooped her up and sat her forlorn, heaving body on his lap in one of Mrs Booth's embroidered and antimacassar-covered armchairs. He stroked her blood-stained hair, trying gently to untangle the gored patches with his thick fingers. He rocked her and eased her sobs to a periodic catch in her throat. Not wanting a return to the uncontrolled panic in her little body he met with before, he dropped out of local dialect so often used for admonitory confrontation and slipped into the more usual speech Poppy responded to usually.

"First, tell me, are you hurt at all?" he started in a quicker more soothing manner.

"No," came her quietly hesitant reply.

"Where has all this blood come from?" he tried again, seeing he wasn't about to be offered an explanation voluntarily.

"Maggie Jenkins," was the sullen, defiant answer.

"But did she have a nose-bleed or a cut?" Joseph asked. "Did she fall? How—?"

"I hit her with my Tossy," Poppy answered.

Joseph paused for a moment's thought. Was he hearing correctly? *His* Poppy? Were they talking about this inoffensive, quiet, happy-go-lucky child who had spent the last eight years growing up in their midst?

"But, why?" Joseph asked, valiantly trying to come to terms, seeking a reason for this outburst of aggression from one so timid before. The look of sullen defiance still played around her features; a defiance that was not open but was lurking beneath the surface ready to declare itself at the slightest provocation. This was Annie at her height. Yet, what had taken *her* sixteen years to cultivate, Poppy had acquired in half the time.

"Why did you hit her?" Joseph insisted. "I must know. Is she hurt?"

"I think she must be … dead!" came Poppy's stark reply. "There was a lot of blood, and…"

It was here that she broke down, and the whole story

flooded out in one torrential outflow.

When he had heard it all, and the storm had subsided enough, he sat, not quite knowing what to do next.

"I know you are upset, my poppet," he went on eventually, groping for the right thing to say. He had never been comfortable with words, finding things difficult enough to remain silent when he felt he had nothing to add. "I know also that you must be sorry for what you did to Maggie, but—"

Her outburst took him completely by surprise. She leapt from his lap and planted herself squarely in front of him, hands on hips, stamping her foot.

"No! No! I am not!" she cried in anger and frustration. "I am *not* sorry! She deserved it, and I'll hate that Maggie Jenkins forever. I hope she's dead because she's spoilt my doll. My Tossy's worth more than *all* her blood."

Here, her outburst stopped as suddenly as it had erupted, with her clutching her doll to her cheek, tears beginning to well again in her eye corners.

"Will they take me away, Unca Joe?" she asked, face finally looking up to his, innocence brimming over with the tears. "For killing Maggie, I mean."

She was calm now, all defiance and anger melting away with the comfort her doll gave her. The battle was over. Annie's character had asserted itself in the child, and never again could Joseph regard her as that quiet bundle of placid innocence. Beneath the surface, dormant until the right stimulus set it in motion, lay the ever-present McIntyre stubbornness and defiance.

"No, my pet," he answered, not too sure what would happen or what the next step should be. "Of course they won't. I won't let them harm you, but we must at least see Maggie's father and tell him what happened. Anyway, where is your grandpa? I left you with him before I went into the Swan to sign off on that mare deal with Tom Garside. He'll know what happened if he saw it all. So—"

"I don't know where he is," Poppy answered dutifully. "He wasn't there. He went off soon after you went to see Mr Garside. Said I'd be all right with the other children."

The pungent bitter-sweet scent of copulation, mingled with the nauseating odour of stale sweat, lay heavy and still in the air. The groans and bestial grunts of the male animal punctuated the already fetid atmosphere as they quickened in their quest for climax.

Theirs no union of mutual love, a delight in exploring each other's body. No. Here was the master and the servant; the taker and the taken; the masterful male over the serving female. He was the minotaur, the great rampant and dominant bull. She was the subservient girl, sacrificing her maidenhood to satisfy his primitive, insatiable desires.

However, this little heifer would not subserve for long. She would give, but not without return. His initial payment would come soon after his climax. A much longer and more bitter payment she would exact later, at her leisure and when she knew it would hurt him most. She knew who he was and wouldn't hesitate to use her knowledge to take from him at least the equal of what she had given.

The explosive finale to this basic scenario startled the consenting female who had mated this particular male before but had never experienced such a violent conclusion. Her gasps were not those of a participating partner, but those of one who endures but does not enjoy the union and were interwoven with more than a little fear. The final rush was one not only of shock but brought considerable relief for her.

Finally, relieved of her burden now snoring next to her like a stag at rut, she disengaged her loins from his, and slid from the rumpled bed along with the love-stained counterpane. She looked for a moment down at the monster sleeping before her who had invaded her body, and quietly vowed again to make him pay for his enjoyment.

No more than fifteen or sixteen years old, her body would have excited any male. Long, firm, shapely legs, rounded buttocks, and belly curving to finely sculptured loins and maidenhair, she was the perfect figure to allure and trap any man. Naked from the waist down, with her white cotton petticoat hem tucked into the bottom of her boned stays, she had perfected her sexual allure in the short months since introduction to its profits.

She remained a moment longer in the half light, fine brown hair cascading over her shoulders, the fine down on them picked out by the dying light from the guttering candle betraying her age. She pulled on her cotton drawers silently, dropped her petticoat and tightened her stays. Her stockings and overdress of plain grey she had replaced in a trice. Looking again at her raptor with contempt to check his sleep, she slid his bulging wallet from his trouser pocket, took out a thick wad of notes, and returned the leather case to its sheath.

She could have emptied his note case just as easily, but she had something which was worth considerably more to her than a sheaf of notes, thick though it was. She had her future safely tucked away which she would produce to confront *him* and elevate *her* when the time was ripe. No. She would bide her time. She had all the time in the world, but time for him was waning. She turned lightly on her booted heels and glided silently to the door. Once there, she paused momentarily to cast a half-glance at his still prostrate form, a sneer of triumph slitting her face as she blew an ironic kiss to his hideousness.

"We will meet again Master Boss Farmer," she whispered. "Until then, sleep well."

The door click, as she left, disturbed his peaceful post-coital slumbers as he turned onto his stomach, ready to resume his subconscious sexual fantasy.

The wagon stood motionless, incongruously outlined in front of the neat, white splendour of the house on the terrace. Nothing moved on the quiet residential cul-de-sac save the swishing of the horse's tail, and the bit in its mouth as its jaws champed uncomfortably against its metal rings. Steam rose in lazy spirals from the animal's back, and its breath spurted downwards thickly from its nostrils in the bitingly cold afternoon air.

The small girl on the passenger seat might have been fashioned in wax had it not been for the slight, almost imperceptible quiver of her eyelashes as the horse's tail flicked within inches of her face. Her shoulders were all but buried by an enormous grey woollen shawl which covered her body shroud-like. Her unseeing eyes gazed steadfastly forward through the steam, out across the cobbled roadway and into the distance, along the terrace of white-dressed houses that had been newly built to commemorate the first couple of decades or so since the new young queen's accession.

Victoria Street, and many more throughout the county like it, was the sign of the arrival of the newly affluent, the nouveaux-riches, the parvenues whose station in life had suddenly become upwardly mobile, following chance fortune in business. Some had been bought by rich farmers, who, aspiring to become gentlemen, had taken a 'town' house to formalise their claim to social recognition.

This particular terrace reflected that new genre of town ownership. All the owners, like the houses they possessed, were as near identical in situation as it was possible to be. The lintels above the doors described precisely the same arch as did the semi hexagonal bays with their identical sash windows. Their plain glasses were like so many square lidless eyes staring out, unblinking and envious, over the cobbles to the detached gothic villas across the narrow street.

The external opulence of these villas reflected the expense lavished on the internal furnishings; arched, stone-dressed and framed windows like flashing gems on a jewelled crown, and chimneys groping for the sky like so many stiff urgent ears of corn. The obligatory glass and iron conservatory stuck out stiffly at the back, resting its brooding bulk among the luxurious foliage that spread part way along its length in the garden.

An iron gate clanged shut somewhere near, rattling iron railings in its anger. The horse stopped its tail in mid-flick, and tossed its head, recognising the firm hand of its master on its rump. The wax statuette at the front of the wagon didn't move as the bulk of someone close eased itself into the driving seat beside her. Reins swished and the horse, eager to be off after champing at the bit for so long, lurched forward, rattling its shoes against the granite cobbles.

"Well, that's that then," came the deep voice of the driver, once under way. "That was John Jenkins I was speaking to just now. Says Maggie is recovering from her ordeal. Lost quite a bit of blood though. Knows she asked for what she got – little Tommy Simpkins said so – and asks you not to worry. She'll be better in a few days, and…"

Uncle Joseph's voice droned on, echoing around Poppy's

head without effort. She heard the noise but didn't register its importance. Maggie Jenkins going to live? That was *not* what she wanted to hear; but what matter now? The episode had had its desired effect. They'd never dare bait her again, and a new light of determination had been kindled within her being. Her *true* being. Her real inner self had at last emerged from its hibernating cocoon. Annie had come back.

"Do you hear me, Lass?" Joseph insisted, becoming a little annoyed at her lack of response.

"Yes, Uncle," she replied vacantly, realising she ought not to antagonise him. Detecting a note of some irritation in his voice. "Yes, Uncle Joseph. I heard you, and I'm grateful. It won't happen again, I can promise."

That was, it wouldn't happen again, until the next time. The next time she would know exactly how to achieve her aim.

Chapter 5

"Nanny?" Poppy asked early in December. "Who are we having for Christmas?"

Nell lifted her hands from the mixture in the enormous brown earthenware mixing bowl, stripping the pastry from her fingers as though she was removing a pair of tight-fitting evening gloves after an evening at the theatre. She preferred to make the mince pies and other pastries, for which she was renowned, herself, even though Mary was an excellent cook in her own right. They got on well, those two, more like sisters than mistress and servant.

They were of an age when fathers had to place their daughters to ensure their future worth and situation. Born a few days apart, they had known each other for most of their lives, being from similar backgrounds. It had been a matter of fate that their positions were as they were. Roles could easily have been reversed had the Master's fancy turned in a different direction.

This wasn't the only thing they had in common. They each had had to endure the unwelcome and unsought sexual advances of the master, one much more than the other; Nell throughout her life and Mary when she was first in employ as a young girl. This had been a further cementing of their spiritual bond; like souls trapped in an earthly hell. Oh, why did women always have to be subservient and suffer in silence at the hands of selfish males?

They had never shared their curse. They simply *knew* what each had had to bear, and *that* simple knowledge had drawn them closer. The opposite results from their respective unions with the same man had had the outcome each would have wished. Mary's barrenness had proved to be a blessing, for, had it been otherwise, she would have become an outcast, and, very likely, have perished, homeless, many years before. As for Nell, her children, what was left of them, had been the comfort she had needed and deserved, giving fruitful purpose to an otherwise barren existence.

"Well, my love," Nell started, pastry gloves finally removed. She turned from the huge deal table which dominated the kitchen, at the other end of which stood Mary, her large pinny like her badge of office wrapped tightly around her spreading frame. She was making enormous stand pies fit to feed the entire army of expected visitors.

"We are expecting about fifteen of our relations," Nell continued. "Let me think now. There'll be my sister Jessie, her Jack and their three, James, Mary and Albert; your grandpa's sister Annie, her husband and their three children, George, John, and Florence who's about your age; Grandpa's brother Alfred and his wife Victoria – they've no children; my brother Frank – now you'll like him. Oh and of course, your Aunt Louisa and Uncle Ernest. She's Jessie's elder daughter. They'll be bringing their son Jonas. He's about ten, I think. I hope you'll get on with him. Now, I know you'll like little Florence, because she's just like you."

"I *do* like Uncle Frank," Poppy interrupted. "I *think* I like him. Didn't he come last year?"

"Yes," Nell answered. "He's the tall, thin one, with wavy black hair. You remember, he made everyone laugh all the time."

"And he mended my Tossy," Poppy said, holding the doll newly cleaned and dressed by Ross. "Yes, of course, I do like him."

"I've put the cooked pies on the stone in the larder, Missus," Mary said, wiping her hands on her pinny as she headed for the kitchen door. "I'm just going for some more eggs from the run. We're right out and I need them for those custards."

Alone with Nell once again in the kitchen, Poppy watched those old, gnarled hands skilfully, magically pinching together the top and side crusts of the pies to form a seal. She sat at the table end, chin on hands, watching, spellbound.

"Nanny," she said disarmingly after some moments of thought. "Why don't you like Grandpa Joss? Why doesn't anyone like him?"

Nell stopped momentarily, taken off guard by the perception of one so naïve.

"What on earth gave you that idea, child?" Nell answered, deciding that ignorance was the best form of defence, a narrow smile hiding her embarrassment.

"Well," Poppy started again slowly, deliberately choosing her words, "ever since Unca Jamie died, I've tried to understand why you and Unca Ross were talking about Grandpa Joss. I didn't understand what you were saying."

Nell, knowing she could prevaricate with the child no longer, finished her last pie and with instruction to Mary, who had just returned with a large basket of eggs, to finish off, she took off her pinny and throwing it behind the door, she ushered the child into the sitting room towards the settee in front of the fire.

She sat down next to her granddaughter, thinking rapidly how best to answer her unexpected, innocent candour. Should she be straight and tell the unabridged truth? But how could you explain emotions, feelings and their death to an eight-year-old? What about not telling her what she suspects? That wouldn't do either. Nell had never lied to Poppy throughout the time she had looked after her. No. it would have to be very discreet, very carefully told, very … She smiled almost imperceptibly.

"I was just eighteen when your grandpa took me from my home to be his wife," Nell started slowly. "So, we have been married thirty-two years. In those days, you see, young women didn't choose their own husbands unless they were very well off. We had to wait until an offer came along, and then our father made the choice for us.

"If I had refused your grandpa's offer, my father would very likely have put me into service at one of the big houses round here. So, you see, I didn't love your grandpa before we were married. I had no choice. If I had had that choice, I would no doubt have waited, in the hope that I might have found someone I could have loved, and who would have loved me. Your grandpa needed a wife, and so he chose me."

Nell paused, her eyes gazing wistfully into the slowly dying fire. She couldn't imagine what her life would have been like without her children, but she would gladly, joyfully have missed the thirty-two years of hell she had spent with Joss. The hell had lessened but the bitterness remained. Her eyes gave life to a tear of sadness at the thought of what she might have shared with the man she *had* loved; a love that had blossomed secretly, briefly, but which had died unseen by any save those that shared it, for want of light, sustenance and a space to spread and grow. She dared not let its bloom flourish for fear of the consequences.

She was young then and had had two children already. Her third she would cherish especially, and would name him carefully, for she had been certain it would be a boy, and she knew what he would grow up to be like … but that was her secret only.

"Nanny, are you all right?" came Poppy's quietly insistent voice, brows heavy with concern.

Nell's dream evaporated as an autumn mist at noon. She removed the gathering tear with her sleeve before it had the chance to follow that same erratic course chosen by those that had greeted all her babies, and those that had helped to expiate the untimely loss of two of them.

"Yes child, I'm all right," Nell answered, all thoughts of her brief, happy past consigned to her subconscious once again. "So, you see, my poppet, Grandpa and I have been together a very long time. As for disliking, I don't think you can say that. He is a hard master to work for and demands hard work for the good money he pays. That's perhaps why some of the men say they don't like him. They have to be right in everything they do, and not make any mistakes. I don't think they would have it any other way, really."

She glanced sideways at her granddaughter, who was also looking into the fire, to see if her explanation had been sufficient. It seemed that Nell's words had had the desired effect, for Poppy had started to rearrange her doll's hair and clothes, all thoughts of human feelings cast to the back of her mind.

Ross was the first one back in for their midday meal, rubbing his hands together as he headed for the fire.

"Hello, you two," he said, crouching by the fire grate to

poke the dying and sullen logs into renewed life. "Winter is really on all right. Snows are just beginning, and it's really parky out there."

There was quite a large bulge in his coat pocket as he stood with his back towards Poppy. She noticed immediately that something was different. There was a slight movement from within, and she pounced on it straight away.

"Uncle Ross?" she started, eyes sparkling with anticipation again as they had done so many times before when she had guessed he had some sort of a present for her, secreted about him. Strangely, it seemed always to be *that* particular old coat he wore, that was about to yield up its treasure. "What have you got in your pocket? Is it a present for me?"

"Eh? What?" was his mock surprised voice, turning on his heels and taking a step towards her. "What's that you were saying? Me? A present for me?"

"No, silly!" she returned, joining in the fun. "You've got one for me. Haven't you?"

"Now where on earth would I find the time to go shopping for you a present, thou young hussy?" Ross said, a half-smile on his face.

"Well, what's that bump in your pocket?" she insisted, leaping to her feet. "There, see, it moved again!"

He half-turned, putting the pocket in question to the other side of her, out of her reach. She followed it around, eyes always on it, until he changed direction suddenly, and took her round the other way. This went on for some minutes, accompanied by whoops of joy from Poppy, all thoughts of her conversation with Nell banished from her mind. Nell watched the game, pleased that Poppy was enjoying herself, and relieved that her questions seemed to have been satisfied, and her mind taken from them.

"All right! All right!" he gasped, flopping into the settee with arms in the air in pretend exhaustion. "You win, only, let me recover my senses and my breath first."

She sat next to him, careful not to get too close to *that* pocket. All the while he was 'recovering' himself, her eyes never left it, detecting now and again a slight quiver. Slowly, deliberately slowly, he drew himself up to a sitting position, and. Looking at her earnest face, he slid his hand gently into his bulging pocket. When it had reached its depth, he stopped.

"Guess," he said finally. "I'll give you three guesses."

"I can't guess! I *can't* guess!" she chanted in wheezing breathlessness. "A ball! A doll! A ... oh dear ... a ... oh, I don't know!"

Recognising her mounting excitement, he withdrew his hand in which could be seen a tiny quivering ball of black and white fur, no bigger than one of Ross's open palms. At this, Poppy leaped from the settee, eyes wide and hands clapped to the lower part of her face. He unfurled his fingers to allow her to see its pathetic, terrified eyes set atop its tiny shivering frame. He held it out to her slowly, inviting her to come closer and take it into her embrace.

"Well?" he encouraged. "Doest thou not want it?"

"Oo yes please!" she insisted, hardly able to contain her joy. "But am I allowed? Grandpa Joss said that anything brought into his house would be allowed to stay only if it earned its keep, and…"

"Of course he can stay," Nell soothed. "Take him sweetheart."

Poppy inched forward a little apprehensively, until her joy overcame her entirely, and then swiftly scooped the bundle to her chest, loving it and covering it with kisses.

"He shall be called 'Toby'," she had decided in an instant.

"I shall love him for ever. May he stay in my room with me. Please Nanny?"

"For now," Nell replied, a pleased smile creeping in. "At least until he is able to cope with the rest of the household."

Here at least was one creature of this world that would never want for love or care, she thought, watching her granddaughter's joy as she wandered around the house, the puppy close to her cheek as she explained where it was and what all the important parts of the house were.

"Tommy Green's bitch had a huge litter a short while ago," Ross explained, anticipating his mother's question, "and rather than have it destroyed, I knew of someone who would give it a good home and lots of love. Jack Russell cross, so it won't grow to be a meat guzzling giant. Don't worry."

"I wasn't," Nell returned. "I know she's often said she'd like a dog, but I just hope it's not going to be a passing phase. After all, her Tossy always came first, and *I* haven't the time."

"True," Ross replied. "But look at her. How could you believe she won't always love it to death?"

The picture of peace and harmony shattered abruptly as the door burst open into the room, followed by Joseph and his father in heated argument about the running of the farm again. Joseph's modern thoughts on keeping the farm up to date in an ever-changing financial climate was always at variance with that of his father. He was acutely aware where the demand for one commodity was often overtaken rapidly by new thinking and the desire for others.

"Don't thee ever forget, lad, that this is *my* farm," Joss growled as he stormed into the room, "and it'll be run as 'ow I think fit."

"And don't thee forget, fatha," Joseph countered equally forcefully, "that it's *my* job to make sure there'll still be a farm here to manage when thy's dead and gone! Changes are happening so rapidly that it's difficult to keep up wi' 'em. We've got to take the best in these new developments to survive. Don't forget we've also got a duty and responsibility for the families that depend on us for work and income. We can't, in all conscience, cast them aside with little thought for their wellbeing."

"All rayt! All rayt!" Joss conceded. "Ye'd better go ahead with that new-fangled threshing machinery for next year, but I don't see as it will justify t'expense. Tha'd better look into Ransome's of Ipswich. I've allus dealt wi' them and can get a good deal."

"Marshall's of Gainsborough is nearer," Joseph interrupted quickly, "and they're much cheaper, I'm told. Horse-drawn harvester will release men for other jobs on the farm to compensate for any shortage of labour hereabouts, and yon new steam-driven thresher will streamline our operation considerably."

"Aye, well, I'll need some convincing," Joss muttered as he sat down in his chair by the fireplace.

"Poppy!" Nell shouted her granddaughter from the back room. "Are you there?"

"Yes, Nanny," she replied as her head popped out from under the stairs, the black and white bundle still clutched close to her cheek. "I'm here."

"I wonder if you'd like to do something with Mary after lunch?" Nell suggested. "Something I think both of you might enjoy."

"Oo, yes please," Poppy enthused, getting quite excited by the approach of one of her favourite times of year. "What is it

Nanny? Is it something to do with Christmas?"

"Uncle Ross is going to choose a Christmas tree from the north field," Nell said in a conspiratorial whisper as if no-one else was supposed to know.

"What's that, Nanny?" Poppy whispered back, sharing the secret.

"It's a decoration for the house, to make it look brighter and more colourful," Nell explained. "You'll see. Would you like to go with him to choose?"

"Can I?" Poppy said in that breathless excited whisper, which showed she was beginning to enjoy the start to this festive season. "And what about Mary? Is she coming with us? You said we were going to something *we* might enjoy."

"No, my love," Nell smiled, casting a comical glance across at Mary, who had thrown her hands up in a gesture of mock horror at the thought of trudging the fields to collect shrubbery and foliage. "She'll be waiting here for you. I've something special I would like you to do. Don't worry. She won't start until you return."

"Can I take my Toby with me?" Poppy pleaded. "Please?"

"Don't you think he's a bit small to be struggling through those fields, poor little dear?" Nell ventured. "He'll be fine here until you get back."

Muffled against the cold, Poppy's mittened hand engulfed by Ross's great paw, they set off down the noisy driveway to cross the farm to the north field where the 'special' trees grew. Poppy didn't know what to expect and was rather taken aback that Uncle Ross was about to cut down a giant tree to take it into their home for Christmas. Just how he would get it through the door she couldn't imagine, let alone stand it upright in the front room.

"Why do we need to take a tree from the forest into our

house, when we can go and see it quite easily when we want to?" she asked innocently.

Ross suppressed a smile at her naïve perception of the new Christmas celebrations, and spent a little time thinking how he might explain to her the reasoning behind it.

"Well, my poppet," he began, "you know that we have a queen to look after us in this wonderful country of ours?"

"Yes, Unca Ross," Poppy replied very solemnly. "She is called Queen Victoria, and she takes care of us all."

Ross's grin grew ever wider as he watched her deliver her serious and important information to him. He couldn't help but remember the serious yet joyous little girl that was Poppy's mother at just such an age; happy and carefree, yet serious enough to understand the gravity of the world around her.

"You know that our queen had a husband who died not too long ago?" he asked, not really sure whether she would understand such concepts as 'husband' and 'died'.

"Yes, of course," she replied, quite matter of fact. "Prince Albert from Germany." She paused for a moment as if considering her response, before saying, "Where's Germany, Unca Ross?"

"It's a country quite a way from us, over the sea" he said. "Although we've always decorated the house at Christmas time with holly, ivy and mistletoe, this will be only the first year we've brought in a tree. Not a large oak, beech or such like I hasten to add, but one about my height, with straight spiky branches. You'll see. It's only over the next hill."

"But why a tree?" she asked, puzzled still.

"That's one of the traditions Prince Albert brought with him from Germany when he married our Queen Victoria," Ross went on.

"Why do we bring in holly and ivy?" Poppy asked, starting

full swing with her almost interminable questions of which there seemed to be an inexhaustible store. "And, what's 'middle toe'?"

Ross laughed at her mispronunciation of the word and proceeded to explain to her where they were to find it, and why it would be especially nice when she was a bit older. "Holly and ivy are supposed to be an ancient protection from evil spirits and an encouragement for the return of spring after winter. So, we need to make sure we get plenty. Grandpa Joss thinks it's all nonsense and superstition, but those old holly trees in the middle field he will have no-one touch, as cutting them down might bring bad luck!"

Poppy gripped his hand even tighter as they skipped through the long grass in the margins between the two fields. The wood glowered moodily on the edge of the north field as they broke through the hedgerow at its thinnest. All the while they luxuriated in each other's company, blissfully unaware that they were not alone. Black, lustful and malevolent eyes ogled Poppy's youthful and innocent form despite her being with her giant of an uncle. They had fixed her frame with longing several times in recent weeks, and now that unquenchable flame licked at his very essence, pushing, prodding his whole being into taking greater risks.

Ross stopped mid-stride, drawing Poppy closer to him, scanning the outer eaves of Boulders Wood, feeling slightly uneasy that there might be someone, something watching them from the impenetrable depths of this place. The events of the time they found Annie flooded his mind and he shuddered at what might have happened to her in this very wood.

"Unca Ross, why have we stopped here?" Poppy's little voice cut into his thoughts. "Is it because of that man I saw at the house the other day?"

"Why do you ask?" he replied, somewhat taken aback. How could she have known what was running through his thoughts?

"Because if it is, I can see him over there, behind that large tree," she said, matter of fact.

She had seen him! How could she have seen him? He had taken great care to cover himself, to hide behind the tree and under cover of the brushwood surrounding it. Was there something supernatural about her, something that no-one else possessed?

"Where?" Ross urged, letting go of her hand and striding out towards the tree. She didn't move, puzzling why her uncle was so eager to try to catch up with him.

"He's gone now," she replied. "He disappeared into the trees."

Ross strode back to her quickly and, scooping her into his arms, he marched off to the north of the field to collect tree, holly, ivy and mistletoe. He threw her over his head to straddle his shoulders, her most favourite ride of all, while bouncing her along the uneven land to great whoops of enduring joy.

All the while this unwelcome and uninvited interloper invaded his thoughts, ever fearful for Poppy's safety as he knew he would be unable to protect her every moment of each day. He vowed he would make it his life's duty to find him and ensure Poppy's enjoyment of a life without fear.

Every time of the year was busy for Nell. Her work was a never ending and constant round of cleaning, preparing, cooking, and looking after the men in her life. This last eight years had offered her another interest, and this one had to be kept in dresses, coats and little shoes. Although something she wouldn't have chosen at her age, she loved Poppy with all her being, as if she were her own daughter. In many ways, she was, of course, and in many ways, she had been given a second chance to correct all the things she hadn't quite managed to get right the first time with her Annie. It was a fine line they all had to tread between firm upbringing and self-serving indulgence. Especially difficult for Nell had been the need to instil into *this* little girl all those values she held dear that she hadn't quite managed with the last one.

For a number of years in Annie's short life, Nell had battled her self-will and defiance, demanding the respect she felt she was due as of right. Those years could have been much easier with hindsight, when a more understanding and compassionate approach might have made truces after battles unnecessary. Would that she had had *this* sort of wisdom then! Perhaps she might even have had her daughter here with her now. How she missed her! She would, she hoped fervently, not make the same mistakes with Poppy.

"Nanny! Nanny! Look what we've got!" a tiny voice burst into the room as the door opened. "We've got a tree an' some holly an' some ivy an' … an' … some middle toe."

Nell smiled broadly at her announcement as she gathered her to her bosom to kiss her forehead. No, she wouldn't be without her for the world, hard work or no hard work.

"Good gracious!" Nell gasped. "And did *you* cut down that tree?"

"No, course not, silly," Poppy replied. "Unca Ross used his chopping thing, but I … I gathered the ivy and some of the middle toe. Couldn't do the holly because it was too prickly."

"I think Uncle Ross knows where to put it for now," Nell told her granddaughter quietly. "Before you went out, I said I would have something for you that I am sure you will enjoy.

Go and take off your outdoor clothes and come back into the kitchen."

Already a wonderful smell of baking had invaded the living room, tantalising her senses, encouraging her to change her clothes at top speed. Poppy had experienced Nanny's Christmases at Boulders Wood several times by now, and she had come to realise there had been developed a pattern which didn't change from year to year. *Knowing* what would happen and when, was all part of the excitement, and being part of the preparation made it all the more poignant for her.

Skipping into the spacious farmhouse kitchen, Poppy's eyes began to widen as Nell held out the heavy cotton pinny she had made specially for her. If Poppy was to be part of their Christmas preparations, she would need to do it properly.

"Nanny, what are we going to do?" Poppy asked eagerly, seeing Mary by the long solid deal table which was scrubbed down with salt and water several times a day. She stood there, elbows pointing outwards as she rested her knuckles on her ample hips, a faint smile playing around her mouth. She remembered a similar scene fifteen or sixteen years before when another little girl with a bright, open and eager face had asked just such a question. The large oil lamps with their burnished copper reflecting disks, topped by newly cleaned glass chimneys, had been lit and placed at intervals around the room because of the fading day. They cast almost eerie half-shadows as the diffused orange light hid behind objects in its path.

Lit for most of each day, the Adams black-leaded range dominated one end of the kitchen, with its angrily glowing coals desperately straining to escape its black cell bars. Nell and Mary knew their range intimately, tending, working and caressing it like a fondly held lover who needed cajoling, stroking and arousing before he would perform.

"It's time we made our plum pudding," Nell replied, almost conspiratorially quietly. "As today is Stir-Up Sunday, *you* need to take a hand."

"What's Stir-Up Sunday, Nanny?" Poppy asked, puzzled at the words she didn't understand.

"When we've mixed in all our pudding ingredients, we must all have a stir and make a wish," Mary said. "Stir it clockwise, mind you, and then your wish will come true sometime in the new year. There."

"What are in … gree … dints, Nanny?" Poppy asked slowly, having trouble pronouncing the word.

"They are what we put into the pudding to make it as delicious as it needs to be," Nell explained. "They are breadcrumbs, currants and raisins, spices, butter, eggs. Mary and I have mixed these in already, and so it's now your turn. Are you ready for this important part?" Nell asked Poppy, whose sleeves she had rolled above elbows in readiness.

"Oo, yes please, Nanny Nell. Yes please!" Poppy answered, excitement rising as she took hold of the great wooden spoon. Plunging it into the rich looking and smelling mixture in the great brown mixing bowl rather after the fashion of a warrior driving a dagger into his enemy's chest, Poppy set to with gusto to try to move the heavy, sticky mixture around. She soon tired, but as she was about to give in, Mary threw three items into the bowl.

"What was that?" she asked, brows knitting, a little perturbed that Mary had dropped hard-looking objects into *her* lovely pudding.

"A ring, a coin and a thimble," they both chorused with a smile.

"But won't it hurt my mouth if I get them?" Poppy

interrupted. "How can I eat my pudding if I know they're in there?"

"Carefully," Nell laughed. "You have to take care not to bite them. If you get the ring in your mouthful, it means you will get married—"

"But I don't want to get married yet!" Poppy protested.

"No, silly," Mary joined in. "Some time in the future when you are older. Besides, *you* might not get any of them. The coin stands for wealth."

"And the thimble for a happy life without being married," Nell finished off the conversation.

"When I was a little girl," Mary said, "I found a thimble in my pudding, and I never married. So, the tradition is true, you see."

"I think that *I* will find the coin *and* the ring in *my* pudding." Poppy said wistfully as she continued to drag the giant wooden spoon through the morass.

Nell and Mary turned towards each other, a look of surprised amusement on their face at the level of sophisticated thinking coming from one so young.

"Well, yes … of course," Nell nodded in agreement. "We shall have to see *if* you get your wish."

A smile of satisfaction crept across Poppy's face, sure in the knowledge that all would be well on Christmas Day, giving the mixture one or two little turns before she dropped the spoon into the bowl. Satisfied she had performed a useful function, she turned from the table, removed her pinny, and walked away sucking the smearings of pudding mix from her hand. Her final comment stunned the two women.

"If you want me, I'll be in the other room where I think Unca Ross needs me to sort out the tree," she said as she passed into the living room.

That day marked the start of the transition from a little girl of eight, whose interests lay only in her doll and anything she might do to help Nanny Nell, into someone who was moving quickly towards trying to be more grown up. Nell understood, but *that* inevitability she had hoped would come later, much later. She wanted to enjoy Poppy's innocent childhood a little longer yet.

Nell followed her out of the kitchen to see her sitting on the huge settee, arranging her Tossy's clothing.

"She's growing up very quickly," Ross observed quietly to his mother as he moved to Nell's side.

A little surprised by her son's appearance, she started slightly as she nodded agreement. "You've noticed too, then?" she added slowly. "I really wanted her to enjoy her childhood a little while longer."

"She will," he replied. "But in a different sort of a way. You can't repair through Poppy the damage that was done to our Annie."

"Damage?" Nell snapped. "What do you mean 'damage'?"

"You know well what I mean, Mother," Ross answered, calming a potentially explosive situation. "You know as well as I do that Annie didn't have as comfortable a childhood as yon bairn. You remember only too well fatha's penchant for anything that might bring back his youth. *That* is the major reason you keep *her* close."

"Ever the gentleman, my son," Nell said quietly and fondly about her boy, with a wry smile. "But, yes, I know only too well your father's filthy habits, and then I was within that much of ridding this family of his odious presence for good. I won't allow it to happen again."

Chapter 6

A thick white blanket of hoar frost lay heavily on Boulders Wood this Christmas Eve morning, its freezing fingers squeezing the life out of anything warm blooded that was inadequately protected against its detached and dispassionate aggression. Dense clouds of grey moisture-laden breath spurted from the horses' nostrils, slowly pursued by large, lazy drops of spittle from mouth corners as they champed on irritating steel bits.

Joss had been up two hours already by the time the rest of the household arose at half past six, to prepare the carriage and pair to pick up his younger brother and sister-in-law. Fred and Victoria McIntyre lived reasonably close to Boulders Wood but had no transport of their own. It was no chore for Joss as he regarded his brother highly, being probably the only one in the family who neither feared nor despised him. Even though he was master and employed others to do for him, he preferred to attend to his horses himself. For them, nothing was too good or too much trouble. They were the power behind many of the functional processes on the farm. *They* did not answer back or give him grief. *They* knew who was master, knew their place, and did as they were bidden. *They* would never let him down, unlike many of the humans around him.

Joss was steadfast in his opposition to this new-fangled machinery being brought in to replace his Shires. Faster it might be, but not as reliable or steady, and it was a sight more costly to maintain and run.

Joss's brother and sister-in-law hadn't had an easy life, much in common with many people in their position. Fred had had his own farrier business where he served all the local farms; not a huge money spinner, but he made a living. His dreadful accident had put an end to that.

The introduction of the self-same machinery that Joss resisted so, had brought its own problems for Fred, in that he had had to move with a rapidly changing scene, or lose out. Trouble was that some of the machinery was so new that artisans such as Fred McIntyre knew precious little about how to service and repair the many excesses and abuses local farmers exposed it to. Job Smith's traction engine up Helmsley way on had toppled over with Fred underneath it, crushing his chest and arm so badly, he had lost use in the limb, and he now found difficulty with his breathing. At the same time, they had discovered that Victoria couldn't have the children she had so badly craved for many years.

Fred had been able to pick up on some of the lighter jobs that weren't affected by his disability, and the rest of his income was subsidised by Joss; this unbeknown to Nell. She liked Victoria and envied her to a certain extent. The difference between them was fundamental. *Her* husband married her because he loved her, and even now, after fourteen years of marriage, they were obviously closer than Nell could ever have hoped – or wished – to be with Joss.

His journey to his brother's was short in distance but long in time, because of the winding nature of the lanes he had to steer his horses through. Because hedgerows either side of the mud tracks were often overgrown, progress was always slow. Much as he regarded his brother, Joss wasn't prepared to jeopardise his beloved horses and carriage even for those meagre ties. Many a careless driver had ridden unseen bends and obstacles only to overturn and ruin precious rigs.

Only the week before, Edward Dawes' son, George, had driven his father's brand-new Landau into the ditch at the bottom of Pineapple Hill because of under-familiarity with the track and over-confidence in his own skill to negotiate it. Because of its size and weight, and the lack of lifting tackle to shift it, it lay where it had overturned for several days. Much more of a blow to Edward was the loss of one of his prize Shires.

Alfred and Victoria's place, in complete contrast to his brother's, was a tiny end-of-terrace white cottage two villages down from Boulders Wood. Fortunately, it came with a small piece of land which they were able to market garden, providing them with produce, and a much-needed small supplement to their already meagre income. At the few month ends where expenditure outstripped income, Joss made up the shortfall.

Joss slowed the horses to a gentle walk as they approached his brother's cottage. The clatter of their iron-shod hooves echoed along the terrace, warning the McIntyres of his arrival.

"Thank ye for coming, Joss," Fred greeted his brother. "It's good of you to come for us, but are you sure we'd—"

"You're my brother," Joss replied gruffly, in an uncharacteristic show of affection. "My door's allus open to you, no matter what. Victoria."

"Joss," she returned, acknowledging his greeting.

"And while we're at it," Joss insisted, thrusting a brown paper package into Fred's unsuspecting pocket. "Tek this."

"What's this?" Fred said, suspecting from its feel that it was a packet of sovereigns. "I can't tek—!"

"Yes, tha can," Joss insisted. "Put it somewhere safe for the next rainy day. Just between thee and me, mind."

"You're too good to us, Joss McIntyre," Victoria uttered as she made a move to hug her brother-in-law.

"Nar then!" he warned. "None o' that, nar. Just tek it wi' mi best wishes, and when you're short agen, just let me know. All rayt? Now, wrap up warm and get into t'cart. It's parky out yonder."

Their journey to Boulders Wood was uneventful if cold and undertaken mostly in silence. Joss wasn't given much to small talk, and his brother respected that. Words had to be to some purpose, otherwise he wouldn't waste his breath.

Poppy was already at the door, wrapped against the cold, to greet her first guests, as the carriage broadcast its approach along the gravel. She had been up since just after first light, unable to contain her excitement any longer. At the arrival of this most magical time of the year.

"Uncle Alfred and Aunt Victoria!" she gasped, clapping her gloved hands. "Welcome to Christmas at Boulders Wood."

Victoria smiled at the invitation from one so young as she scooped her to her bosom, thinking about the daughter she would have liked but was never able to have.

"Well, thank you very much for the warm welcome, Poppy McIntyre," she answered. "We are delighted to be here."

Looking past her great aunt and uncle's arrival as she ushered them into the much warmer interior of the house, she had already noticed another carriage and pair approaching slowly from beyond the outer gate.

"Nanny!" she called, turning towards the kitchen. "Nanny Nell!"

"Yes, my lovely," Nell replied as she put her arm around her granddaughter's shoulders. "What is it?"

"There's a carriage on its way towards the house," Poppy said, a puzzled look drawing down her youthful brow. "I can see only a man holding the reins of two big black horses, and … nobody else. Is there—?"

"Someone inside the carriage?" Nell said, finishing her question with a knowing smile.

"Nanny?" Poppy went on more puzzled than ever.

"I recognise the horses, poppet," Nell explained, grinning broadly. "They are thoroughbred Shires. Beautiful creatures."

"But, Nanny, I don't remember inviting two *horses* to our parties," Poppy replied seriously. "Are there any humans in the box behind the driver?"

"Indeed, there are," Nell said, a heart-felt laugh escaping her lips. "They will be Grandpa's sister Annie and her husband Ned. There will also be their three children – George who is twenty, John who is sixteen and—"

"Come on, Nanny," Poppy insisted, jiggling her legs impatiently. "They're almost here! And—?"

"You're going to love their youngest," Nell continued slowly, almost in a conspiratorial whisper. "She is eight-year-old Florence, and she is … just … like … you!"

"Oh goody!" Poppy screeched, clapping her little hands quickly in front of her face. "Somebody I can play with – at last!"

The carriage drew to a crunchy halt on the gravel before the porticoed entrance that Poppy now occupied in feet-shuffling excitement. Horses' hooves marked noisy time as their tails swished and spurts of breath rushed downward from impatient but relieved nostrils, like slowing engine pistons.

Poppy could wait no longer. As the doors of the Landau began to open slowly, she shot to its side, scattering gravel as she skidded to a halt, clapping her hands and jiggling her feet as she did so. Unable to contain her excitement any longer, she burst into her welcome.

"Glad you could come to our Christmas at Boulders Wood," she started. "Welcome Aunt … Annie? … And…?"

She stopped abruptly, realising that she didn't really know who these people were, what relation she was to them, or why one of them bore her mother's name. Tears sprang to her eyes as a seriously puzzled look invaded her face.

Nell recognised her upset immediately and drew her confused body to her as it began to heave. The fact that Cousin Annie bore the same name as the mamma Poppy never met or knew was beginning to take its toll on her emotions, that she had managed to keep in check up to now.

"It's the name, Annie," Nell explained. "You bear the name of the mother she never knew, and the realisation has only just hit her."

They all moved slowly towards the warmth of the sitting room out of the sharply cold air that was starting to pepper them with stinging pellets of hail. As they reached the front door, Poppy stopped, feeling a small warm hand in hers. Turning around, she caught the smiling, understanding face next to her, and it was then she knew instantly that she and her Cousin Florence would be very close friends … forever.

As they pushed open the door, a bundle of black and white fur surrounding four clod-hopping paws bowled into them, seeking love and attention from both girls. He was no fool, recognising immediately that there would now be twice the affection and attention for the taking.

"Florence," Poppy explained, "may I introduce you to my best friend – up to now, that is – and he's called Toby. He stays with me all day, except when I go to school, of course."

"School?" Florence asked, not knowing the meaning of the word she had never encountered before. "What is 'school'?"

"It's a place just down the road from Boulders Wood where we learn things like how to add up numbers and how to read and write," Poppy began to explain. "I could do all of those things beforehand, because my Nanny taught me. Lots of other children don't know, though. I help them when the teacher asks me to."

"There is a voluntary church school not far from us, which is going to be a Board School after Christmas," Annie butted in. "Florence will have to join in then. We've taught her all she needs to know up to now, but come January's end, the law says she will have to attend."

"Not sure whether I want to go," Florence said, an unsure grimace growing on her face.

"The new Education Bill says you have to, I'm afraid," a familiar deep voice followed them into the room.

"Unca Ross!" Poppy squealed joyfully as she turned and threw herself at him.

He groaned playfully, pretending to be weighed down as he threw her into the air and caught her at his knee level. She loved the way he played, making her screech in joy and excitement, all the while watching Toby bounce around, wanting to get in on the action.

"More! More!" Poppy demanded, almost too giddy to stop. "And Florence too!"

Florence stood and watched in awe at what she had neither seen nor experienced in her short life. But then, her father was a dour, staid Yorkshireman that had never given rein to his inner childish emotions – not even when he was a child. Dour Yorkshire males didn't indulge either their youngsters or themselves. It just wasn't done, being an expectation that they wouldn't show themselves up. Ross, however, had been cast from a different mould. He had loved his sister to distraction and, by association, *her* daughter, too. He had been convinced almost from Poppy's appearance on this earth that she was Annie's reincarnation – too much like her for it not to be so. This one he needed to look after, so woe betide anyone who tried to hurt her. If they did, they would feel the full weight of his retribution.

"You will be sharing my room with me over the next few days, Florence," Poppy said as they munched their way through a home-made and home-baked ham sandwich that was built like the proverbial doorstep. Nothing in this household was ever bought from a shop – something Poppy would show to her new best friend before they would have to go home after Boxing Day tea.

All this was new to Florence, as *her* father wasn't a farmer, and they didn't live in the countryside like Poppy. He worked as a carpenter for a local furniture maker in a village, a bit of a distance away from Boulders Wood, where there had been problems with the creation of a local school board after 1870. Consequently, the school that was supposed to have been built to cater for children over five, was still at sod level.

"Nanny?" Poppy had asked earlier. "Would it be all right if Florence came to school with me, please?"

"Not my decision, sweetie," Nell had replied, "and I don't know. Perhaps your uncle Ross might be able to tell you. Ross?"

"I've a feeling Florence might live too far away from here

to be allowed," he replied after a moment or two's thought. "You are allowed to go to *your* school, Poppy, because you live just round the corner from a school that belonged to our local church, and that has been here for a long time. Even if the School Board said 'yes', she would have to travel every day, and that might be too much, particularly in the winter."

Not the sort of answer Poppy had wanted, as disappointment hung in her eyes. Her uncle always had *all* the answers she wanted to hear, and perhaps he might find an answer that she could hang on to.

"Tell you what," Ross offered to the girls. "How about if I tell you a story when you've settled your stuff in your bedroom?"

"Yes, please!" they answered eagerly as they leaped to their feet and raced to the stairs.

"No longer than ten minutes, mind," he shouted after their scurrying feet as they rattled the oaken stair treads.

"Why ten minutes?" Nell asked him as she slipped her pinny straps over her head. "What's the story? I didn't have you down as a story-teller."

"It's one I used to like when I was younger," Ross answered. "'*A Christmas Carol*'. Remember? Written in 1843 by Maestro Charles Dickens? You read it to me several times every Christmas."

"Yes, I remember," she laughed. "You used to pester the life out of me until Christmas was over. Ten minutes?"

"I need to be out to see to the horses in three quarters of an hour," he replied with a shrug. "I need them to be back down here as soon as—"

"Here they come," Nell warned as she turned to join Mary in the kitchen, followed by a whirlwind of arms and legs. "Not in here, girls! *We've* got work to do. I assume you would like to eat today?"

The whirlwind settled in the living room on the settee opposite Ross's favourite chair, book in hand, opened at the appropriate page.

"Ready?" he asked quietly.

"Yes, Unca Ross," Poppy replied.

"Yes, please," Florence joined in, shuffling back into the poofy cushions.

"'Marley was dead'," he started, to rapt children's faces desperate to hear it all, and then hear it all again…

"There's big changes acoming, si thi," Tom Garside had said in earnest conversation with neighbour Joseph McIntyre at the Black Bull's Farmers' Ordinary, Christmas Eve morning.

"Tell me about it Tom!" Joseph replied. "Getting father to accept and agree is like pulling camel's teeth, tha knows."

"I can understand that," Tom agreed. "Don't forget that I knew 'is father before 'im – dour Scot that *'e* was."

"Now, here's a thought," Joseph offered as he drained his tankard.

"I'm all ears," Tom butted in quickly, fully aware of Joseph's clever ideas and sensible schemes.

"I shouldn't worry about it Tom," Joseph replied, a serious look on his face. "They're not *that* big, no matter what anybody might say."

Tom burst into a fit of belly wobbling guffaws, almost choking on the mouthful of ale trying to finds its way down his throat.

"Ee," he added once he had wiped the escaped froth from his chin. "Thee and thy sense of yooma! Any road, tha were saying?"

"As two experienced farmers offering the produce to

our consumers that we know they need and expect," Joseph began to explain, "we tend to do similar stuff – in competition almost."

"Tha's rayt," Tom agreed. "It's become a bit on a worry for me as to how far we need to go developin' areas that seem to be comin' up. I mean, I know we both are into arable in a big way, and—"

"At Boulders Wood, we've invested heavily in a new steam-driven thresher," Joseph interrupted sharply. "This is allowing us to free up workers to do other stuff that's becoming neglected."

"Marshall's of Gainsborough?" Tom added. "Aye. We've looked at that. Not cheap, but necessary, eh?"

"Back to my original idea?" Joseph said, shifting back to his train of thought. "I've been pondering for a bit now, as to whether thy might be open to sharing t'markets available to us."

"Tell me more," Tom replied eagerly, shuffling forward in his seat. "What does tha mean by 'sharin'?"

"Well, here's the thing," Joseph began. "We both know full well that market for beef, poultry, milk and cheese are on the up, and neither on us does much in them areas. It seems daft both farms are into arable in a big way and are not even starting to consider the advent o' t'other stuff that might become big business."

"I think I know where tha's goin' wi' this," Tom replied, a grin beginning to show through in his stubbly face.

"If we – thee and me – sit down together after Boxing Day and decide on areas where we can become mutually supportive—," Joseph continued.

"Any thoughts on a controlled merger, Joseph?" Tom threw into the conversation unexpectedly, rocking his companion back on his chair.

"My God!" Joseph gasped. "Who snitched? Has thy been reading my mind, Tom Garside? That's been wandering round in my head for a while since I caught the rising demand for the stuff *we* don't do much of. Look, Tom, can we get together soon and throw about a few ideas to our mutual benefit? Mi father will tek some talking round, but I think we'll be able to persuade him that this is t'onny way."

"Too rayt, Our Joseph," Tom agreed, draining his tankard and getting ready to move. "My place, day after Boxin' Day eleven in t'mornin'?"

The two men shook hands and left The Bull in opposite directions, both buzzing from the expression of common thoughts and ideas.

Chapter 7

Snow had been falling steadily over night, with the humans snug in bed oblivious to the worsening conditions outside. Both Nell and Mary were up early ready to prepare the feast for the day ahead, to be confronted by Joseph sitting by the fire he had laid and lit an hour before, a steaming tea mug in his hand.

"Joseph?" Nell said, surprised to see the back of his curly head, as she rounded the newell post at the bottom of the stairs. "Are you all right?"

"Aye, Mother," he said, relinquishing his seat to embrace her. "A few things on my mind that needed thinking through and sorting, stopped me from sleeping."

She was the most important person in his life, and he would always make space and time for her. He was aware how hard she worked to keep the household together, and he knew what a difficult time she had had with Joseph's nasty father – in more ways than one. A hard demanding and intractable task master both with family and staff alike, Joss was loth to give an inch in any circumstance, and he bore not an ounce of compassion or feeling for anyone but himself.

"Sorted, then, my son?" she asked as she tied her pinny, ready for the real business of the day. "Your father about?"

"He's been and gone for an hour or more – goodness knows where in this snow ," he replied with a shrug of his ample shoulders. "I've sorted out most of my problems with satisfactory results, I think. I'll let you know the outcomes when everything is ready for putting into place."

"Sounds exciting," she said with a smile, knowing he would have any improvements to the running of their livelihood ready soon enough. In the meantime, she had a lot to do.

"Ross and I will lay and decorate the table for one of your wonderful feasts this afternoon," he said. "In the meantime, we have some youngsters to entertain – when they decide to rise. All the presents and stuff are around the tree that Ross decorated – never seen it looking so attractively festive. I like the new idea of hanging those large stockings from the mantle shelf, with children's names embroidered on them."

"Mary and I made them ourselves," Nell said proudly as Mary joined them. "You'll have to wait and see what they contain."

"Fresh mince pies, Missus?" Mary asked, although she knew the procedure of old.

"Aye, Mary," Nell replied to her sister-in-arms. "I've no idea what I'd do without you."

"You'd make fewer pies and ask fewer people to join you," Mary laughed as she returned to the kitchen to start her chores for the day.

"Nanny! Nanny!" the voices from two excited girls echoed down the stairs as Nell was about to join Mary in the kitchen. "Merry Christmas, Nanny."

"The tree and all the presents are over—" Poppy gabbled.

"Have you seen what's hanging from the mantlepiece?" Florence interrupted, her eyes and mouth becoming saucer-shaped as she caught sight of the enormous stocking bearing her name.

"Into the kitchen you two," Nell ordered. "Breakfast time."

Joseph smiled and beckoned his brother to join him in the back room as he came in from the blizzarding snow.

"Subterfuge, eh, Brother?" Ross said, as Joseph clicked the door behind them.

"A few more people yet to come," Joseph explained, "although I'm not sure how they're going to make it in this snow. Anyway, when everybody's here and settled, *we* are going to help them all celebrate the festivities.

"You are going to be Father Christmas," he went on, thrusting a large brown paper package into his ample hands. "At the same time, I will be Santa Claus."

"Aren't they one and the same?" Ross puzzled, a frown clouding his features.

"Almost," his brother explained. "The former, apparently, is much older, being the celebration also of approaching Spring, as you'll see from the costume you have under your arm. Santa Claus came across to us with Prince Albert, who, unfortunately, is no more. You will notice the difference in *my* costume."

"Yo ho ho! And all that?" Ross bellowed, a grin accompanying his merriment.

"Not so loud, Brother," Joseph warned. "All this is supposed to be a surprise."

"No peeking yet," Nell warned her granddaughter and Joss's great niece, as they crept under the tree to find where their presents were hiding. "Time enough for all that when the rest of the family is here."

Meantime, Joss had returned from wherever and was toasting his more than ample backside in front of the fire, watching the two little girls keenly under hooded unblinking lids. Fred and Victoria McIntyre, and Joss's sister Annie and her husband, Ned, were finishing a hearty breakfast, but their sons, George and John, were still snoring the morning away after a late-night carousing with the other adults. This was the only time in the year they were allowed to join in.

The outside door swung open unexpectedly, ushering in several other large and small figures wrapped against the inclement weather of the season.

Nell poked her head round the kitchen jamb, alerted by the slamming of the outside door.

"We're here!" Nell's brother Frank's unmistakable voice announced. "Anybody home?"

Nell rushed out, wiping her hands on her pinny as she shed it on the nearest chair, to embrace sister Jessie and her Jack, along with children James and Mary.

"Do I deserve a cuddle little sister?" Frank's voice insisted again. "There is a fantastic smell oozing from yon kitchen."

"All to be released in the not-too-distant future, Uncle Frank," Joseph offered, wringing his uncle's hand fit to pull it from his arm. "Good to see you again, despite what others might say."

"Ha ha!" Frank replied, laughing loudly. "You always were a card, young Joseph. Goodness! And young Ross, eh? You've grown another six feet since last I saw you, I do declare.

"And these young urchins over here must be Poppy and … Florence?" he went on. "My word! My lord! Merry Christmas, I do say!"

Uncle Frank had always been loud and merry, despite his being tall and thin. Nothing like the round bellied Christmas character he ought to have been.

Louisa, Jessie's elder daughter, ushered her soon-to-be eleven-year-old son Jonas, to the fore to introduce him to the household and especially to his great aunt Nell, whom he had seen only once before. He was polite but quiet as adults weren't to his taste. His gaze shifted immediately to the two young girls of about his age that were scrambling about under the tree, contemplating but not touching the wrapped presents.

All this time, Joss had neither moved from in front of the fire nor said anything to anyone. The only people of interest to him were his brother and *his* wife, his niece her husband, and, of course, especially the two young girls, Poppy and Florence.

"Tha'd mek a better door than a winder," Frank announced as he moved towards the fireplace to speak to his brother-in-law, who ignored his comment entirely and didn't offer to move.

"Bloody 'ell, Joss," Frank went on almost in a whisper for him, "Tha doesn't get any more sociable the older tha becomes."

"It's not about me, or thee for that matter," Joss growled. "It's family time for once a year, and tha'll have to tek it as it comes. So, either get thissen a tot from t'sideboard ower yonder, or sit thissen down and stop thi rattle."

Lunch time was a joyous and festive affair with everyone present eating and drinking in moderation as they prepared themselves for the main event of the day – full Christmas dinner that Nell and Mary had been preparing non-stop for days.

The front sitting room cum dining area was more than

large enough to seat and entertain a family twice the size of the McIntyres. The table was already set for dinner, decorated with evergreens, holly and ivy, and the best crockery settings for twenty, including Mary. She had always been regarded as part of the family.

And what a feast it proved to be!

Standing rib of beef, the largest cooked goose ever to have waddled the fields of The North Riding, potatoes and several varieties of vegetables. Afters consisted of plum pudding that Poppy had had a hand in mixing on Stir-Up Sunday, which was carried into the room by Ross in his Father Christmas suit of greens and reds and whites. His flowing white beard and hair were made from horsehair and wool, tucked into his red hood. "Ho ho ho!" he chuckled in true Christmas fashion.

He was followed by Joseph dressed in *his* Santa Claus outfit which was simply a floppy red suit with a large cushion stuffed under his tunic to make him seem to have a fat belly, fastened off with a large black belt to keep the cushion in place. He carried a huge silver tray of newly introduced Christmas crackers which were a huge success, with their cracks and bangs showering the pullers with coloured paper-wrapped sweets, mottos, small toys and paper hats. Poppy, Florence and Jonas shrieked and whooped with delight at receiving 'extra' presents from them.

This of course wasn't the end of the meal, as last of all, after a belly resting hiatus, Christmas cake and mince pies were ushered into the room. That proved to be *too* much for the older folk, as, once they had settled into settees and chairs around the fire to open cards and presents which had been largely hand-made by the givers, very full bellies urged brains to contemplate snooze time for a while. This gave Nell and Mary, along with Ross and Joseph, the time to clear all vestiges of feasting and over-indulgence back to the kitchen, in readiness for a few games to be played. These were usually things like charades, theatricals and blind man's buff, although these didn't last for too long.

Throughout this time, Joss interacted little, but watched much, particularly as the two young girls played with their new dolls, books, and clockwork toys, planning what his next moves might be. He, too, was the only person to see the dishevelled, matted hair framed dirty face looking in at the small window by the front door, desire and lust in his red, staring eyes. One blink and he was gone. Joss said nothing and made no move to alert his sons, because he knew what their reaction would have been. *He* knew who the peeper was but wasn't prepared to divulge. He wasn't the only one to have seen the spectre, though.

Poppy, too, had seen him, and although a shiver crept down her spine, she said nothing.

"Why are we going out in the cold snow, Unca Ross?" Poppy asked the next morning. "It's nice and warm inside, and why have we got all these small boxes to hand out?"

"Today is called 'Boxing Day,'" he explained. "These boxes all contain some money that we will take and give to each of our farm workers as a thank you for all their hard work in the year just gone."

"But why, Unca Ross?" Poppy asked again, her frown betraying her puzzlement at such a strange way of paying their workers. "Don't they get paid at any other time? How can they afford to live? Is all the food they eat free? Does—?"

"Woa, Tiger!" he said smiling at her pert questions. "They all receive a weekly pay packet with money in it according to what they have done during the week. *This* money in *this* box is an extra to thank them for all their hard work. Understand?"

"I think so," she replied slowly.

As they turned around to set off on their errand of mercy, he noticed six deep footprints by the small window to the side of the front door. There was none leading to and from because of the evening before's snow fall, but the ones he *did* notice had obviously been sheltered by the porticoed veranda, allowing them not to be obliterated by the heavy snowfall. He said nothing to Poppy so as not to frighten her, but she knew. She had seen their visitor the evening before, just like she has seen him those two previous times both at the house and at the edge of the forest, beyond the top field when they went to collect the Christmas tree.

"Did your friend Florence not want to come along?" Ross asked as they reached the by now silent gravel driveway. "I thought she might have enjoyed a walk out in the snow."

"She's still tired from the journey the day before," Poppy replied. "Besides, she says she doesn't like snow."

"What do you think about Jonas?" he went on as they reached the first worker's cottage.

"Don't know," she said. "Not met him before. Last Christmas and the one the time before, Nanny said he was poorly, and they didn't come."

"I thought you said you didn't know him," Ross added with a smirk.

"I asked Nanny before we went to bed last night, you see," she replied, her pert answer making Ross smile.

"And your name is—?" Jonas asked.

"Florence," she replied quickly.

"My name's—" he answered, trying to start up a conversation.

"Jonas," she butted in. "I know already, and I know also that you are about ten years old."

"That's astounding," he replied. "And, how—?"

"For me to know and for you, perhaps, to find out," she said, with a cheeky, indulgent smile as she turned and walked away; "if you are clever enough."

Jonas was a young man who exuded quiet self-confidence that others might have mistaken for arrogance and was quite taken aback by Florence's attitude and sharp comments. She was a *girl*, when all said and done, and shouldn't be able to talk to him like that. After all, he was a boy, and boys were more useful, more employable, and even … superior to mere girls. Weren't they? That is what he had always been led to believe, and he was going to become a professional man. He might even join the Foreign Office or become a lawyer or indeed … a gentleman farmer.

Should he follow her and explain his position, and get her to explain herself? Maybe not. She seemed different from the other young girls he had met, but they had been few and far between anyway. Did he really *want* to even *try* to understand them, or would it be better to deal with them on a superficial level just as … inferior beings? Probably. But he wasn't so sure now.

By the time Ross and Poppy had returned to Boulders Wood, everyone had risen and breakfasted, ready for either another day there, or for preparing to return home. Uncle Frank had already departed to attend to urgent business in Northallerton that couldn't wait another day, and Nell's sister and her three were ready to leave by lunchtime. Her boys, James and Albert, were back at work the following day and daughter Mary was preparing for her wedding to Boris the Banker in late January.

Although Nell's sister and *her* son, Jonas, were staying another day, her husband Ernest had to return to *their* home in Richmond to re-open his veterinary surgery. No doubt there would be a lengthy queue of people with poorly pooches and ill pussies galore.

"Nanny! Nanny!" Poppy enthused as she rushed into the kitchen, her slippers once again on her feet.

"What is it my lovely?" Nell replied as she turned from the pastry table where she was making left-over pies for lunch and dinner. "My word, your nose *is* red, and your cheeks are so rosy that I could swear that you were cold!"

"I am now very warm," she said, stripping off her outer coat and jumper. "We've been giving out Boxing Day boxes to our workers on the estate. They were very pleased to find that the boxes weren't empty."

Nell smiled at her endearing naivety, and it filled her with joy to see that it pleased her to be helping those less affluent than her.

"Florence!" Poppy whooped as her cousin and friend reached the bottom of the stairs from their shared room. "You should have been there. It was wonderful to see their faces as they opened their Boxing Day boxes with all that money inside. I think Uncle Joseph had put extras in them so they might have a jolly Christmas. Shall we go out and make a snowman?"

"I don't think so," Florence grimaced. "I don't like snow. It's too cold, wet and it makes my hands and feet cold. I quite like the look of it and the ideas behind it, but why can't it come in the summer when it's warm?"

She shivered visibly as she looked out of the window in the sitting room, at the thought of trudging through all that white nightmarish stuff.

"I think it might melt in the summer," Poppy said in all seriousness. "Besides, I like to run about and take Toby for walks into the fields and woods. He's not been out lately because he doesn't like the cold or wet. He likes to be where he is now, curled up in front of the fire, snoozing the day away. What a life, eh?"

"Shall we go and play with our toys instead?" Florence suggested. "I've no doubt it will be lunchtime soon."

"Yay!" Poppy cheered quietly, throwing her hands into the air, as they both clattered up the stairs to their room. Poppy had never had people of her own age to play with before, so this was a time to relish and hold on to. She knew in her heart that they would be very close friends forever.

"What do you think about Jonas?" Florence asked once they had rearranged their dolls in particular. "I found him a little strange once you and Uncle Ross had gone out to deliver your Christmas Boxes."

"Not sure," Poppy replied, her brows furrowing in ignorance. "I've met him only for the first time when they walked through the door yesterday. He gives me the impression that he—"

"Thinks he is better than us?" Florence butted in, a grimace underlining her feelings.

"Exactly," Poppy agreed. "Couldn't have put it better myself. He is very similar in attitude to Maggie Jenkins."

"Is she the one you whacked with your Tossy the other week?" Florence asked. "Why *did* you hit her?"

"She was making fun of me in front of her friends," Poppy started, defiance taking its stance in her face and clenched fists.

"I couldn't have her doing that. She won't be doing it again."

"Good for you!" Florence added. "Not sure whether I would have had the courage to do what you did. Did you think you'd ... killed her?"

"I was *sure* I had," Poppy replied emphatically. "Hoped I had. I was overcome by a feeling of ... disappointment when Unca Joseph told me she was going to survive after a few days or so of recuperation. If she tries it again, woe betide, because I'll be ready for her next time. I do wish you and I lived closer."

"I wonder if mother and Nanny Nell would allow me to stay here with you for a while longer?" Florence put forward tentatively. "I don't have to go to school because ... there isn't one!"

"Sounds like a good idea," Poppy agreed, jiggling her feet as she spoke. "Shall we go and ask now?"

They rushed out on to the landing and virtually slid down the bannister. They rounded the newell post and headed for the kitchen, where Nell and Florence's mother, Annie, were sitting at the huge kitchen table, drinking tea and eating mince pies.

Ross woke with a start. His stiff arm was numb, and his neck ached because they both slipped into unnatural positions when he had fallen asleep on the settee in front of a guttering, sullenly dull and barely alive fire. He had stayed up to think through the situation with his father and his future at Boulders Wood.

Most of the Christmas guests had departed before the end of the day, except for Louisa and Jonas, and Annie and Florence. Jonas had fallen ill and had been confined to his room to recover. Annie had allowed Florence to fulfil her request to spend a few more days with Poppy.

He stretched his aching limbs, to be brought to full consciousness by the smell of acrid smoke. Searching the room, he caught a glimpse of whisps of smoke creeping from under the closed door of the back room. Rubbing his eyes and suppressing a rasping cough, he realised what had happened in these early hours. A guttering wax candle on the Christmas tree they had moved into the back room to create more space for games in the sitting room, had been caused to reignite by a gentle breeze from a loose-fitting small window.

On opening the door, Ross was met with a burning fir tree, causing thick smoke to gather at the top of the room. Instinctively, he dashed into the kitchen, filled a galvanised bucket from the huge water tap, and, putting a second one to fill, he threw the first bucketful onto the seat of the flames.

By this time, Joseph had joined him, and together they doused the flames completely, amidst coughing and retching at their smoke inhalation. Fortunately, Ross had caught the fire in time preventing it from spreading into the ceiling and the floor joists above, otherwise, being mostly wood, the house would have lit up like an enormous torch, taking its inhabitants with it.

Joseph raised the household, while his brother staggered to the front door to let much needed cold air flood the house, and his lungs.

"What on earth's going on? Ross?" Joss bellowed angrily, as he stamped downstairs and bulldozed his way into the back room. He didn't stay in there long as the smoke was still choking, although clearing through the back window urged along by a stiff cold breeze from the front door.

"Isn't it obvious what's happened, Father," Joseph snapped back. "A candle's been left smouldering in t'back room on t'tree, and without Ross's swift action at the expense of his own safety, we'd all a gone up in smoke. It's all out and safe now, but t'room's bin gutted. Still, we were about to refurbish in t'new year."

Joss turned and stamped out of the room without a word, knowing full well who hadn't extinguished the errant candle properly, leaving it to his sons to sort things out, one of whom was still finding difficulty breathing.

"Mother, Louisa and Annie, if you'd take yon bairns back to bed," Joseph suggested. "Ross and I will see to things down here. It's all safe now. If you would make sure all bedroom doors are fastened and windows are open a crack, it would ensure any lurking smoke is dispersed quickly."

"You all right, Brother?" he went on once the room had been cleared, although Mary had remained behind to rustle up tea for the young men.

"Aye," Ross replied, coughing less seriously once he felt the hot liquid coursing down his throat. "Be rayt."

"Mary?" Joseph asked turning to her.

"I am that, Master Joseph," she replied, a look of stark fear in her face. "Except that I had decided to sleep in there tonight to relinquish my room for the stayers over, but Missus wouldn't hear of it. I'm really rather glad she insisted."

"He didn't believe a word and would have none of it, Tom," Joseph said as he sat drinking tea with Tom Garside in the Garside farm sitting room.

"As we expected, eh, Joseph?" Tom replied. "Despite all the facts that are staring all on us in the face. I was talking to Harry Smith at Broke's Farm ower Richmond way on, and he says the same. Town folk are almost demanding a bigger choice in farm produce – meat, milk, cheese, poultry, for example.

As individual farmers, we don't have the expertise or finance to be able to offer all of that individually."

"As I said to father t'other day," Joseph agreed, "we must either diversify and merge or go out of business. I'd rather merge wi' thee, Tom Garside, and…"

He paused for a moment, almost stopping breathing as Tom's eldest daughter, Lilly Victoria, entered the room to offer tea and home-made scones. A beautiful and elegant young lady of about Joseph's age, his heart almost stopped beating, he was so captivated by her. Sensing this, she too was taken by this astoundingly good-looking man.

"Tea and scones, Mr McIntyre?" she said demurely, not allowing him to see the slightly quivering hands that set down the tray on the coffee table next to her father. Joseph may not have caught her reaction, but her father noticed how they reacted to each other's presence, not allowing them to see his covert smile.

"Thank you, Miss Garside," Joseph replied hesitantly. "That would be … lovely."

As she turned to go, Joseph's unblinking gaze followed her out of the room, exhaling slowly and quietly as she closed the door behind her.

"And develop our business interests together," Joseph went on, finishing what he had started to say, with a flush growing around his throat and neck.

"I tek it tha's niver met my eldest daughter, Lilly Victoria, Joseph?" Tom asked, suppressing a knowing grin.

"Er," he stammered. "I don't think, er, I have had the … pleasure."

"So, we need to decide pretty soon what we are to do next, perhaps?" Tom continued.

"We do that!" Joseph replied eagerly. "As soon as we might,

even if we don't have mi father's blessing … yet. I'll work on him and get some sort of an agreement from him. Once we've done that, we can draw up plans for reorganisation and reimplementation. Does thy agree with that, Tom?"

"Certainly do, Joseph," Tom agreed, rubbing his hands together gleefully. "Can't wait."

Joseph stood up ready to leave, shaking his host's hand, as the kitchen door opened, and Lilly Victoria entered, throwing a cursory glance at Joseph McIntyre. He froze, watching her, and stopped breathing as she passed through, still gripping Tom's hand. Once the outer door closed behind her, Joseph exhaled slowly, released Tom's hand from his iron grip, and bade farewell.

"Well," Tom said to his wife, once Joseph had left, "I do believe Joseph is tekken by our Lilly Victoria."

"And she with him," his wife, Lilly, said in return.

"Watch this space, eh, lass?" he replied with a satisfied grin. "There'll be more in our merger than farms and farm produce, me thinks."

Heart thumping in the pony and trap, Joseph couldn't get Lilly Victoria's lovely form out of his head. What should his next move be? He had no idea how to talk to or to treat the opposite sex. Should he ask the only person he would trust as to what he ought to do? Yes. He felt sure his mother would know, but how would he broach it with her? The first mention, and she would know what he should do.

Should he ask his mother? Or maybe his brother?

Chapter 8

Ross had always had the deep-down feeling that he hadn't been sired by the brute he called father, convinced there was no way they bore the same make up. He was nothing like the man, physically nor mentally – but then, neither was his brother Joseph. Although *they* spent little time together because of work, they were close. He would do anything for his brother, in the same way that he would have done with his mother and little sister. His father? He wouldn't cross the street to pick him out of the gutter.

If Joss *wasn't* his father, how—?

"Penny for your thoughts, my son?" Nell's voice interrupted his reverie. Every time she saw him deep in thought, she was transported back to his making, to the only time in her life she was truly happy, and then—

"Just daydreaming, really," he replied slowly, a huge yawn escaping his lungs, "and thinking about Father."

"You?" she gasped, aghast at the suggestion. "Thinking about the man you hate more than anyone else in the world? Now, *that's* a turn up!"

"Yeah! Right!" he scoffed. "No, I mean, I was thinking about how two people of the same blood could be so different and still come from the same source."

Careful Nell! The thought ran quickly through her brain that he ought to know, but now perhaps wasn't the time. Maybe some time … soon? Maybe. She had to be careful not to let her boy, her beautiful boy, see that she hesitated, that there was perhaps something he should know about *his* relationship with Joss, and so, his origins.

"Just feeling tired, I suppose," he added. "What with the fire, Christmas and the season where there's not as much to do around the farm. I need to work to keep my mind active."

"Where *is* your father, anyway?" Nell asked, more out of curiosity than need.

"Went into town, *he* said, about an hour or so ago in the pony and trap," Ross replied through another yawn. "Business, he said, but I think we probably know what that means."

"Nanny! Unca Ross!" a little voice swept in from the ajar front door. "Quick!"

Nell and Ross looked at each other as they recognised Poppy's urgent little voice needing their assistance. Ross reached the door before his mother, flinging it wide as he did so. Jonas was almost out on his feet, hanging onto Poppy and Florence for dear life as they reached the portico.

"For goodness' sake!" Nell gasped. "What's happened?"

Ross had relieved them of their burden, scooping the boy into his huge arms and transporting him to the room upstairs he had occupied since before Christmas. Jonas's mother rustled out of the kitchen where she had been helping Mary with another batch of baking, to see her son being carried upstairs quickly.

"What's happened?" she asked, a worried tone to her voice. "Has he hurt himself? What's he been doing?"

"The three of us decided to take Toby for a walk into and through the wood by the top field," Poppy replied slowly. "It was lovely and fresh, and Toby was having such a good time. Anyway, as we turned onto the top path to bring us back to Boulders Wood, somebody leaped out from a group of bushes and took hold of me."

By this time Ross had joined them mid-tale, his eyes fired with the retribution he was about to visit on the unsuspecting attacker.

"It was Maggie Jenkins' brother, John," Poppy explained. "Said he was going to give me some of what I did to his sister. I kicked him on the shin which made him yelp, but he didn't let go; until, that is, Jonas pulled him off and socked him in the jaw. He went down like a ton of silage – spark out. Knock out with one punch. He's my new hero, is my cousin Jonas. But it took it out of him with his being so poorly, and we had to help him back home. We left Maggie Jenkins' brother where he fell, making sure, of course, that he wasn't face down. Is Jonas going to be all right, Unca Ross? He's not going to … die, is he?"

"No, my sweetie," Jonas's mother piped in from the foot of the stairs. "He'll be all right. He's fast asleep now and will be right as rain in a little while. In the meantime, anyone tell me who this 'Maggie Jenkins' is?"

There was a brief silence in the room while Ross explained the course of events, when a chorus of 'oohs' and 'ahs' broke out.

"The nasty girl deserved what she got," Louisa said as she brought another tray of freshly baked hot mince pies and a delicious-looking and smelling Christmas cake. Mary and Nell followed with a huge metal teapot, cups and saucers, and a large mug for Ross.

"Looks like I'm just in time," Joseph's deeply gravelly voice joined them from the front door. "I could just do with some tea and the odd pie and piece of cake."

He shut out the cold behind him and pried off his big boots at the door, making a bee line for the fire and plates of goodies to the side of it.

"Been anywhere interesting, Brother?" Ross said quietly, sitting together at the dining table, as the other adults gossiped, and the children played noisily.

"Aye," he replied, eying a chunk of cake and a piece of cheese big enough to form a door stop. "Just come from Tom Garside's place."

"Isn't that three times in as many days?" Ross asked, a great grin growing. "Something attracting you there? Lilly Victoria, perhaps? Or one of her three sisters, Martha, Charity and Florence, maybe?"

"I know of the first one," Joseph replied, "but I'd no idea she had three sisters."

"Then, Lilly Victoria it is," Ross pronounced, to his brother's embarrassment. "Don't be embarrassed, Joseph. She's a lovely woman."

"How do you know about Tom's family, anyway, little Brother?" Joseph replied quickly.

"Aha!" Ross said, touching the side of his nose with his forefinger. "I make it my business to know, which, at your age, you should do, too. Don't leave the tekking of a wife until tha's too old, Joseph."

They laughed together that easy laugh that close brothers always share, leaning on and supporting each other throughout troubles, trials *and* treasures. Perhaps Joseph ought to confide in his brother, as he seemed to know the whys and wherefores of how to treat females. Perhaps he could wait a while longer and work it out for himself.

"So," Ross persisted, "is it purely about female attraction, or is it something else underlying?"

"Well," Joseph started to explain slowly, looking around to check that no-one else could overhear. The more he explained, the higher up his forehead Ross's eyebrows rose, until they almost became lost in his very thick hairline.

"That's a very brave and clever solution to a knotty problem we are all beginning to experience, oh Brother mine," Ross said, exhaling sharply as he sat back in his chair. "There's nobody I'd rather have links with than Tom Garside. Sound as a sovereign, wi' his head screwed on rayt well. Spoken to father about this yet?"

"Not in so many words," Joseph replied, a grimace betraying his feelings. "We've had words – very heated words I might add – about the way we should move forward, taking into account how the markets are moving for produce like corn, meat and milk."

"His response, I assume, has not been as positive as we need it to be," Ross offered with a knowing inclination of the head.

"Let's say he's not as enthusiastic as he ought to be in the present circumstance," Joseph said with a shrug. "It's a crying shame, because if he doesn't drag himself out of the 1850s when corn was king, we *will* go under. However, I've not finished with him yet. I've warned him that he has to give on this, or I will leave and take on with another competitor – and there are plenty of them around."

"Bit between the teeth, eh, Brother?" Ross whistled.

"Is Jonas going to be all right, Nanny?" Poppy asked. "Only, he didn't seem as well as he should have been."

Nell smiled at the pert maturity her granddaughter was beginning to show. She would hold that thought for a little while until some other pressing question shouldered it out of her mind. This question, however, she had returned to several times since he and his mother, Louisa, had departed back to Richmond a week or two before. She felt a certain degree of ambivalence towards him – liking his company but not his thoughts on females and their place in his circle in general.

From where and how his philosophy on life and his place in it had developed, had surprised his mother to the point of shock, because at no time in his short life to date had he been subjected to such extreme thoughts within the family. Was it a phase he was passing through that had descended upon him from the ether and that he would shed before long, or was it something more sinister that would take over his life? Louisa and her husband Ernest could only hope … and pray.

"Did you like Florence?" Nell asked as she tidied the sitting room.

"I wish she lived around the corner," Poppy replied as she rearranged her doll, Tossy. "We could then play together all the time, and we could go to school together. She has as many friends where she lives as I do here – none," Poppy replied with a profound harrumph.

The snow by now had begun to melt around the farm, and to recede to the foot of the hills beyond the wood. Nell had avowed on many occasions over the last year or two that Januarys were becoming milder and the hard snows of yesteryear less frequent. Ross had put it down to normal shifting weather patterns that came and went over the years in a cycle.

Because it was natural, it was hard to predict with any degree of accuracy.

When not playing with Poppy, Toby spent a goodly part of his day laying by the front door sniffing the cool air creeping under and around its edges, longing to be outside gambolling and running about as if there would be no tomorrow.

"Going out to the stable, Nanny, to feed the new chicks, to take Toby for a little walk, and to see to Tabby's new kittens," Poppy shouted as she unsnecked the huge oak front doors.

"Wrap up Poppy!" Nell shouted back. "It's still a bit parky out yonder, and you might catch your death of cold if you're not careful."

The sun put in the occasional appearance through torn grey clouds, and where it did, spirals of steam rose lazily from annoying puddles blocking the paths around the house and yard. The barn was surprisingly warm, particularly where the tortoiseshell cat Tabby had scooped out her nest to give succour to her five-day old mewling kittens.

"Hello, Poppy," a rough gravelly voice startled her as she stroked the two kittens she had nestled in her arms.

She turned with a start to find Joss's threatening bulk blocking the exit to the stall in which she was sitting cross-legged.

"Grandpa," she gasped. "You startled me. Are we going to keep these beautiful kittens?"

"If you wish, my little one," he replied, as he shuffled closer to her, a deeply malevolent look in his eyes. He reached down to take hold of her wrist, scattering the kittens without thought.

"Grandpa!" she shouted, as she tried to struggle free from his iron grasp. "You're hurting me. What are you doing?"

He drew her resisting and squirming young body to his, fondling her all the while he drew her in. That she was his granddaughter was irrelevant to him. She was new, young flesh with which, according to his warped morality, he had the right to do as he wished. Seigneurial rights were his to dispense as and when he desired.

She tried to wriggle free, finally understanding what he was trying to do.

"Get away from her, you filthy owd bugger!" Nell's voice intervened as she swiped him across the back with the egg basket she had come out to fill.

His surprise at hearing her voice and feeling her wrath, made him lose his grip on Poppy's arm, allowing her to dash behind her Nanny, dress unbuttoned, trembling and weeping.

"Get thee away, wife," he snarled as he inched forward. "She is in my house and is my property to do with as I will."

"Keep away," Nell hissed as she snatched a twin pronged pitchfork from the byre close by and pointed it at him. "If you come a foot closer, I'll stick your disgusting hide with this."

New young flesh almost within his grasp, he lunged at them, tripped over the cat that had shot in fear between his feet, impaling himself as he fell forward on the pitchfork Nell held in front of her. With a last desperately anguished cry he collapsed, hands grasping still, with lifeless eyes glazed and staring.

Both Ross and Joseph who were doing maintenance work close by, dashed into the barn to see what all the commotion was about. Although Nell often wished to be free of the vile beast that had been her husband, it was an undeniable shock to witness his demise – impaled through the heart by a common pitchfork. Joseph advised her to take the distraught and traumatised Poppy into the house, and they would take care of matters here.

"My God!" Ross gasped "T'owd bugger's seen himself off at last. It was onny a matter of time before something like this happened, but not at Mother's hands."

"We need to establish in everyone's mind what obviously happened here," Joseph insisted. "He was rushing about as far as we could tell, tripped over the cat, and fell onto the pitchfork. There must be no mention of Poppy and Mother's involvement at all. It would only complicate matters. This needs to be over and done with as quickly as possible."

"I'll take the pony and trap to the village police station to report the accident," Ross offered. "This will allow the police to do their job, and then we can have an end to the whole sordid affair. Leave him where he is, Joseph, so they can see that everything is above board."

The road to town was a fraught and difficult one, with piles of snow blocking the way, and deep puddles of melted slush warning travellers to proceed at their peril. Ross, however, made it as quickly as conditions would allow.

"I need to report an accidental death, Sergeant," he said as the desk officer lifted his face to the newcomer.

"Who, where, when and how?" Detective Sergeant Shaw, a member of the newly formed Criminal Investigation Department, asked as soon as he had drawn the ledger from its drawer beneath the ledge where Ross was standing.

"It's mi father Joss McIntyre," Ross started to explain. "He was in the barn sorting out the farm cat's kittens when we heard an almighty commotion and yell. When we got inside the barn, we found he had impaled himself on a pitchfork, and was most definitely … dead."

"All right," the sergeant said. "I'll come over as soon as—"

"If you would like, I'll take you over and bring you back, as I have a pony and trap outside," Ross offered.

"That's uncommonly good of you to offer, sir," the sergeant said with a nod. "We are very short of appropriate transportation at the moment. So, that would allow me to come straight away."

"Thank you," Ross said patiently politely. "It won't take us long. I know you are very busy."

Because the snow and slush were clearing rapidly, the journey took them fifteen minutes less than it took Ross to get *to* the police station. Once back at Boulders Wood, the policeman asked to see the scene where he examined the body and, after a few moments of perfunctory questioning about circumstance, timing and who found the body which Nell answered eruditely and succinctly over a cup of strong tea and a plateful of freshly baked farmhouse goodies in front of a roaring log fire, he pronounced the death to have been a terrible accident.

"And don't forget, Fred Shaw, that any time you are in the area, don't forget to call in," Nell said as he and Ross made for the door with a parcel of home baking under his arm. "You will always be welcome and there will always be a hot drink, a roaring fire and some of my home baking for you to try."

"Do you know, Missus," he replied, metaphorically licking his lips again, "that I love home baking, and my wife's a fantastic baker. Unfortunately, we don't get much chance to do it as my £73 a year wage won't often stretch that far,"

"All the more reason for you to call in with your wife to do some baking with Mary and me," Nell answered. "You will always be welcome."

"Have we done the right thing, Ross?" Nell said, a hand covering the grimace on her shocked face. "Shouldn't we have told the truth?"

"But we have told the truth, Mother," he replied earnestly. "Father lunged to attack you after he had tried to molest his *own granddaughter*, for goodness' sake! How gross is that? In his haste to brush you aside in the stable stall to continue his disgusting violation of a ten-year-old child, he stumbled and fell, impaling himself on a pitchfork. Now, whose fault was that?"

"But I was holding the pitchfork to—" she muttered almost unheeding her son's words.

"To defend your granddaughter by warning him off!" Ross insisted. "We needn't – as we all agreed yesterday – mention your involvement in the deed for fear of doing further damage to an already traumatised little girl. The police sergeant was satisfied yesterday that it was an unfortunate and regrettable accident. Does Poppy really need the case to be reopened and re-examined now? Just think of the damage it could do to her after such an in-depth investigation. Best let sleeping dogs lie."

Nell sat on the settee, nodding and staring quietly into the distance, a strong cup of tea to hand that Joseph had just brought for her.

"We now have to arrange for the funeral and for a period of respectful mourning," he advised.

"You needn't think for a moment that I will be wearing that black stiff crape material for a year, along with full black widow's weeds and my face covered by a weeping veil!" Nell insisted. "I'm rid of the foul bugger, and that, after a decent time of a week or two, brings me back to life. A time for rejoicing in the family. *Poppy* needs our attention, not some outdated expensive social expectation."

"You are in charge, Mother," Joseph said in support of her stance. "You will do whatever you think necessary. The only thing we must do is to contact an undertaker cum jobmaster who can not only make a coffin but also arrange for the burial. I have found four in the local Gazette; two in Northallerton – Weatherells and Samuel Dottridge – and two in Richmond, who are Thomas Leeson and Ernest Bragshore. I'll take the trap and visit them all today to see what our next step has to be."

"And what about—?" Nell began slowly.

"The body?" Ross suggested.

"It can stay where it is," Joseph said sternly. "The pitchfork has been removed, and the body laid out in the byre, and covered. It's very cold out there so there'll be no change to it for a good many days.

"In the meantime, the farm has to be managed," Joseph went on after warming his hands around a huge mug of tea. "In that respect, life has to go on as normal."

"Along with seeing to Poppy," Nell added, "I will write to all our extended family to spread the news, and to let them know when the funeral will be. This new-fangled mail will let them know quicker than we can get around."

"How about putting a piece in the local newspapers?" Ross suggested. "The Yorkshire Gazette is the one that the farming community up here uses quite a lot, and then there's the Craven Herald and the Wensleydale Standard. I think also we need to send one of the stable lads with the other pony and trap to the closest funeral people, asking them to come over as a matter of urgency."

"The dreadful thing is that Poppy knew what the filthy bugger was trying to do," Nell went on almost reluctantly. "*That* will take a lot of time to recover from. The horrors of the real world, eh? Now, if you'll excuse me, I have a granddaughter to see to, and a household to run, neither of which will see to itself."

Taking the tea things into the kitchen and leaving Mary in charge, Nell climbed the stairs to give succour to her only granddaughter in *her* hour of need.

Chapter 9

The morning of the funeral dawned clear but very cold, as a major ground frost had descended overnight and laid a thick hoar carpet, raising concerns about travelling in horse-drawn vehicles to the graveyard. At least Nell wouldn't be cold in her thick black crape clothing.

She had felt it would be inappropriate and unnecessary for Poppy to attend the funeral, so she asked Mary to keep her in the house with her; perhaps helping in the kitchen to distract and occupy her mind. The poor girl had been somewhat withdrawn since the event, saying nothing and mooching about, doll attached to her cheek, a distant look in her eyes, and the dog at her heel. It had been only a few days, and it would take even a child longer to recover from such overpowering trauma.

At ten o'clock sharp, so as not to waste the day, everyone had gathered in Boulders Wood front room to await, as the two eight-seater carriages, each drawn by two black Shires, crunched through the frosty gravel to the front door. The body had been collected two days before for preparation, ready for burial, and the hearse, duly loaded, headed the cortege.

Nell had rejected the undertaker's notions on a glass-sided hearse and coaches, sable and crape shawls and ridiculously tall black silk hats as being unnecessarily expensive, over-elaborate and overtly papist, in favour of simple, respectful and non-hypocritical.

Joss's sister, Annie, and brother-in-law, along with their two children, and Joss's brother Fred and his wife were to ride in the first black mourning coach along with Joseph and Ross. The second coach was to carry Nell, her sister, Jessie, and *her* husband, along with their three children, and her elder daughter, Louisa, and her husband. Nell's brother, Frank, was unable to make it because of work commitments.

The younger children – Poppy, Florence and Jonas – were to stay at the farm in Mary's charge, doing something largely useful and enjoyable.

"This is a dreadfully sad time," Fred McIntyre chuntered as he helped his wife into their carriage. "I can't understand how it could have happened."

"None of us can, Uncle Fred," Joseph replied, casting a quick glance at his brother. "One minute he slammed out of the front door, and what seemed like only moments later, the squealing cat and howling hound warned us that something was amiss. As I was first on the scene, imagine my shock at seeing a pitchfork through his chest, keeping him propped up as if her were about to sit down."

"We can only guess that he tripped over the cat's new kittens, overbalanced and impaled himself as he tippled over," Ross added. "It's the last thing we would have wanted to happen, especially after such a wonderful gathering at Christmas."

"And we will be coming back to the house to take some sustenance," Nell said to *her* carriageful. "It's what Joss would have wanted."

They all knew that *that* was *not* what he would have wanted at all! He got on with his own family, to a point, but never had much time for Nell's. He would often slam out of the house if any of them called socially, without so much as by-your-leave, to return only when they had gone. So, there was no love lost on either side. They would never go so far as to say, 'Good riddance!' but it was to become a commonly-held sentiment.

The pair of leading Shires strained to set the hearse moving after a light flick to their ample backsides from the hearse-master's whip, setting the whole cortege in motion. The funeral director, with ribboned black top hat, walked just ahead of the hearse, marking time regally with his ornate mace-topped staff, through the village where most of his work force lived. Nigh on everyone turned out to pay last respects at his passing. Bare headed with heads bowed, they stood until the cortege had passed, many of them no doubt hoping for a new freer, healthier style of management from Joseph, the man they all admired, and everyone respected.

"Are you all right, Poppy?" Florence asked quietly as they sat playing with their dolls in the corner of the living room. The back room was locked, ready for it to be cleaned and refurbished following the fire. This had meant, of course, that Poppy's dog had now to sleep in her room with her, which pleased her no end.

"Not really," Poppy replied, almost in a whisper. "Grandpa's … gone, and—"

"That's life, I'm afraid old girl," a young boy's arrogant and patronising voice interrupted the girls' conversation. "I know it's hard for you emotional girls to accept that you've to get on with it, and not crawl around the house moping and crying endlessly."

"You're such a prig and an idiot, Jonas Pearson," Florence replied sharply. She didn't like him; felt he was rude and too much up himself to be able to mix sociably with real people. "I can't see you *ever* living a normal life with *real* people. What right-thinking person would want to live with a toss pot like you?"

"Oh, I say!" Jonas replied, taken aback more than somewhat. "Bit sharp, don't you think?"

His mother and father, Louisa and Ernest, couldn't for the life of them work out how he had developed either this attitude or manner of expressing his views. They often said that he could only have *inherited* it from his great-great-uncle Albert, whom he had obviously never met, because he had died before Jonas was born. There was a significant debate at the moment surrounding the question of inherited tendencies in society at large, with the for and against factions equally vehement. But such issues played no significant part in ordinary country folks' everyday life.

In a perverse sort of a way, Poppy quite liked Jonas. There was something strangely different but attractive about him – a view that certainly was *not* shared by her close friend, Florence. She had taken an instant dislike to him the moment she clapped eyes on him for the first time at the Christmas celebrations.

Poppy, however, could never forget how he had saved her from the clutches of Maggie Jenkins' brother, John, who was intent on revenge and retribution for what Poppy had done to his sister. One punch, eh? How wonderfully brave was that? No matter what others might think of him, he would always be her hero.

"Are you all right you three?" Ross asked as he breezed back into the sitting room.

"Only Jonas and me, Uncle Ross," Florence replied. "Poppy's upset in her room."

"Hungry you two?" he asked, a look of concern invading his face about Poppy.

"Not so bad, Uncle Ross," Jonas replied, not at all concerned about Poppy's well-being. After all, she was a girl. "We've had a few tit bits from the serving wench in the kitchen. Mary, is it?"

"That 'serving wench', young man, is a close member of *this* family," Nell butted in firmly. "You'd better remember that if you want to be welcomed into this house again."

"Are you all right, Victoria?" she went on, turning towards her sister-in-law, who was by now sitting by the fire. "You look a little … peeky."

"I know it's probably an inappropriate time to mention this," Victoria replied, a flush creeping up her face. "Fred's brother gone, and all that. But …" she gripped her husband's hand and smiled at him – almost in excitement, "I believe I am expecting, after all these years."

Fred's jaw dropped slowly, and a puzzled, confused stare became fixed in his eyes.

"Victoria!" Nell said with a smile of genuine congratulation, as she flung her arms around her. "At last! Wonderful news."

"How long has tha known this?" her husband stammered, at last regaining a modicum of speech. "Tha didn't tell *me*!"

"Not official, Husband," she replied demurely. "At the moment, just a woman's … intuition."

"I know those feelings well," her niece Annie added. "After all this time, you must take care of yourself. Uncle Fred?"

"She will that!" Fred agreed. "And we will have the

wherewithal to mek it happen. *My* news is that I heard yesterday that I have secured a permanent job with t'Stockton-Darlington Railway as a supervisor. Good money as well.

"Good news wi' sad news, eh?" Fred added after a moment or two's silent reflection. "Today of all days."

"New job, you say, Fred?" Ross added as they sat down close to the table where Mary had set out all sorts of food goodies for the funeral guests.

"Aye, lad," his uncle replied, a note of pride in his voice. "Stockton and Darlington Railway, under John Anderson, their resident engineer. I'm to work on a new pier and cliff hoist at Saltburn. T'iron work's coming from t'Ormesby Foundry in Middlesbrough."

"Sounds interesting, and much better than the farm engineering work around here," Joseph added. "Although, *we* will be needing you to work on the new machinery we are getting in here."

"We?" Fred asked, a little puzzled. "I thought your dad was dead against such stuff for Boulders Wood, if you'll pardon the expression."

"He was initially, until I pointed out all the advantages in this new age," Joseph replied confidently. "He did eventually recognise the benefits to the business and to our local work force. We *did* have the occasional head-to-head about what he called 'wasting money', though, I have to admit. A hard man sometimes, your brother."

"I have to say, though," Fred went on, "he wor allus kind to us – ever since mi accident."

"And rightly so," Joseph replied. "It's what all families should be doing. I've got to admire your tenacity, Uncle Fred. Many men would have given up, but it's wonderful that you are moving confidently into a new era."

"This spread is wonderful, Nell," her sister said, through a mouthful of meat pie. "I thought it was Christmas again."

"You've Mary to thank for all of this," Nell replied. "I couldn't have managed a household over the years we've been together without her. Force of circumstance, eh? Things could have been so different."

Mary blushed as she sat down with her cup of tea and nibble. She was glad things had turned out as they had, although she hadn't wished t'Master any harm. She just wished he had been ... different.

"I traipsed all the way to Settle this morning," Joseph said over a late dinner with his family a week after the funeral, to call in on Charlesworths, the solicitors."

"To see about reading Father's will?" Ross ventured.

"And that's just the point," Joseph replied with a hefty sigh. "It can't be read."

"Can't be—?" Nell asked, not sure what he meant.

"Because there isn't one, is there, Brother?" Ross butted in, a knowing frown beginning to grow.

"He didn't leave one," Joseph added. "The solicitor has advised, it seems - several times – but he never got round to it."

"And what does that mean, pray?" Nell asked, completely at a loss as to what was to happen now.

"Well," Joseph replied slowly," the solicitor told me that legally, in all such cases, the deceased's estate would pass to—"

"Oh no!" Nell groaned, expecting the worst.

"The eldest son," Joseph grinned. "And as the eldest son, I have had the papers drawn up, and all you have to do, Mother, is to sign on the dotted line."

He pushed over a large, buff envelope that bore a

grand-looking red wax seal, proving it was legal.

"And what is this?" she gasped, very much in the dark as to its meaning.

"You need to read it some stage, Mother," Joseph explained, smiling hugely. "Basically, it says that you, Nell McIntyre, are now the owner of Boulders Wood Farm and all that is contained therein."

"But…" she stammered, at a loss what to say.

"I've had title deed signed over to you, as the short-lived owner myself," he went on. "Ross and I will continue to manage all its affairs, if that sits well with you, with only one proviso."

"Which is?" she exhaled slowly, with a relieved smile.

"That Ross and I will keep our jobs," Joseph said, a mock-serious look hiding his joy.

They all laughed that easy laugh that all close families share, understanding that, finally, *this* family would be able to function as a family should, and the farm would hopefully grow from strength to strength under Joseph's capable guidance, without hindrance or impediment.

"And when I die?" Nell asked, drawing them back to reality. "What then?"

"You either make a will, or you let inheritance run its course again," Joseph replied without hesitation. "It makes no difference to us. Your choice, Mother, that nobody can gainsay. Mistress McIntyre! Lady of the Manor!"

"And my first request as such would be that you remove all vestiges of that owd bugger's existence as quickly as you are able," she said, with a toss of her hair. "You and Ross together will take all executive decisions concerning the successful running of this farm and all else. I need *only* to be informed. You take all the necessary decisions – including co-operation with our neighbours, Tom and Lilly Garside."

"And how did you work that one out?" Joseph said with a puzzled frown.

"I'm your mother, Joseph, and mothers know everything about their sons," she replied with a self-satisfied nod. "Be forewarned. Tom and Lilly have four lovely daughters, too, but no doubt you know that already."

"How did you work that one out?" he gasped, a seriously shocked look overtaking his eyes, with more than enough underlying embarrassment.

Ross laughed heartily as he left the table to sit in his favourite chair by the fire, which was once his father's most favoured seat. No point in waste!

"No impediment now then, Joseph?" Tom Garside said as his fellow farmer walked through the door into the Garside front room.

"Impediment, Tom?" Joseph replied, a little perplexed by his friend's reference, as his eyes tried not to stray to the beautiful form of Lilly Victoria sitting sewing on the settee with her younger sister, Martha. The older daughter's eyes latched on to Joseph's face several times, to see if he was indeed looking at her, almost as if they were arranging a secret assignation. Each time she did this, all other thoughts fled from her mind.

Tom recognised this instinctively and amused himself trying to draw his friend back to the question at hand.

"Co-operation/amalgamation of our two farms into one business?" Tom suggested again, trying his hardest to secure Joseph's attention for longer than an eyelash flutter from his eldest daughter. "Can I show thee summat, aht side in t'barn? Joseph?"

"Mmm?" the younger man muttered.

"Get thi coyt," Tom suggested with a grin. "I've summat to show thee."

"Now then, Tom," Joseph asked as they approached the hay barn. "What have you got to show me?"

"Nowt, Joseph," the older man replied with a grin. "I just wanted to get thee ahtside so thy concentration might escape from the face of my eldest daughter, for a minute or two."

"I'm sorry, Tom," Joseph apologised, turning a pale shade of pink around the gills. "But—"

"Niver thee mind, Joseph," Tom laughed. "We're having t'same trouble wi' our Lilly Victoria. Why doesn't thy ask her out? You're definitely smitten wi' each other."

"I'd love to, Tom, but I've never asked a lass out before," Joseph replied, vaguely embarrassed at the suggestion. "Don't I need to ask your permission before—?"

"Nay, lad," his companion assured him. "I think I've known thee long enough. Besides, she's old enough to mek up her own mind. She won't be persuaded to do summat as she doesn't want to do. I've had to cope wi' all of that since she wor born."

"So, then, how do I go about … broaching it with … her, like?" Joseph asked after a bit of a pause and a sharp intake of farmyard air into his more than ample lungs.

"Come back ower to t'house in ten minutes, and I'll have cleared t'way for thi, so to speak," Tom replied.

"And then what?" Joseph asked almost in a panic. "Will she—?"

"She'll listen to thee politely, and ifn she likes what thy 'as to say, she'll gi thee a straight answer," Tom assured him. "No shilly shallying abaht, like. T'rest is up to thee. All rayt? Once tha's got that off thi chest. T'next time tha comes round to see me, I'll mek sure she's not in t'room, and then we can get down to business."

"Hello, Lilly Victoria," Joseph said slowly, heart pounding and mouth so dry he could hardly speak or breath. "I'm, er—"

"Joseph McIntyre," she said, aware of how he felt because she was experiencing similar feelings, though she was coping better with them, appearing calm and much more in control. "I know. You've been here before."

"Er, so I have," he muttered, trying to lick his lips. "Your dad, er, Tom—"

"Yes?" she said, trying to move him along. "Has what?"

"Has, erm," he said again hesitantly, "suggested … said … that it would be all right by him to—"

"Yes, I will," she butted in, not wanting to wait.

"Ask you—" he continued. "Sorry, did you say—?"

"Yes, I will walk out with you," she repeated. "It is what you were about to ask, isn't it?"

"It is," he replied. "You must have gathered that I have not—"

"Done this before?" she said, beginning to smile. "Yes. I could tell."

"I don't even know what to do, or where to take you," he admitted to her slowly and in a whisper, relief just around the corner.

"Perhaps a nice little carriage ride into the country might do fine for a first 'walking out'," she suggested. "You might gather that I haven't done this sort of thing before either."

"A ride for half an hour or so allowing us to become better acquainted?" he asked.

"Sounds about right," she agreed.

"Next Saturday, perhaps?" Joseph suggested. "How about a bite to eat in Richmond, too?"

"At twelve noon?" she said, with controlled excitement, but not wanting to show *too* much enthusiasm. "Here?"

"Perfect," he said with a nervous smile as she left the room. Now what had he gone and done? Agreed to walk out – for the first time – with a beautiful young woman. Is that what he truly wanted? To spend time with—? You're damned right it was!

He walked back to his pony and trap, an excited smile plastered across his face, as the sun's rays peeled back the covering cloud, promising a better day. He could smell dampness in the air, but he was confident it wasn't going to rain today. How could it after the news he had just been offered?

What to do next? He would have to see what Saturday might bring. That would either enhance or dash his hopes and aspirations.

The following Monday, Joseph had arranged to visit Tom Garside to wander over some of the possible ways they might implement mutual improvements to the running of both farms. Tom's farm was half the size of Boulders Wood, with fewer mechanical machines that might make his practices easier both to manage and to take to profitability.

"I don't know whether you read the article in the Yorkshire Gazette about trends and traits in farming," Joseph said, as Tom brought a couple of tankards of strong tea to the table in his front room.

"I did that!" Tom replied, eager to carry on what he hoped would be an illuminating conversation. "I've bin saying for long enough that we need to move away from wheat and arable in general and convert to some extent to producing other stuff as what folks in town are asking for."

"And that's one of the bitterest arguments I had wi mi father," Joseph replied vehemently. "He always said that it was *his* farm and *his* decision to stick with wheat when I urged him to diversify into meat and or milk and cheese. I threatened to walk away at one stage – not long before he died – and—"

"I wish thy had, Joseph, to have walked through *my* gate," Tom interrupted. "We could have been up and runnin', ahead o t'game by now."

"Aye, me too, but he relented enough to have me stay," Joseph replied. "It was always going to be too little too late with him. Now we have a God-given chance to move forward reasonably quickly."

"We've had t'best times as far as returns on wheat investment's concerned, ower t'last ten years or thereabouts," Tom added. "We're now down to scrattin' for a livin', and not onny us. T'workers we employ are feelin' t'pinch as well, and we can't let that continue. I'm afearin' that we might start to lose us best workers in t'jobs market this coming spring."

"Research and training and investment are all needed if we're to move forward for our businesses and our families," Joseph said with conviction.

"Talking of which," Tom replied, changing direction a little. "'Ow did tha get on wi' our Lilly Victoria, Saturday last?"

"Does tha know, Tom, it wor a lovely day out," Joseph said, a softer smile replacing the earnest look on his face. "We had a little run out into t'countryside Richmond way on and then stopped for a bit to eat at the King's Head. I've asked her out again, and she's said yes. It can't have been too bad for her, because we talked a lot about all sorts of stuff. Can I ask you a bit of a difficult question?"

"Fire away, Old Man," Tom offered with a shrug.

"Don't know whether this is too impertinent to ask," he started quietly. "Onny, if I were to ask … Lilly Victoria if she would—"

"Yes, Joseph, and that is…?" Tom said with a grin, knowing what was coming next.

"Well, if she might agree to … to be my … to marry me—?" he stammered.

"And?" Tom went along with the question, knowing what both question and answer would be, enjoying watching his embarrassed squirm.

"Would you give your permission?" Joseph blurted out, the words dropping from his mouth en masse.

"It's not me thy 'as to ask, Joseph," Tom replied. "She is her own person, and she will say it as she sees it and feels it – with the utmost honesty. But if it were up to me, I'd say 'Go for it', in a heartbeat."

"Thanks for that, Tom," Joseph said with a grimace. "I'll have to think about what my next moves might be, then."

"Don't leave it *too* long, mind," Tom replied, with an enthusiastically knowing nod, as Joseph headed for the door, with Tom's words weighing heavily on his mind. What would he say when he decided to pop the question, and what would he do if she knocked him back? Hmm.

Poppy had had an enormous shock once she had realised what her Grandpa Joss was trying to do to her, and that had forced her into a period if introspection and withdrawal. She couldn't tell anyone what she had experienced, bearing in mind the way he was stopped. Her nanny had saved her from the worst thing that could have happened to her, but she now viewed the ignominy and shame as a punishment for the bad person she must have been.

Nell had given her as much reassurance as she was able, but because Poppy had become so introverted and unresponsive, she felt she could only go so far. Poppy's Uncle Ross was the only person to whom she responded at all, and he only had a certain window of opportunity each day because of work commitments.

"You realise, of course, my little poppet, that Grandpa was a sick man who didn't like many people," he said to her as they sat side by side on the settee. "Because of that, he upset a good many people, as your Nanny once told you."

"I know, Unca Ross," she replied quietly, her eyes averted from his. "But I feel I *deserved* punishing for being bad."

"Bad?" he said, not really understanding where that was coming from. "How do you make that one out? You've *never* been—"

"Maggie Jenkins?" she pointed out, almost talking into her cardigan. "Do you remember what I did to her? At the time, because of the hurt she had caused me, I wanted her to be … dead, and would have rejoiced if she had been. I can remember the feelings of disappointment when Unca Joseph said she would recover and be none the worse for what I'd done. Doesn't that have to be worthy of punishment?"

He couldn't believe how she had grown in mental maturity but was unable to see beyond a tit-for-tat reasoning for how she was feeling at that point. Yet, she was only just gone ten, and would need time to understand fully. Gentle, loving chats were the way forward, he felt, and he *had* to make the time for that purpose.

The only other way was to bring her close friend, Florence, to the farm as regularly as possible, which was fine for Florence as she didn't go to school yet. There were plans to have her school up and functioning, but for now, there were problems to overcome. He wasn't too sure either whether Poppy might be ready to go back to her school once the world had returned to normal after its Christmas celebrations.

"You seem to be very deep in thought these days, Brother," Ross said as he sat down with a mug of tea.

"Working out the feasibility of merging certain farming functions with our neighbour, Tom Garside," he replied. "Then we can put in place the changes we needed to make when Father was alive."

"Agreed," Ross said. "That's not all, though, is it Joseph?"

"I don't know what you mean," his brother cut in sharply. "There isn't—"

"Lilly Victoria, for example?" Ross interrupted with a knowing smile. "Come on, Joseph. We've always been able to confide and share. 'A problem shared is a problem halved'. Isn't that the saying?"

Joseph closed his notebook slowly and, settling down into his high-backed armchair with his tea, he sighed, a look of almost despair in his eyes.

"You've decided you would like to marry her, haven't you?" Ross said slowly, looking for some sort of reaction from his brother. When he didn't notice any, he continued, "Or is it something more important than marrying the woman you have come to love?"

"Right, as ever, Brother," Joseph sighed deeply, as he prepared to tell all to his younger sibling. "I just don't know how to go about it or what to say. I've had words wi' Tom, but all he said was to ask her sooner rather than later."

"Then why don't you do as he has advised?" Ross suggested urgently. "He's the one who knows – as far as any man *can* know a woman. Take her out to one of your favourite places – I'm sure there must be a good choice of those – and simply take the bull by the horns and ask her. Not that I'm saying, of course, that she looks like a - you know what I mean."

"Common sense tells me you're right," Joseph agreed, hesitating.

"I can detect a 'but' holding up proceedings here," Ross said.

"But," his brother answered with a slight grimace, "I'm afraid what she might say; that she might reject my offer, perhaps."

"Let's be honest, Brother, you do scrub up reasonably well when you have a mind," Ross replied. "What young woman would get a better offer from a young, good-looking farmer, apart from me?"

They both laughed after Joseph had thrown his napkin at his brother's head. Straight talking is what he needed to put him into a right frame of mind.

"Well?" Ross went on. "Decision time, before we break out the silage?"

"I'll think on it," his brother's answer entered the room slowly.

Chapter 10

Mid-summer brought early mornings and late evenings for Boulders Wood. The first dairy cows introduced by Tom and Joseph had been installed in Tom's new milking parlour, along with perfunctory cheese-making equipment. Joseph's beef production had taken a leap forward with a fresh birth of calves from a newly bought herd of highland stock – and a top-class bull.

Joseph himself had been walking out with Lilly Victoria, but since Tom's warning, he hadn't dared to broach the question of marriage with her, despite desperately wanting to. She was patient in the extreme, and didn't want to rush him, although, as far as she was concerned, he was the man she wanted to spend the rest of her life with. She had even decided where they would live and bring up their family.

"Joseph?" Ross asked one bright early-July morning as they were taking a break from working in the fields. "May I ask a question?"

"Of course you may, Brother," he replied, knowing he *would* ask, whether he gave permission or not.

"How is Lilly Victoria these days?" Ross started slowly. He had decided that it was time that his brother, whom he knew was smitten by Tom Garside's beautiful daughter, was thinking of their future together.

"You know," Joseph replied with a shrug, as he gazed into the distance. "Why?"

"Well," Ross said, turning to look his brother squarely in the eyes, "don't you think it's about time you married the girl before she is snapped up by some other lucky chap? I know you both want to be married, but your shilly shallying is putting a bit of a stopper on it. Afraid or summat?"

"You *know* how it is," his brother replied hesitantly. "What with farm and business and all. It's—"

"An excuse, Brother," Ross answered, metaphorically poking him in the ribs. "You know as well as I do that you're putting it off for some ridiculous reason. It's time you stopped being evasive and lying to yourself.

"I tell you what," he went on after a moment or two's quiet. "If you don't get a move on, I will keep on badgering publicly until you do. Understood?"

"I understand perfectly well, Brother," Joseph growled, eyes flashing angrily. "You are interfering in business that is nothing to do with you. I'll ask her – if I want to ask her – in my own good time."

"Then don't come bleating to me if it blows up in your face," Ross snarled as he rounded on Joseph.

With that he stormed out of the byre and away back to his work for the day. What a bloody idiot his brother was, unable to see what was under his nose. If he didn't gather Lilly Victoria to his arms soon, she would become tired of waiting, and some other lucky man would.

Joseph knew that his brother talked sense, but was he

prepared to take the next, frightening step to secure the woman he loved desperately? If he did ask her, what would her answer be? Would she take him on as her husband without question? Would she say, 'Thank you, but no thank you'? Questions he pondered long and hard as he walked across to talk to Tom about their new highland cattle.

His neighbour's yard was quieter than usual. Then, probably the hands were out in the fields at their daily tasks.

"Joseph?" a melodic voice wafted over as he passed the hay barn.

His heart lurched as he recognised that voice instantly. Turning slowly towards the barn, his heart lurched again as he saw the beautiful form of Lilly Victoria silhouetted in the doorway, a large basket of fresh eggs under her right arm resting on her lovely hip.

She waved at him to join her.

"Good morning Lilly Victoria," he said quietly as he neared her. She hadn't moved as, with a welcoming smile, she watched his muscular frame approach her.

"Hello Joseph," she said pleasantly. "On your way to see Father?"

Every time he was in her company, Joseph's mouth became dry and he experienced a sinking feeling in the pit of his stomach. Why couldn't he just—?

"Are you all right, Joseph?" she asked with a concerned look when he hadn't answered her. She took one step towards him that finally tipped him over the edge. Pulling out a small box that had seen better days, from his waistcoat pocket next to his Albert, he took her hand, thrust the box into it and blurted out, "Lilly Victoria, will you do me the honour of—?"

"I will," she replied quickly with a smile, making to open the box.

"Becoming my—?" he continued. "What did you say?"

"I will," she repeated a little more loudly.

"Does that mean—?" he gasped, still unable to believe his luck.

"Yes, Joseph McIntyre, I *will* become your wife," she went on unabashed.

He simply stood, eyes bulging in shock and lips open in a little circle of delight. He pulled her to him as she made to open the box, to find the most astonishingly beautiful engagement ring that drew an excited gasp from her.

"At last!" she sighed.

"What next?" Joseph asked naively. "Shall I organise a preacher to come out next week and—?"

"I don't *think* so, Mr Joseph McIntyre," she replied with a snort. "There's a lot of organising to be set in motion, and that is no work for a … man. The women in the family – me, my mother, your mother, and perhaps my sisters to a lesser degree – will sort everything out."

"And me and your dad?" Joseph butted in finally.

"Just be ready with your wallets," she said with a giggle.

"I love thee, Lilly Victoria," he said quietly as he drew her unprotesting body to his to kiss and to hold tenderly.

"Now, you need to get on with your business with Dad, or we'll never get round to our wedding day," she insisted after a few moments of bliss and heaven.

"At last!" Tom whooped, clapping his hands. "Excellent!"

"I had thought that we might just nip out and—" Joseph said to Tom.

"Does tha want to commit suicide, Lad?" Tom interrupted in shock. "Is tha tired o livin'?"

"No," Joseph stammered in puzzled response. "Why? I just thought—"

"Women do the thinking," Tom explained with a wise and self-satisfied smile. "We do as we are told. It'll be all rayt, don't thee fret. They'll sort it all aht, an' we'll have a few snifters to celebrate."

Joseph's introduction to the workings of the female mind in matters such as this was timely if surprising, because he believed it was a man's world where all decisions were taken by men. However, behind each powerful man there always lurked an even more powerful woman. *Her* power lay in *his* belief that *he* was in charge – a mistake that most men held to their cost.

Joseph, however, didn't care. Whatever the decisions about their impending nuptials Lilly Victoria and her mother made, were all right by him. Because he was smitten, the only thing that mattered was their becoming husband and wife – whenever that was to happen.

"I think we ought to up the ante as far as reorganisation is concerned," Tom said as they sat at the table in the front room.

"How do you mean, Tom?" Joseph replied. Not sure at the reference. "Heard something new?"

"Aye, I have that!" Tom said emphatically. "Tha knows we've done rayt well out o t'price o corn ower t'last few years, persuading a lot o t'farmers further south to expand."

"Something that's persuaded many of 'em to do nothing else, I've heard," Joseph agreed.

"Well, I've heard as t'foreigners are tryin' to flood t'market wi' cheap grain which'll push t'prices down," Tom explained. "There is a growing demand, apparently in towns for more dairy and more meat, both of which we are beginning to cover."

"So, by the end of this year and well into t'next we need to have upped our output of milk and cheese and beef?"

Joseph added.

"Aye," his partner agreed. "I'm looking into sheep as well, and what they might do for us."

"I still think, though, that we need to keep a significant foothold in wheat and barley," Joseph pointed out. "Bottom's not going to fall out of the market overnight. I've also priced up t'costs of sending stuff like dairy and beef to wider markets by these new-fangled railway trains, and, does tha know that it's a hell of a sight cheaper than by track and road?"

"So," Tom started to add, "we'll—"

"Father," a female voice cut gently into the conversation. "Look what I've got."

"And what's this tha's showin' me now, Lilly Victoria?" Tom replied with a chuckle as he inspected the diamond and sapphire ring on her engagement finger. "Has somebody asked thee to marry 'im? Do I know 'im? Has he asked my permission?"

"Since when did anyone need thy permission, Husband?" his wife asked with a smile. "Joseph McIntyre, thank you for wishing to become part of our family, and we look forward to greeting grandchildren."

"Mother!" Lilly Victoria sighed. "We're only just engaged! Give us time."

Cousin Florence didn't understand why Poppy was so upset and not the Poppy she met at their Christmas gathering. She enjoyed visiting to be with her cousin, but not as much as the last time she was there. She had, of course, other things to occupy her mind, because the old village church hall where she lived, had finally by law been turned into a proper school room. They had a proper teacher and proper school stuff like chalking slates and proper wrought iron desks with wooden tops and tip-up seats.

She shared hers with Effie, who lived only a few doors from her in their village. Effie wasn't very good at reading, 'riting or 'rithmetic, but then she did her best. She liked to bring her doll to school in her over-sized school bag, but Florence considered *she* was too old for all that.

Florence didn't have any friends in her village really, and that was one of the reasons why she liked to visit Cousin Poppy as often as she was allowed. It didn't happen very often because it was too far to walk on her own, and her father was often too busy to take her in his small pony and trap. Consequently, Ross would take Poppy to stay the occasional weekend with Florence, and vice versa.

The constant attention he gave to Poppy, made a huge difference to her well-being. He did more things with her than he had been used to doing; took her out on walks with her dog, Toby, both before and after her school sessions, and generally took her out of herself, allowing her to recover gently from the episode with her grandfather.

"Who is that black man over by the trees at the edge of the wood?" Florence said to Poppy on one of their walks with Unca Ross.

"The one with the long black beard and raggy hair?" Poppy replied in a whisper her uncle couldn't have heard as he was a few yards behind them. "I've seen him once or twice before. He gives me the creeps. Don't tell Unca Ross, or he'll be off after him, and then we'll be on our own."

"Let's wait for your uncle to catch up," Florence suggested. "Then we can stay close. I wouldn't walk up here on my own."

"Me neither," Poppy agreed with a shudder.

"I saw that dirty, raggy vagabond again this morning," Ross warned his brother quietly. "He was up in the woods as I was walking with the girls."

"They didn't see him, did they?" Joseph asked, his voice dropping to a whisper as he put his accounts book down on the settee next to him.

"Don't think so," Ross replied. "They were chattering happily together, and the figure was gone in a trice. I wonder if he lives in one of the derelict cottages out towards the Black Lake."

"And where would he get enough food to live on?" Joseph said, giving his full attention to his brother's concerns. "Perhaps we need to have a look one of these days … soon."

"Good idea," Ross agreed, rubbing his hands together. "I don't like the idea of his being around when Poppy's out and about. You never know what anybody like that is capable of."

"It's bad enough that she was accosted by her own grandpa, for God's sake!" Joseph replied, almost turning a deep shade of purple at the thought. "She's taking some time to get over it."

"She'll never get over it," Ross replied seriously. "She'll only learn to control t'feelings and t'thoughts with our help. I think little Florence has been a big help so far.

"If Mother hadn't skewered t'owd dog, I might have done it missen," he went on.

"Hello?" a questioning little voice crept up to them as they paused for a drink of tea. "Could you tell me where I might find Mr Joss McIntyre, please?"

"Who wants him, young lady?" Joseph asked warily.

"My name is Jenny Bott," she replied. "This is my three-year-old son, Toby, who was sired after many matings with the master of this household, Joss McIntyre. I need to speak to him about his responsibilities for *our* son."

"I'm sorry to have to tell you this, Miss Bott, but Mr Joss McIntyre is no more," Joseph replied rather tersely. "He had an unfortunate fatal accident a while ago. So, he won't be able to see anyone until the next life. Good day."

"But…" she stammered, nonplussed, not knowing what to say next. "Dead? But he can't be!"

All her plans for a better life for her and her son hinged around the 'stipend' Joss had been paying, anonymously, for a small cottage in the village. Once the payments had stopped, she made it in her way to find out who her benefactor might be, as she had been threatened with eviction for non-payment of rent. In the meantime, she had had to revert to her old means of earning enough to keep a meagre roof over her son's head.

"We're sorry, but we can't be of any help to you. Good day," Ross butted in.

Jenny Bott stopped moving and talking, keeping a tight hold on her son's hand while she thought what her next move might be. Lost, again, this time by ignorance and … death.

Perhaps not just … yet.

"Did we *have* to come to town, Nanny?" Poppy asked, becoming rather tired by the tedious business Nell was conducting – whatever it was.

"Are you tired or bored, Poppy?" Nell asked, more than a little perplexed at her granddaughter's attitude. Normally, a trip into town would have been received with more than a little excitement and anticipation at what her nanny was going to buy for her. "Look, here's your Uncle Ross now. I'll ask him to take you for a drink and a bun to Mrs Sharples tea shop. Would that be all right for you?"

"I suppose so," Poppy said, her dour and lifeless response not fitting with Poppy's usual good humour.

"Ross?" Nell said as she beckoned her son. "Would you—?"

"Of course I will," he replied. "I heard what you both said, and I'd be delighted to have my beautiful niece buy me a cup of tea and a pastry."

"But I never—!" she protested, but then laughed at the face he pulled, linking his arm and skipping as they headed for a sit down and a drink.

"Children, eh?" she muttered with a smile as she turned around.

"Problem, aren't they," a male voice stopped her in her tracks.

Recognising that voice instantly, she stumbled backwards against a shop wall that prevented her suddenly wobbly legs from pitching her onto the floor.

A strong hand gripped her helpless elbow and, hoisting her back to her feet, led her towards *her* favourite tea shop around the corner from where she had been shopping.

"I'd know that voice anywhere," she said.

"And I'd know that hand anywhere, too," he replied quietly.

"Ross Booth," Nell said with a sigh, looking into his deep green eyes. "I thought you had gone to live in the Antipodes, with your wife, on a sheep farm?"

"I had," he replied. "But marry in haste, as they say. It was a mistake from the start, because she was an alcoholic who drank herself into the grave, and now – I'm back. Do I hear your husband is no longer with us?"

"I never heard from you in all those years," she said, almost blaming him for their time apart, as she ignored his question.

"You do realise what would have happened to both of us had your husband found out, of course?" he countered. "What we had I kept in my heart and my head all those years, wishing I had known you first, and now—. How is my son?"

"Ross is a lovely man, and is just like his father," she said. "He doesn't know, by the way, and I would like it to stay that way – for now at least. May I have your word on that?"

"Need you ask, Nell?" he replied, a look of disappointment leaping into his eyes. "I would never do anything to cause you upset or worry. I just need you to know that I've sold the sheep farm, and I'm … back – permanently."

As soon as he'd thrust his business card into her hand, he turned on his heels and was gone, setting Nell's mind and emotions whirring. Seeing him took her back almost three decades, along with the excitement and fear that clandestine meetings brought. Still, living on the rim of a potential volcano made her feel alive, until her pregnancy warned them that they *had* to step back from the brink. They wanted to be together desperately, but he had no money, and she didn't have the courage to walk out on her bullying boorish brute of a husband. Consequently, the lovers went their separate ways – he to Australia and she back to her humdrum life in the wilds of the North Riding, to bring her beloved son into her unforgiving world.

How she wished they had been together throughout the intervening decades – her onetime true love! The brutalising years she had spent under Joss's heel had gradually ground away almost all of her memories of their time together – almost, but not quite … all. She was reminded every day of the love they had shared, by a son that was the image of his true father.

"Nanny!" an excited child's voice brought her back from her haunting dream. "Nanny, we've had a lovely time, Unca Ross and me. Who was that man I saw you talking to just now?"

"Just someone I used to know many years ago," Nell stammered after a few moments of stunned silence. "I knew him when I was a young girl, just before Grandpa Joss took me for his wife, when I lived with my mother and father. It seems he has been living overseas for quite a long time, as a farmer in a country called Australia, at the other side of the world."

She had to be careful to tell a qualified truth for fear of being caught out by an unexpected lie, and she had always vowed not to lie to her granddaughter.

"It's funny," Poppy said, as she did a twirl of happiness on her toes. " He looked just like Unca Ross."

Chapter 11

Tom Garside was a bluff, straight-talking, no nonsense Yorkshireman that called a spade a spade, never told lies nor romanced, and could be relied upon in any crisis. These were the reasons Joseph liked him. He would gladly have had Tom as his father, although, if he had, he wouldn't be marrying Lilly Victoria in the near future. *That* date hadn't been set up to this point, as the females in the family hadn't finalised plans yet, which, on occasion, caused Joseph to feel rising impatience.

Ross would often ask him why he was delaying needlessly.

"I wonder if we ever *will* be husband and wife," Joseph used to say to his brother's pointed questioning, much to Ross's delight. *He* enjoyed making fun of his impatience, but tried hard not show his amusement, knowing full well it would happen sooner or later.

"Have patience. You won't hurry one woman along, let alone a whole bunch of 'em," was Ross's usual answer.

Joseph tried to rationalise, but it was no good. Wedding planning was most definitely women's work.

He had wondered, too, how Tom had maintained his equilibrium and even his sanity, living in the middle of a family of five females, with no adult male to share time with. In fact, unbeknown to Joseph, this was one of the reasons why Tom liked *him*, because *he* also stood no nonsense in his dealings with his fellows and spoke pragmatic sense.

"And why are you spending so much brass on yon milking parlour and dairy, pray?" Tom's wife said, the morning after Nell's visit to town with Poppy. "Are you thinking of taking in paying guests to consume all the extra milk and cheese you are to produce?"

"Nay, Lass," Tom replied with a sigh. "Hasn't tha bin listening to t'other five times I've already told thee? Well, 'ere it comes again. We're going into production – Joseph and me – because of the high demand for dairy produce, and the much lower demand for corn and barley. In other words, we are amalgamating our strengths – at no extra cost I have to tell thee – to best serve out two farms. Meks sense also, now that Joseph and our Lilly Victoria are to be wed."

"And where's all this going to take place, pray?" she replied as if not really understanding – or even believing – what he was saying.

"Perhaps you haven't noticed, my little chickpea, that yon owd barn where we stored bales of fodder for t'few cows we 'ad, was set up as both recently," he started to explain with a heart-felt sigh. "So, milking and cheese *and* butter making can go on under t'same roof."

"Short of laying out more money we likely can't afford, who will work all these contraptions?" his wife, Lilly, answered with disdain.

"*You* will, my lovely sweet pea," Tom said, a benign smile overlaying his face. "That is, you and our girls. You will, of course, be overseen by Nell McIntyre until you have all learned what to do. She has been doing this sort of stuff for quite some time."

"But we can't—!" Lilly complained, a look of panic in her face.

"If you don't, it could mean selling the farm," he explained seriously. "Then, all we have worked for ower t'last thirty years or so, will be set at nought. It won't take you long, I'm sure, because you and our lasses are t'best there is at working stuff out – you've told me that often enough ower t'last umpteen years. Now's your chance to back up your words."

As far as he was concerned, Tom was destined to live his life surrounded by females and had resigned himself to that inevitability. On his youngest daughter's eleventh birthday, however his wife Lilly had given birth to a boy, whom Tom insisted on calling George, with due deference to the patron saint. Although he was delighted that at last a male had appeared to support him, he vowed that this would be his last offspring.

George was a quiet, unadventurous lad who entered the world on the same day in the same year as next-door neighbour Poppy. Although her birth was difficult and lengthy in the extreme, George arrived quickly and with the minimum of fuss. Poppy was unenviably lively and very inquisitive about everything life presented to her, whereas George was quiet, well-behaved and placid.

During their early years Poppy and George spent time together – when they were allowed. This was quite often dictated by her Grandpa Joss, unless he was out on 'business', allowing Unca Ross to take her for an hour or so to play with George in the Garside's barn.

When Joss finally met his end, their playing times became more regular – unless, that is, Jonas was there. George didn't like Jonas's way of talking to Poppy and Florence, so he made it in his way to be otherwise engaged when there was the slightest hint Jonas might be around. Although it was difficult to arouse anger in him usually, George soon became irritated when the older young lad invaded *his* space, to the point that his mother ushered him into the house out of ire's way.

"But what is it about Cousin Jonas that you don't like?" Poppy asked her friend.

"Don't know really," George's answer came back slowly. "Perhaps it's his foppish way or his rudeness or…" and then he would descend into a sometimes pointed sometimes meandering diatribe about why he didn't like Jonas's company – much to Poppy's amusement. She liked George, but she also liked his nemesis, Jonas.

Summer was a tremendous time for the three friends – Poppy, Florence and George – when they played out in the warmth for most of the daylight hours. They all, of course, had to take into account the new education law on schooling. Generally, Poppy and George had become used to its intrusion into their lives, because they had been going to the same school for some time – they even sat together in class. The cast iron frame that their double-seated desk was attached to, could be unforgiving if you were clumsy enough to bang your knee on it when you were sitting or rising.

Florence's school, however, although partly built and now in use for some children, was still in process of being altered, and so she enjoyed minimal benefit from the sort of education on offer.

Yet, she wasn't best impressed by its intrusion into her weekdays, or even her life in general. Many of the children of her age around the village where she lived, had not yet started school, despite the new Education Act, because their farm-working parents needed the income they generated by working in the fields, for their families to be able to live. Goodness knows how their families would survive when they were obliged by law to go to school.

George and Poppy quite enjoyed their time at school, although there were things they both weren't so keen on. Poppy loved the little blue slate chalk tablets upon which she was able to draw pictures before erasing them with no trace, before doing her sums or practising how to form her letters which she had done at home for as long as she could remember.

George, on the other hand, found difficulty managing those tiny pieces of white chalk well enough to make any coherent signs on *his* slate. He never had been the most dextrous of children. He was quite a bright boy, able to talk his way into or out of difficult situations but explaining his thoughts on slate was a different matter altogether.

Florence was a very smart young lady. She was quiet usually, but deep and intuitive. She had been taught to read from a very early age by her mother, Annie, and so books were to prove to be a life-long passion. Of the three, she was probably the sharpest and smartest. She loved her cousin Poppy because they were so alike, and yet, *so* different.

When Florence stayed with Poppy on weekends at the height of summer, George always asked his dad to bring him to Boulders Wood so they could play together. By this time, Poppy had more or less pushed the incident with Joss to the back of her mind, although there was still the occasional nightmare. It hadn't been so much the death of her grandpa that had hit her – in this age early death was a fact they had to live with – but now she fully understood what he was trying to do to her. This in itself wasn't anything she could share, even with her closest friend, Florence, but she had to try to push it to the back of her mind and to … cope with it.

Indeed, life had become doubly difficult for Poppy. One of those difficulties had been removed, but still there was the question of the startling image of the frighteningly dishevelled tramp that she had seen on at least three occasions in recent history. Her Unca Ross was aware of him and had become more concerned to keep her safe whenever she was outside. Both George and Florence knew nothing about this dangerous-looking figure.

As she had noted a remarkable resemblance to Grandpa Joss, speculation grew that he was a long-lost close relative who had, somehow, been drawn to Boulders Wood by blood. Those who could not bear the thought he might be Joss's kin suggested the vision was nothing but a figment of Poppy's over fertile imagination. Still, Ross had seen him too.

Because of this unquantifiable danger, they had been ordered to stay within the confines of the front of the house. This gave them hedges, trees, a small stretch of water, and plenty of space to run off energy, and to give rein to imaginative play.

The only problem was Poppy's wilfulness that drove her to break most of Ross's guidelines that should safeguard her. She was her mother's daughter – almost a reincarnation of Annie.

The question of Poppy's father still remained unanswered – a mystery that may well remain so for the rest of eternity. Yet, Ross thought that his mother *must* have some knowledge of shady family history; most families had the odd hiding skeleton, or so it would seem. Would she know, or more pertinent, would she be prepared to share?

―⁓―

School for Poppy gradually became an imposition. Her question to her nanny was constant.

"Why do I have to go, Nanny?" she would say at the beginning of most days. "I can do already all the things the teachers want me to do, and so I don't learn anything new. You have taught me how to do sums and how to write and read already, and I do the last two all the time at home."

"You *have* to go every day," her nanny would explain. "The authorities say so, my lovely, and we can't disobey them now, can we."

"But I didn't have to go when Grandpa Joss … died," Poppy insisted, the first Monday in June. "Did I?"

"That was a special day, poppet," Nell replied, more than a little taken aback. This was the first time since his burial that Poppy had mentioned his name.

"I think I know what Grandpa Joss was trying to do," Poppy said slowly, a tear beginning to well in her eye corners as her lips started to quiver. "But … why? Why me?"

"That is a very hard question to answer," Nell replied guardedly, almost at a loss as to how to answer her searching question.

"Had I done something wrong, Nanny?" Poppy said as Nell pulled her unprotesting body to her bosom. "Was he … ill?"

"He'd been ill for quite some time, truth be known," Nell started slowly, searching for the right words that the bairn could understand. "Do you remember some time ago when I explained how and why I married him?"

"Yes, Nanny Nell," Poppy replied, a smile growing. "You

said that you couldn't afford not to, in a nutshell."

"That's a very good way of putting it, my poppet," Nell said, laughing at her turn of phrase. My, hadn't she grown up in those few short years!

"Grandpa Joss always preferred younger girls around him," Nell explained carefully. "He felt it kept him younger, and that was always considered to be his illness."

"Did he do what he did to me, then, because I was getting too old?" Poppy asked, her voice almost dropping to a heavy whisper.

"No, my lovely," her nanny replied seriously. "You were just the right age – for him. But it wasn't *right* at all."

"I know, then, why he left me alone when I clattered Maggie Jenkins with my doll," Poppy said, the light of innocence guttering in her eyes.

"Is it time, Nanny, for a cup of tea and a buttered scone, please?" Nell's granddaughter asked, dropping out of their serious conversation.

"That sounds just about right," Ross's deep voice startled her as he closed the front door quietly behind him. "Shall *I* make the tea, Mother?"

"No, my son," Nell replied as she headed for the kitchen. "I'll—"

"No need, Missus," Mary's voice stopped her in her tracks, as *she* backed out of the kitchen bearing a laden tray. "I thought you might be ready."

"Can you make that one more please, then, Mary?" he asked as he hung up his outer coat.

"Already done, Master Ross," Mary replied quickly with a smile.

"I know that, Our Mary, but the other one has to be for you," he bantered. "Please join us. You have always been as much part of this family as any of us."

"I don't—" she stammered, looking nervously over at Nell.

"You know how I feel about you, Mary," Nell began. "We've been here together from the start, and we've both been through the same experiences from day one. Nobody deserves to sit here with us as part of the family more than you."

"George?" Poppy asked her friend as he was skimming flattish pebbles across the pond towards the side of the house and well below the forest eaves.

"I don't know, Poppy," he replied, almost dismissively.

"I haven't asked you anything yet!" she protested.

"I know that, but you usually ask such difficult questions that I never know the answers to," he sighed.

"I wasn't going to ask you one of *those* sorts of questions," she laughed. "What I was going to ask was, do you see that figure almost at the edge of the forest's tree line? By the track leading down to the house?"

"I saw him slope out of the forest about a quarter of an hour ago," he replied. "He looks like a tramp, whatever one of those is. Creepy."

"He seems to be looking over this way," Poppy said, moving closer to her friend, "and—"

"I've seen him too," a new, deeper voice joined the conversation. "That is the reason why you need to stay close to the house. We don't know who he is – and now, he's gone."

"Uncle Ross!" Poppy gasped. "You startled me!"

"Just wanted to let you know that it's time to eat," he said, putting his arms around both children. "Coming George? Mary's done a lovely spread. Uncle Joseph's going over to see your dad, so he could tell him you're with us."

"Love to, Mr McIntyre," George answered, a big smile licking his lips. He knew of the legendary spreads Mary produced, and, as he loved his vittles, he thought it would be rude to refuse.

Two sunken unblinking eyes watched them turn into the house, through a dirty, matted and unkempt mass of facial and cranial hair, with a burning unnatural desire that needed to be quenched. Once the front door had clicked shut, he turned and melted into the forest to await an opportunity that he knew would present itself sooner or later. He had waited this long since the last time he had pounced, but he would have to be very careful this time bearing in mind what had happened to the master of *that* household.

"We wouldn't wish to be skewered by a pitchfork, would we?" he muttered to himself gruffly. Then his dark and grizzly form was swallowed by the threatening forest as the sun dipped slowly behind the trees, casting its crushing cloak over all.

Chapter 12

"Father's death really was a turning point for you, wasn't it Mother?" Ross said quietly as mother and son sat together in front of the living room fire; she a cup of tea to hand and he a small tumbler of malt whisky. "It seems like the weight of eternity was lifted from your shoulders with his passing."

"I can't say I wouldn't have preferred to become married to someone I loved and who loved me in return," she replied, comfortable in his company. "I have to say that I am glad to be free from the shackles that being married to him fitted me with. Yet, I wasn't *glad* to see him die, particularly in the way he did."

"I never loved him as a son *should* love his father," Ross went on. "He never courted emotion and close feelings from anybody, I would venture. It never seemed to me either that he treated me like his son because—"

"You weren't *his* son, Ross," Nell said quietly as she gazed into the fire. "You bore neither his looks nor his temperament."

Ross sat next to her quietly watching the flames playing up the fire back as he sipped his whisky, quietly accepting the bombshell that she had just dropped in his lap.

"Why does that not shock me and fill me with surprise?" he said calmly quietly.

"Probably because, deep inside, you … knew?" she replied, taking hold of his hand gently. He let go and, putting his arm around her shoulder, drew her head to his chest, lovingly kissing the top of her head.

"It doesn't really matter, Mother, because the only person I needed to have near me was you," he said. "I knew deep inside that I wasn't of Joss McIntyre's blood, and I knew that one day we would be rid of that abomination that blighted our life for such a long time.

"Tell me about him, please," Ross asked after a moment or two's pause. "Tell me about my real father, and why he's not here now."

Nell sat for a little while in silence, watching the red and yellow tongues fighting their way around the fire grate in their eager quest for liberation.

"You know of my early life as your father's 'wife', and what a torture he put me through," she started slowly. "I already had Joseph and Jamie, who were the lights of my otherwise dire existence. Joss was a hard taskmaster and a very demanding husband which I had to accept; that is until I found out about his many dalliances with much younger females."

"That must have been hard to take, you poor thing," he replied, stroking her hair.

"It was surprisingly liberating, actually," she explained with a relieved sigh. "He began to leave me alone more often, which was a blessing.

"Then, on a visit to one of our outlying villages, I met your real father. He was tall and handsome, with sandy hair, and the sunlight danced in his piercingly green eyes. As time went on, we talked about running away together, and what we would do as a couple. I fell pregnant and he urged me to leave Joss who was too busy with his floosies to notice. I couldn't leave Joseph and Jamie, who were only little, and he had no money for us to live by. So, I decided to break off our relationship and return to Joss. The baby I brought into the world – you – he thought was his, and so my humdrum life ground on. The one light amidst the darkness? I had you to remind me of the love we shared."

"What happened to my father?" he asked, now searching her eyes keenly. "Does he live around here still?"

"Poor man!" Nell sighed. "He couldn't stand to see me regularly having *his* child brought up by another man, so he sailed to Australia two weeks later."

"Still alive in … Australia?" Ross asked tentatively. "But then you wouldn't know, would—"

"He is still alive," she answered, deliberately slowly. "And he is back. He lives in Richmond."

"How do you know that, pray, if you haven't—?" he scoffed.

"Do you remember our going into town the other week with Poppy?" Nell explained. "She saw me talking to a man whom I said was an old friend. Do you remember?"

"And?" he asked, a puzzled look playing around his eyes.

"That was your father," she murmured, almost apologetically. "His name is … Ross. Ross Booth. Ever since that day, his face hasn't left my mind."

They sat for a while; mother and son, now joined by another, more urgent bond.

"I think I need to meet this Ross Booth," her son muttered, almost to himself. "Finally, either to give me purpose or to ensure closure."

"Are you telling me that we two share a common purpose?"

Nell said as she turned to face her son. "To find the man that gave me you, my beautiful little boy?"

"I am that, Mother!" he replied more firmly." After all, he is the father I never had, and I need to place myself into some sort of a context before I embrace *my* future and spread *my* seed."

"You haven't anyone in mind, have you?" she said, not sure whether that might be some sort of a hint.

"I might," he added with a tantalising chortle, "or perhaps I might ... not."

"I'll make us a cup of tea," she offered as she got to her feet slowly. She had begun to develop signs of arthritis in her joints that stopped her from leaping into action at any time.

"Thank you, Mother," Joseph's deeply resonant voice joined them quickly in front of the gloriously glowing fire. "Parky out yonder."

"How are things going with – you know – wedding arrangements?" Ross asked, with more than a tone of mischief in his voice. "Will it be any time soon; maybe even before the turn of the century?"

"Don't even go there, Brother!" Joseph answered, shaking his head slowly. "I have been assured by both Lilly Victoria and her mother that the arrangements will have been made ... soon."

"So," Ross chortled, "are we to expect an announcement imminently *soon*? Or as *soon* as *they* decide which—?"

"Could be next year," Joseph sighed. "Or even the next decade!

"I have to tell you though, that you have an admirer," he went on conspiratorially quietly looking over both shoulders to make sure no-one else was eaves-dropping.

"Go on with you!" Ross scoffed, a pale pink suffusing his

throat and cheeks. "Who could possibly admire a big lump like me?"

"Hey, don't run yourself down," Joseph interrupted, pleased not to have the glaring spotlight shining in his eyes for a change. "Martha, Lilly Victoria's younger sister, is a beautiful young lady of twenty-five, and in her eyes, so Lilly Victoria tells me, you can do no wrong. Perhaps time that you were thinking of taking a wife, eh?"

"It shouldn't be too long now," Nell said as she put the tray on the occasional table by the chimney breast.

"What won't, Mother?" Ross asked, puzzled by her announcement.

"Your brother's wedding, of course," she replied with a smile. "All the notifications and announcements have been arranged, everyone that *is* anyone knows about it, and the pastor at St Bede's Church will be asking to see you soon."

"Are you sure about this?" Nell said quietly to her son as they sat at the window table in Richmond's Cornucopia Tea Rooms. "I mean—"

"Never surer, Mother," Ross replied, a resolute smile on his face. "He's my natural father, the one person I've never had in my life – until now, hopefully."

"Hello, Nell," a deep voice wrapped around them. "And you must be Ross."

Nell turned sharply as her son stood up, to be met by a large man with a ruddy complexion and sandy hair, little shorter than Ross himself.

"Hello … Father," Ross replied shaking his hand warmly. "Long time, no see."

They all laughed heartily in what seemed like was going

to be a comfortable meeting. Nell would never have believed that she would now be sitting in the company of two men whom she loved for different reasons, and who she had been convinced would never meet each other. And now—.

"Of course, it was a dreadful blow to me not to be with the woman I loved, who was carrying my child," Ross Booth explained once their conversation had focused on joint personal matters. "But I had to understand that I wouldn't have been able to provide for them. Consequently, I had to accept the inevitable. Australia seemed the only option."

"But why Australia?" Ross asked. "You weren't a criminal … were you?"

His father laughed at the thought and said, "No, but I met plenty of people that were. My journey by ship took four weeks, and I ended up at a small sheep farm in a little town called Ballarat. I didn't sheep farm for long, not because it was hard work, but in the early 1850s gold was discovered in the alluvial deposits surrounding the area. I moved in to prospect and that was where I made my fortune. Now, here I am with not an inconsiderable amount of money in my bank. Unfortunately, however, it's too late for me to use my wealth for my son's benefit."

"Did you ever marry and have other children?" Ross asked, intrigued with his story.

"I did marry, but unbeknown to me, she was an alcoholic," he replied, a sadness descending to his face. "She died from alcohol poisoning ten years after we were wed. Because of the drink, we were unable to have children, unfortunately. Consequently, my son, you alone will inherit my estate."

"If you are looking to invest, you need to talk to my brother, Joseph," Ross suggested. "It all depends, I suppose, on how much you have spare."

"Ross!" Nell gasped at his presumptuousness. "You can't say that!"

"Why not, Nell?" Ross Booth asked. "I have more money than I know what to do with. I would welcome the opportunity to invest in a worthwhile project. Do you know of one?"

"Mother now owns the large farm we work," Ross went on eagerly. "As the bottom has all but fallen out of the grain market that provides our staple income, because of foreign imports, my older brother, Joseph, has entered into a partnership with a smaller neighbour to diversify. But, you would need to talk to him."

"Come around to our farm at the weekend, and then you can talk to him and his soon-to-be wife," Nell suggested, almost reluctantly.

"Wonderful!" he enthused, standing up to leave. "I'll do that with pleasure. Unfortunately, as I've several bits of business to attend to hereabouts, I must take my leave. Thank you for inviting me. It's been the realisation of a long-held dream – to meet my son finally, and, of course, to see you again, Nell."

He kissed Nell on the cheek and shook Ross's hand warmly before heading for the tea shop door. One final wave, and he was gone.

"Well, what a to-do," Nell sighed. "Ross?"

"Nice chap who still holds a candle for you, Mother," he replied.

"Get away!" she said with a wave of the hand, a pink flush suffusing her cheeks. "How can you say that? You don't—"

"Trust me, Mamma," Ross assured her. "Anyway, a proper father at last ... hopefully?"

Sleep, that deft night-time ambusher, was elusive for Ross

senior that night. He was shocked how his emotions had meted out a significant kicking, when he had expected to treat the day's meeting pragmatically. He hadn't realised how deeply Ross and Nell were embedded in his subconscious, and how he had shut away for all those years the feelings that had just resurfaced.

He didn't even know that his offspring had survived the birth let alone what it would be like growing up. Throughout his first years away his thoughts had been consumed with guilt that he had walked away, and with emotion that he would play no further part in their lives. And now…

Nell, too, found it difficult to sleep. She had often been used to waking several times each night, until, that is, Joss had met his end. *That* night she slept throughout, without waking, relieved at being able to lead an ordinary, normal life. With Ross strolling back into her life, her emotions had swamped her, taking her back to relive those dreadful times as the love of her life was forced to walk away.

Pragmatic and practical to the last, she had consigned those upsetting thoughts to the inner recesses of her mind, to be drawn only in times of rest and peace. Unfortunately, they were precious few with Joss as her master. Late to bed and early to rise, he was a creature of habit, which affected her considerably both physically and mentally. That is, until later in life – and after Joss's death.

What was he to do? What was *she* to do? Ross Booth would marry her like a shot, but she was wary. She had been bitten rather badly the first time. Would she be prepared to risk that again? Her problem was that although she loved him when her Ross had been conceived, *that* was almost three decades ago. She would need time to get to know him again, because next time, barring ill health and accidents, she would want it to be for life.

She couldn't do with unresolvable thoughts churning around in her head, and even though the clock hadn't reached three yet, she was up, wrapped snugly against the chill. She had gone into the sitting room to waft the fire's embers back to life and to make—

"Cup of tea, Mother?" Ross's voice joined her from the kitchen doorway. "Couldn't sleep either?"

"Memories wouldn't let me, my son," she replied, a rueful smile heralding her disappointment. "You?"

"I couldn't believe how much I am like my father," he said sipping his tea.

"Physically, yes, but temperamentally?" she agreed. "I wouldn't like to guess."

"Cards on table time, eh, Mother?" Ross advised boldly. "Are you going to see more of him?"

"I don't know ... yet," she answered. As she sipped her tea, a faraway look drifted into her face. So many years, so little time to recapture her lost dreams.

"Be ever mindful that our life on this earth isn't unending," her son reminded her. "If you have any dreams left after your life with Joss, you owe it to yourself at least to explore them. I'm sure Ross Booth will feel the same whatever you decide. He cares about you. I could see it in his eyes, and in how he looked at you."

"So, the wedding has been arranged?" Joseph asked his fiancée. "Is there anything I need to know?"

"Of course there is," Lilly Victoria assured him with a proud smile. "You're the groom, and the groom has the most important part to play of all – except for the bride, that is."

"Your dad warned me that the only people playing any part in the organising and arranging would be you, your mother and your sisters," he said, pursing his lips.

"He was having you on," she laughed. "He's a fine joker is my father. We *have* made all the arrangements, but it's now up to you to see the pastor once I have given you the dates. According to Mother, as a couple we need to speak to him a time or two to put the service into order."

"Oh," Joseph replied with a mischievous grin. " I thought I was to be led into the ceremony blindfolded."

She laughed heartily at the image he had created in her mind. She kissed him passionately and, looking into his eyes, she murmured, "I love you Joseph McIntyre. Not long to go now until our first night together."

A concerned look crossed his face, reinforcing his thoughts and feelings about what would be expected of him. He had never slept with a woman before let alone a beautiful woman like Lilly Victoria. He was pretty sure *she* had never slept with another man either. They were both moral people, believing that sex wasn't just a function to be shared between consenting adults, but between consenting adults who were married – to each other. This was a lesson both had learned growing up in a loving family. The question had spent a lot of time teasing his mind recently – whether or not he would know what to do when the moment was upon him.

"Don't worry," she said, a gentle smile trying to reassure him. "We'll work something out."

Although concerned about proceedings surrounding his impending nuptials, that was the least of his worries. It the present climate in the farming world, where single produce grain farms were finding it increasingly difficult to function properly, Joseph and his partner, Tom Garside, had made their best decisions in the current market. However, even they were feeling the economic pinch.

"This bloody Tory government, unfortunately, wants nobody to have any say in how trades are done and prices are stacked," Tom grumbled often. "That is, unless tha's got so much money tha doesn't need any of that."

"Aye," Joseph would reply, "but times are changing, my friend. Once votes are allowed to us ordinary folk under the new law amendments, power for change might shift to where it's due."

"We're niver abaht to return to t'corn laws of t'early part of this century, but there must be some leeway for us to survive?" Tom argued scratching his head.

"How many markets must there be across t'North Riding, then?" Joseph asked rhetorically, throwing a new thought into the ring.

"'Ow does tha mean?" Tom said, not sure where his friend's line of reasoning was taking him.

"Well, if we were to visit even fifty per cent of them weekly, to sell our meat, chickens, milk and butter, we would make enough to tide us over until business picks up," Joseph answered him, with a raise of his eyebrows.

"I think tha's got summat there!" Tom went on, excited at the thought. "We wouldn't have to up t'production of t'milk and butter and cheese, and we'd still have enough to sell in bulk to our present outlets."

"You could get your lasses involved, and I'll try to get Poppy interested," Joseph went on, building up an excited head of steam. "She needs something to stop her getting bored at weekends."

"Dad!" Tom's youngest daughter shouted almost hysterically. "Dad! Come quickly! It's urgent!"

"What is it, Lass?" Tom urged as he and Joseph rushed to their aid. "Has somebody died?"

As they reached the milking parlour, they found Tom's wife pacing about in something of a state, sighing and wringing her hands alarmingly.

"What is it, my lovely?" Tom asked again, a little more sharply this time. "What's happened?"

"You're going to have to do something about these ruffians, Father," his wife argued, in a state. "It just won't do!"

"Seen a ghost or something?" Tom sighed, realising he wasn't about to get much out of his wife.

"We were in the back of the milking parlour, when something told me to look around," Martha, Tom's second daughter explained. "That's when I saw this ... this wild face at the little window – staring red eyes, huge black beard and long unkempt hair, dirty face – close up against the glass, just watching. When he saw me looking at him, he vanished; nowhere to be seen even when we chased out of the side door. Who is he, Dad?"

"Do you have any idea what that ... thing was, Joseph?" Tom asked, puzzled as to what and why.

"He's been seen two or three times around Boulders Wood recently," his friend replied slowly. "I haven't seen him myself, but Ross, here, has."

"Poppy brought it to our notice a while ago, too," Ross added, grim faced. "I think for safety's sake we ought to investigate more closely, instead of passing it off. He might be dangerous, and as such, that puts all our folks at risk. It's beginning to seem to me like a bit of a coincidence that he appears to live in or about the woods. What about our Annie...?"

"We'll explore that later," Joseph replied, making surreptitious signs to his brother that enough had been said already.

Chapter 13

"I just wanted to know what *you* thought, Missus," Mary asked over a cup of tea with Nell in the kitchen. "Should I accept, or shouldn't I? If you say no, I'll—"

"Of course, you should do it, Mary!" Nell replied with gusto. "How long have we known each other? And how many times have we either had words or a disagreement?"

"Well – none," Mary said slowly, not sure what she was trying to say.

"Then my advice to you is to take up the offer – from Gough's of Richmond you say?" Nell went on, smiling broadly. "Your baking is second to none in this area, and they would be very lucky to have you baking for them. Your apple pies are legendary, after all."

"I'll supply them – all at my own expense of course – with a few at a time to see how they go," Mary offered. "In my own time, you understand."

"And did this ... offer just come out of the blue because of your reputation?" Nell puzzled, unsure how this state of affairs had arisen.

"I knew they were having problems replacing Mrs Grimshaw when she left to look after her husband, Alf, who had been crippled by a runaway horse a little while ago," Mary explained. "So I offered to step in – not literally, you understand – by taking them one or two pies to fill in, so to speak."

"Well?" Nell asked when her friend had stopped talking. "Come on! How did they go down?"

"They disappeared literally in minutes, with praise from everyone," Mary replied, showing her embarrassment at praising herself.

"Excellent," Nell said, drawing her friend to her – something she had always wanted to do but never had either the incentive or the space to do it. "*That* has to be developed, and I know the very man to become involved."

"Man? Involved?" Mary puzzled "But how, and more to the point, why?"

"Leave it to me, Mary," Nell advised. "You need someone with money and the will to support you to ensure you are able to deliver what the shop needs."

"Am I to ... leave Boulders Wood then?" she replied, a horrified frightened look invading her usually placid and sure face.

"No fear!" Nell assured her. "This is your home for as long as you need and want it. Because we no longer have a demanding and overbearing master to gainsay everything we want to do, *we* can decide on how long you need to prepare to produce. One? Two? Three days? More?"

"No, Missus," Mary said, having regained her composure at last. "I only need a day to bake and deliver. But how will I be able to afford it? My wage—"

"Will be exactly the same as it is now," Nell assured her again. "You will use some of the money you earn from supplying the shop, to buy ingredients for the next, or you might use ours and replace it at the end of the month. Whatever suits you best."

"I am so grateful, Missus, for—" Mary began.

"Just think of everything *you've* done while you've been here, my girl!" Nell reminded her. "Whatever I can do to help, I will do."

Ross had noticed wispy swirls of smoke lazily spiralling upwards from the middle of the forest above the lake, on several occasions when he had been working the water's edge. It appeared only during winter months, and never more than once or twice. His biggest concern was that some careless fool would let this campfire turn into a conflagration, destroying *their* forest that harboured many native species – red squirrel, pine marten, tawny owl, crayfish.

Although he knew these woods well, he had never encountered the remains of campfires, burned undergrowth or clearings where ragamuffins or ne'er-do-wells might encamp. There were no derelict buildings to his knowledge either that such a person might call 'home'. Then he had caught a fleeting glimpse of that figure before Christmas as he and Poppy collected foliage for the festivities – a gaunt black figure whose features he couldn't make out because of the distance.

Poppy's description of its face faded slowly into mind – with its grizzled looks, dirty face and matted black hair and beard. Where could he be from? Did he have any association with anyone in the area – family, friends, acquaintances, farm workers? These were nebulous questions for which there were no answers, unless he was able to talk to him face to face.

Him? Surely it *was* a male. No female would be able to

survive living in the wild. And then there was the facial hair. Surely not!

One of these days he would track him down … one of these days … but not today.

"Far away, my soon to be brother-in-law?" Lilly Victoria said quietly, not wishing to intrude into his thoughts as she placed his large mug of tea before him in her parents' front room.

"Thank you, Lilly Victoria," Ross answered. "I'm just waiting for your dad. One or two things I need to run by him."

A slight smile flickered across her face because she had a slight inkling about his main reason for calling – and it wasn't anything to do with farming. She left him to drink his tea and to wait for her father, who was attending to some knotty problem in the pig pen out back.

"Who'd be a farmer, or a father for that matter, eh?" Tom Garside said, shutting the front door with a clatter. "Good to si thi, Ross, lad. What can I do thee for?"

"Well, a couple of things, really," Ross said with a slightly embarrassed cough, as they both settled to armchairs by the fire.

"Let's get t'personal stuff out o t'way first, shall we?" Tom jumped in, with more than an idea of why he was here. "And my answer is a resounding 'yes'."

"How did thy—?" Ross asked, a perplexed look invading his face.

"I'm a father," Tom replied with a cackle, "and fathers know about such stuff. It's bin obvious for some time that tha's had a liking for mi second daughter, Martha, and she allus goes red and a bit quiet whenever tha's in t'room. Two and two."

"Mekking fower, eh, Tom, you owd bugger," Ross laughed heartily. "So, do I have thi blessing to ask her if she would do me the honour of … walking out with me?"

"Of course tha does," Tom said, leaping to his feet to wring the lad's hand. One more off his list – only two left to go. Taking all amusement apart, he couldn't have a better prospective husband for his lass if he'd made the choice himself. "A father couldn't have had two better prospective sons-in-law than thee and thi brother, Joseph."

"The second thing I wanted to talk to you about concerns sheep, Tom," Ross said moving on to the business of the day. "I've had it on good authority that, asides t'obvious meat implications, sheep's wool is making a move."

"'Ow does tha mean?" Tom asked, lifting his flat cap to scratch his sparsely covered scalp.

"It's becoming more popular to make into clothing and such like," Ross explained. "T'West Riding wool trade is growing, and factories are sprouting like mushrooms, apparently, I was just thinking as it might be a good idea to increase our flocks to meet these increasing markets."

"Good idea," Tom replied enthusiastically. "'As tha spoken to Joseph about it?"

"It was him as suggested I speak to you," Ross said, a satisfied smile growing as he settled back into his chair.

"Can I let thee look into it further, then?" Tom suggested. "Then we can get summat done about it. Got to go I'm afraid, Ross," he continued, getting to his feet. "Got Joe Cartwright coming to talk to me about yon underperforming bull."

As Ross finished his tea and Tom had departed, Martha entered the room quietly, almost as if a bell in the kitchen had prompted her.

He jumped to his feet, knocking over his mug, which, fortunately he had drained the moment before. This brought a grin to her face and redness to his cheeks. She walked across to say hello, as her two younger sisters followed from the kitchen, huddling together and giggling quietly behind their hands, while casting glances as Ross and their sister spoke to each other nervously.

Throughout the time since her grandpa's death, the realisation that he had died because of her had struck a note in Poppy's head, despite all her nanny's best efforts to instil into her that the blame was not hers, she had become unable to reconcile the facts that she was still alive and he ... wasn't.

"Your grandpa wasn't a nice man, Poppy," Nell had said to her granddaughter quietly. "Lots of people disliked him for what he did to them and for what he stood for. You've got to remember that *he* attacked *you*, and I shudder to think what he would have done had I not been there."

Poppy remained quiet and introspective, her face very downcast and unhappy. She didn't understand and hadn't done so since the happening.

"Nanny?" she asked

"Yes, lovely?" Nell replied.

"Will I be punished?" Poppy said slowly, a very confused air about her.

"For what, for goodness' sake?" Nell assured her, slipping her arm around her slumped shoulders. "No, of course not. We do, however, need to get you back to your happy and joyful self. Do you think we might be able to do that?"

"I think so, Nanny," Poppy replied hesitantly. "But I still can't get Grandpa's face out of my head. Will I ever?"

"You will if you put your mind to it, love," Nell explained. "You have to remember that you are young, and you *will* get over it, but you have to decide that *that* is what you want to do."

They sat down at the kitchen table together with a cup of tea and a sandwich; something they had not done for some time. Nell had begun to worry about the child; about her not eating well enough to keep body and soul together, and about the depressions that had settled on her daily. She needed to be taken out of herself, to be provided with a distraction, another interest that she could immerse herself in.

"Hello, you two," Ross's voice introduced his entry. "My, those sandwiches look good. Going to share yours with me, Poppy."

"Decidedly not, Unca Ross," Poppy replied without looking up, her second bite now on its way down to her stomach. "You'll have to make your own, I'm afraid."

Nell grinned, relieved that she has started to answer back, and recognised that the Poppy of old was perhaps beginning to re-emerge more regularly.

"Monday today, so what's on the agenda?" Ross asked once he had joined them at the table with *his* sandwich and tea. "School, young lady?"

"No, Unca Ross," she replied with a frown. "Probably next Monday."

She thought for a while, and, eying his lunch she said, to her Nanny's laughter, "You do realise that your sandwich would probably feed the *whole* of the village, don't you?"

Ross laughed to see that she was returning to normal, albeit slowly.

"Ross!" Joseph's raucously loud voice yelled from the farmyard. "Ross! Get out here fast!"

The sense of urgency in that call dragged him to and through the front door, where his eyes met a bloodied brother, a prostrate and immobile body with a shotgun close by on the cobbled yard floor, with a further two young lads cornered between the house and the attached barn. When the cornered two saw Ross, fear rose in their face and they tried to bolt, to be caught by the brothers who knocked the thieves unconscious.

"Can't be more than seventeen or eighteen these two," Joseph said, clenching and unclenching his fist as he wiped away the blood.

"What are they and why are they here?" Ross replied, not too sure of method or motive. "Were they after thieving the shotgun, or…?"

"I think they were after the chickens," his brother said to the groans of the two youngsters who were now sitting, cradling their jaws.

"Aye, lad," Joseph continued, rounding on them. "It's possibly broken. Tha's not about to have *that* one mended in a hurry. T'last lad I saw as had his jaw broken died because he couldn't eat. So, what's the story? Were you after yon chickens, or what…?"

"Well, if tha's not off to speak, we'll have to lock thee up in yon woodshed until we can speak to t'local constabulary," Ross butted in. "That could tek anything up to three days, and by that time all sorts of nasty complications might well have set in, causing untold agony."

"We were med to do it," one lad uttered, holding shut the lower half of his battered jaw.

"And?" Ross persisted, his threatening presence exerting more pressure on the pair. "Who did the mekking?"

"Yon, ower yonder," the other lad mumbled as he spat out blood and a broken tooth in his attempt to relieve the agony that was causing him so much grief.

"And he is…?" Ross went on.

"Don't know," the first lad replied. "Met 'im t'other day."

"Then my last question, before we throw you into t'back of yon cart is … why?" Ross said.

"No job, no munny, no food … hungry," the first lad muttered, head in hands, feeling very sorry for himself.

By this time Joseph had shackled the older man securely with a length of rusty and pitted chain, hands and feet, tethered to an iron hoop set into the wall, used mostly for securing their bull. He was beginning to rouse slowly, trying not to let them see he was regaining consciousness. He tested the chains once or twice and, realising there was no way he could release himself ready for escape, he took stock of his situation. Joseph had noticed this, a grim grin forming.

"Hey mister!" the chained man growled. "Why am I chained like an animal? I have rights and I have—"

"Tried your darnedest to rob us and kill me," Joseph replied. "That shotgun is definitely not mine. Looking very much like the one that was stolen from my neighbour the other evening. I have every right to beat you within an inch of your scrawny life."

The man protested his innocence unconvincingly.

"You're lucky it wasn't my brother here that caught you," he went on. "*He* would have beaten you to a pulp. *He* is unforgiving, as will be my neighbour when I let him know where his gun is."

"Good gracious!" Nell's voice cut into the scene. "What's going on? What's …? Ned? Ned Sparrow?"

"You know him, Mother?" Joseph asked incredulously.

"Aye, I do that!" she answered. "Ned Sparrow is Jenny and Henry's son. They have a small holding a couple of miles away, and a lovelier couple you couldn't hope to meet. What's going on, and why is he here?"

"He's a villain, Mother," Ross added, once he'd brought

the other two youngsters across. "Forced these two lads, whom he doesn't know, to come along and … rob. As far as I can gather, *they* are late teenage, with no means of providing for themselves, or their mother and four sisters. Brothers obviously … hungry brothers."

"Is that true lads?" she said, turning towards their hanging heads.

"Yes, Missus," Alan, the older of the two muttered. "Sorry for all the bother we've caused. We—"

"Can have a job here if you're interested," Nell offered. "Initially to provide food for you and your family, until we decide if you are worth employing full time. Conditions are that you work hard and cause no more trouble. Then, we'll think about paying you."

The lads looked shocked, not expecting to be treated so kindly. They thought they would have ended up in the cells at the local clink, nursing their injuries and looking towards spending time away from home.

"Take them into the shed to get cleaned up, please Ross," Nell went on. "Then take them into Mary to get some food inside them."

"But Missus, we tried to rob you," Jack, the younger lad insisted.

"And for that you've been punished. Do you like losing teeth and having an injured face?" Nell asked, receiving no reply. "I thought not. Will you do as I ask?"

"We certainly will, Missus!" Alan assured her, a painful smile reminding him of the reward for breaking the law, as he nudged his brother in the ribs. "Would it be all right if we took the food you said you'd feed us now, home instead? Our mam and sisters haven't eaten for a bit."

"How long?" Nell asked. "Come on now! Truth."

"Three days," Alan replied, almost in tears.

"Then *you* shall eat here, now, and then you'll take food home for your family," Nell explained. "Agreed?"

"Yes please!" they both said with tears running down their cheeks.

"Mary here will put some food on the table for when you're clean and patched up," Nell assured them. "So, be off, and we'll see you tomorrow morning at eight."

When Ross had led them into the shed to clean up, Joseph turned to his mother and said, "Do you think they'll be here tomorrow? I mean, most ruffians would take the hit and run. Can you afford to trust them?"

"Well, if I don't, they'll be dead within the week, and so will their family," his mother replied with a grimace. "I can't have their demise on *my* shoulders. Besides, it's the Christian thing to do. We'll see."

"And this reprobate?" Joseph added "What'll we do with him?"

"Nothing's been lost or stolen or destroyed, so, as I know his parents, how about if we take him to them and let *them* deal with him," Nell replied with a satisfied smile. "We'll give *them* the choice."

Chapter 14

Lilly Victoria's choice of home to move into after they were married, had surprised Joseph. He had thought she might have wanted to live either with in-laws or with her parents as a temporary measure until they could afford to build. The small virtually derelict cottage a hundred yards from the porticoed front of Boulders Wood would not have been his ideal. It cost them nothing to acquire because it had been a farm worker's tied cottage that had lain empty for a number of years.

Her cousin Albert was a stone mason with whom she used to play as a child, and he had offered to renovate the property as a wedding present – with one proviso. They were not allowed to watch its progress back to life and would know what it was like only on the day Joseph carried her over the threshold for the first time. Although she was a very patient woman, she was excited to see what she would be living in from their wedding day.

"Have we decided what's going to happen and when?" Joseph asked one day at the meeting her mother had called between both families to finalise all arrangements.

"Everything is in order," Lilly Victoria's mother said with an air of pride. "All the dresses have been chosen and made – including the bridesmaids' – and the reception is booked at the King's Head in Richmond."

"King's Head?" Nell added with a sage nod. "We could have had it at Boulders Wood. It would have been a darned less expensive."

"It's something different, Nell," Lilly replied, dismissively. "A special place for a special event that happens only once."

"And our other three daughters?" Tom said quietly so as not to attract attention from his wife. The look she threw in his direction assured him he had been unsuccessful.

"Wednesday 23rd of June, at St Michael and All Angels Church in Hudswell." Lilly Victoria interrupted, nodding at her soon-to-be-husband. "As it's only weeks away we must speak to the rector as soon as possible, Joseph."

"I've some business to attend to in Richmond , and as it's onny a mile or two beyond Hudswell, I'll call in to arrange our visit," Joseph said. "Wednesday? June? What's wrong wi' Sat'di?"

Horrified 'Oos!' and 'Ahs!' rattled round the gathered sisters as a pregnant silence descended.

"As June is the luckiest month because it was named after the Roman Goddess Juno, who was the goddess of love and marriage, no other month will do, I'm afraid," Tom's wife chipped in. "You have no other choice.

"As far as the day is concerned," she went on after a slight pause…

"Monday for wealth
Tuesday for health
Wednesday the best day of all
Thursday for losses

Friday for crosses…"

"Saturday for no luck at all!" Lilly Victoria's three sisters chimed in as they descended to a bout of mild giggling.

"We have to collect dresses for the bride and bridesmaids on the Monday of wedding week," Mother Lilly added after taking a deep breath.

"Collect dresses?" Joseph said, a serious look of confusion invading his mere male face, much to his brother's amusement. "Why do they all have to be the same colour? Are the bridesmaids getting married as well?"

The tittering giggling of Joseph's sisters-in-law-to-be surrounded and compounded his confusion.

"You do know why the bride wears a veil, I assume?" his future mother-in-law ventured with a patronising smile on her face. "No? Of course you don't. After all, you're only a man. Well, although a white veil these days shows chastity and purity, in Roman times it was felt that the veil would disguise the bride to outwit any malevolent spirits."

"Same colour for bridesmaids' dresses carries on that tradition," Lilly Victoria added. "For tradition is all that it is. We don't actually *believe* that anymore."

Tom cringed inwardly at his friend's obvious confusion and embarrassment at the hands of his womenfolk. He had experienced this sort of genteel ambushing on more occasion than he cared to remember – age and 'memory loss' being great healers. Now he had become inured to its gentle barbs. There were far more important things in his life than taking umbrage; bringing a good enough return from his farming to provide for *their* not inconsiderable needs, for example. Joseph would get over it with time and take on the mantle of chief provider for one of his soon-to-be smaller flock.

"At least we will contribute to alleviate the expense the

King's Head will try to heap on your shoulders, Tom," Nell added sharply. "No-one should be asked to bear that sort of a burden."

"That's extremely decent of—" Tom started to say, a grin reinforcing his joy to hear those words.

"Oh no, you won't!" his wife insisted indignantly. "That is *our* responsibility, and one we will not shirk."

"But, sweet pea, don't forget that we have three other daughters to arrange for, and—" her husband protested quietly.

Lilly turned slowly on her husband, giving him a withering look no man could ignore. Tom held up his hands in capitulating supplication, knowing she would not be gainsaid. He would have to find the money somehow. His friend Joseph looked on him with pity and sympathy, knowing all the while that he and his father-in-law-to-be would come to some financially amicable arrangement that Tom's wife would never know about.

Tom understood Joseph's almost imperceptible nod, agreeing with a similar surreptitious raising of an eyebrow.

"This is getting to be a bit worrying to say the least," Joseph said to his brother as they clambered over fallen trees and scrambled through undergrowth of short stubby bushes and dense brambles of Boulders Wood. "He's been seen four or five times close to houses now."

"The most worrying for me is the children," Ross replied. "They can't play and be anywhere without supervision. Not natural or right."

"The last time I noticed thin, spiralling smoke from what I can work out, was ower yonder by yon dense copse of beech saplings, ower-grown by those wicked-looking brambles,"

Joseph added. "Surely he's going to be—"

"Look what I've found!" Ross gasped, a hoarse whisper escaping his shocked face. Out of a dense spiky thorn bush, he pulled and held aloft a black locket and broken chain. "If I'm not very much mistaken, it's—"

"Our Annie's favourite necklace!" Joseph interrupted. "I'd recognise it's heart shape and engraving anywhere. I bought it for her tenth birthday from Whitby."

"But it's jet black," Ross noticed, a note of surprised disbelief in his voice. "Why would it have become so ... black over the years?"

"Because it's made from Whitby black jet," Joseph explained. "The origin of the saying – jet black. She wouldn't have left it *anywhere* voluntarily. So, this is where she must have been on that fateful night. I wonder…"

"If our blackguard might have had anything to do—!" Ross went on.

"Ssh!" Joseph urged almost in a whisper, dropping to one knee behind a thorn bush and dragging Ross with him. "Cracking twigs over … there."

He pointed to a wide expanse of very dense undergrowth where an almost imperceptible tremor suggested someone might have been watching them. He waved to his brother to circle around to their right as *he* moved in the other direction, intending to surround whatever – whoever – was there.

"Nothing?" Joseph gasped as the brothers met. "I could have sworn—"

"Me too," Ross agreed, scratching his head, puzzled at what they hadn't found.

"Look!" Joseph said, pointing to a broken bush twig with a strip of what looked like human mucus dangling from its end. "That's not been snapped by any animal *I* know."

"Bugger!" Ross cussed. "He's been watching us all the time. Apart from this disgusting residue, has he left any tracks so that we might follow him? I would dearly like to meet him."

"Me too, but there's nothing we can detect, short of bringing in a red Indian tracker from—" Joseph started.

"The local red Indian tracking shop?" Ross suggested, a slightly mocking smile invading his face. "Bloodhounds?"

"All right, funny beggar," Joseph chided his brother's humour as he moved off. Ross's big hand on his arm stayed his forward movement and urged silence. Pointing to a derelict building he could just make out through the trees and bushes closely growing cheek by jowl with scarcely an inch between.

Joseph moved off to the right as Ross carried on as silently as he could, dragging his huge frame through the tearing thorns. He drew that fateful time back to his mind almost ten years before, when they found Annie's barely alive body, mauled and hardly breathing not too far from this spot. He clenched his fists the closer he came to the building, ready for anything. He still couldn't reconcile the loss of his beautiful if wayward sister all those years before. He would have done anything to get her back, but at this point, finding the cause for her demise for now would do nicely.

"Anything?" Joseph asked as the brothers came together again.

"No," Ross replied. "This place has been abandoned for some time, although there are signs of human activity at the back of the building. The interesting thing, though, is that it shouldn't be here at all. I know the plan of Boulders Wood pretty well, and *this* building features nowhere on it."

"Then, why is it here?" Joseph asked rhetorically, knowing his brother would have no answer.

"Squatters?" Ross suggested tentatively. "If you notice, it

isn't really a proper building, because the stones giving it shape and form, are laid loosely one on the others."

Human detritus lay scattered, discarded when of no further use – a filthy cloth napkin here, an abused tartan neck scarf there. These were all meaningless to the brothers as they had neither seen nor known their origins before.

"This vagabond is either a figment of our overactive imagination, or he has moved on to irritate, annoy and threaten elsewhere," Joseph said with a shrug.

A dirty but very strong arm wrapped itself around his neck from behind pulling him backwards and all but stifling any sound. Ross turned sharply to see a filthy, semi-clothed body with seriously overgrown and matted head and facial hair trying to throttle his brother. Wild demented eyes burned through the matting, ready to wipe out anything that stood in its way.

Ross's automatic reaction on seeing his brother being almost choked to oblivion was to lash out with his huge knot of a fist at the assailant. That punch would have destroyed any normal human being, but his target simply shook his head and did not loosen his grasp on Joseph's neck and throat. His third punch in quick succession knocked the attacker backwards, enough to allow his brother to drop to his knees.

After checking quickly that Joseph was all right, Ross turned to attend to their assailant, to find that he had disappeared. In this area of overgrown and impenetrable undergrowth, he couldn't even tell which way the attacker had fled.

"You all right, Joseph?" Ross asked as he returned to his brother, who by now was sitting on a fallen tree stump, gasping for breath as he nodded to his brother.

"I think we found him," he replied, glad to feel the air filling his lungs once again. "Did you see which way he went?

I'd like to reacquaint myself with yon fellow."

"Could have been anywhere, I'm afraid," Ross said. "He's obviously a madman, but there is no question in my mind that we have found Annie's assailant."

"The question is, though, was he our Poppy's sire?" Joseph wondered. "Or was it somebody else before she was chased down?"

"Best not go there," his brother added quickly. "Besides, we'll never find out for sure, and we wouldn't wish to put Poppy through that. I think she's had enough to cope with in her short life. Don't you think?"

"Agreed," Joseph said, a sage nod accompanying a wry smile. "Our main priority now is to find yon vagrant, and *deal* with him. He's been on the loose for far too long, and we can't have him being a danger to all our youngsters, including t'workers' bairns."

"And how do you propose we do that – find him I mean?" Ross asked with a shrug. "After all, he had you banged to rights, and we didn't see *that* coming. If I hadn't been here, you might not have survived the encounter."

"All the more reason why we have to find him," Joseph added sharply. "Can you imagine what he *could* do to one of our young'uns? I won't allow what happened to Annie to happen to Poppy."

"Miss Poppy McIntyre?" Miss O'Reilly asked, turning to face Poppy as she stood at her tall wooden teacher's desk. "Are you with us today?"

The thin squeak of a voice didn't match the teacher's tall thin frame but had the desired effect of jerking Poppy out of her distant daydream.

"Er … yes Miss … O'Reilly," the child replied haltingly, not quite up to speed as to where she was in this dingy, dull and dourly drab schoolroom, where daylight barely crept through its small windows. Oh, how she longed for the open fields of freedom at Boulders Wood!

"Have you finished your writing, young lady? Only—" the tall thin voice went on.

"Yes, Miss O'Reilly," Poppy replied immediately confidently.

"Bring it to me then, young lady," the teacher piped, a disbelieving sneer hanging around her thin pinched features.

For some reason, *this* teacher had taken a dislike to the strikingly pretty ten-year-old as soon as she had clapped eyes on her. She had caught her distantly daydreaming on many occasions which she always took pleasure in exposing. Yet, the more she drew attention to Poppy, the more Poppy proved her wrong in her assumptions that she was slow and lazy.

The work she had been forced to do up to now had been much too easy, as she had learned to read and write at home, largely encouraged and developed by her Uncle Ross. She had kept a running and detailed diary since she was six, so schoolwork was dour and dull in the extreme, having moved from chalk and slate to quill and paper recently. If anyone could have managed her already busy and productive life without school, it was Poppy.

Almost imperiously, Poppy took her work to the teacher, written in beautiful copper plate on one full foolscap sheet of paper.

"Well," the teacher said, trying not to show her disappointment at not having anything to be sarcastic about. "I won't be able to teach you anything then."

"Probably not," Poppy replied confidently, recognising the teacher's attempted sarcasm.

"So, how did you learn so much in such a short life?" the teacher asked, with eyebrows raised in surprise at her pert response. "Were you born with so much cleverness?"

"My grandmother taught me, Miss O'Reilly," Poppy said, ignoring the teacher's comment. "I learned also how to do sums, including division and multiplication."

"Then, perhaps I should appoint you as one of my monitors?" the teacher replied.

"No thank you," Poppy answered, after a moment's thought. "I don't think that would be fair on all the other children. Do you?"

That mature observation rocked Miss O'Reilly back on her brogue-shod heels. Poppy turned and strode back to her cast iron-legged wooden desk, next to the village children that hadn't been as fortunate as her to have been taught by smart family members.

George Garside had to cover his face as he looked down at his desk lid to hide his growing smirk. He didn't like Miss O'Reilly either, but he would never have been brave enough to speak to her like his friend Poppy had. He was placid and accepting and wouldn't cause waves that might swamp him in the future.

The bell for the end of their afternoon session pushed all thoughts of school into the distance as they left the claustrophobic little room and its clouds of white chalk dust hanging in the air.

"Thank God that's done for another week!" George sighed. "Don't you like Miss O'Reilly? I mean—"

"She is of no concern to me," Poppy replied as they strolled home. "I just don't like wasting my time on someone that knows less about school stuff than my nanny."

By this time George had picked up a largish branch from

beneath a small oak tree that had been battered by recent gales, by the apothecary's cottage at the edge of the village and was hitting stones with it as he walked along a little way behind Poppy.

As soon as she had turned the corner of the lane that led to Boulders Wood, she was stopped in her tracks from behind by an incredibly strong arm around her waist that lifted her off her feet as if she weighed no more than her doll, Tossy. Unable to scream because of fear and the dirty hand that covered her mouth, fear overcame her as she lost consciousness.

Chapter 15

"Would you like to hit these stones with me, Poppy?" George called in hope as he rounded the corner. "Here, catch!"

The sight that hit his eyes stopped him in his tracks. The sound of George's voice miraculously startled Poppy into consciousness as he ran towards her captor.

"Hey! You! Scraggy man!" he shouted, incensed at the sight. "Let go of my friend! Now!"

The ruffian turned his head and snarled at George, showing two rows of broken and decaying teeth, "Get away, boy! Or you'll get the same!"

Shocked into life by all of this, Poppy's reaction was to sink her white teeth into her assailant's filthy hand, drawing blood and a screech of pain. At the same moment, George swung his make-shift club at him, catching a hefty blow on his leg. That blow drew a further yowl and blood from a gash torn into the side of his knee.

Poppy struggled free from his loosened grasp, and grabbing George by the hand, hot-footed it around the next corner where she ran into her Uncle Ross.

"What is it?" Ross urged

"Round that corner, Uncle Ross," George shouted. "An ugly, dirty man. Quick!"

Ross shot round the corner to find … a blood trail into the undergrowth. His urge was to follow, but he turned back to the two children to make sure they weren't hurt or injured in any way.

"George?" he said as he tended to a dazed and upset little girl.

"We were on our way home from school, Poppy a bit in front of me," George began slowly. "When I got round the corner, this … lump of a man had hold of Poppy. She bit the hand that was covering her mouth and I whacked his knee. There must have been a sharp lump on my branch because his knee started pouring blood. He took off into the undergrowth."

"He was the image of Grandpa Joss," Poppy whispered from the tree stump she was sitting on.

"Sorry?" Ross said. "What did you say?"

"It was like Grandpa Joss, but with lots of hair," she replied. "Can we go home now, Unca Ross, please?"

"And this young man stepped up to the plate and saved her life," Ross explained to the gathered group as he put his arm around George's shoulders. "Didn't think of himself at all and whacked her attacker hard enough to draw blood and make the miscreant drop our Poppy long enough for them to escape. By the time I got there, he had vanished, but leaving a significant trail of blood."

"I think we ought to do something about this … molester,"

Tom Garside urged. "Your Poppy was lucky our George was around, otherwise … God knows what might have happened."

"I'm sure we can guess what would have happened, Tom," Joseph insisted. "He's a monster and must be caught. We need to inform the police, but, because they don't have enough manpower, we need to take matters into our *own* hands, along with as many of our work force as we can muster."

"He's right," his brother agreed. "The problem is that he seems to move about a lot and never stays in the same place long enough for us to track him down. We need to flush him out."

"Harry Townley and his brothers Sam and Stan have six bloodhounds between them," Tom interrupted. "I'm sure they'd be more than happy to bring 'em along on a hunt once we've agreed a procedure."

"We've got twenty workers between us," Ross added. "I'm sure they would be eager to track him down, bearing in mind how many bairns they have between 'em."

"Along with ten men I know in Richmond that would be delighted to join in," Mary said from the kitchen door.

"That makes thirty-six plus six dogs so far," Joseph added. "The number of policemen would depend on how far their superiors allowed them to join us."

"Hows abaht we consult wi' all t'folks we've just mentioned, come together and decide on a plan of attack later this week?" Tom Garside suggested. "All rayt?"

"Sounds like a plan," Joseph agreed. "We should arrange for all on us to meet at Boulders Wood in, say, a week from today. In t'meantime, we need to keep our bairns close, no matter how much they might complain."

"The blood trail should provide enough scent for t'hounds," Ross added. "Unless it rains during the next week, of course."

As they were turning to disperse, Poppy walked over to George, put her arms around his neck, kissed him on the cheek and said quietly, "You're my hero, George Garside, and I'll never forget what you did for me."

George's grin told the world how much those words meant to him.

"Do you know anything about a brother that Joss McIntyre might have had, Mam?" Ross asked Nell the following afternoon over a mug of strong tea, when they were alone together in the living room. "Only, Poppy insisted yesterday that her attacker *was* her grandpa with hair."

"I don't know about that," Nell replied quietly, staring into the flames before them, as she sipped her steaming tea.

"Come on, Mother! You *must* know something," he insisted. "I can tell by your reticence that—"

"Look, Ross, I above all others would love to settle this … this person's threat once and for all, but I know only this," she said. "Your - Joseph's - father did have a brother – a twin brother to be exact – who disappeared when they were teenage. Joss never talked about him, as you would expect, but his other siblings were not reticent about it. There have been one or two sightings, but rarely. Rumours have abounded as to his whereabouts, but nothing of substance."

"So, is it possible then that—?" Ross said.

"Possible, but if it were so, I have no reason to believe why he might attack Poppy," Nell interrupted.

"Our Annie, too?" Ross added. "Is it possible – if it is him – that he might have attacked our Annie, too?"

"I don't have the answers to any of these questions, Ross," she replied quietly. "I wish I did."

Realising she was becoming upset, he redirected the conversation to something less poignant and raw.

"Can I take it that we don't know anything more about Joseph and Lilly Victoria's wedding?" he said. "He's said nothing to me about it."

"Remiss of him, because it's only two weeks away," she replied. "Wednesday 23rd June. Has he given you the ring?"

"Yes," he said, with a frown flicking around his forehead. "Somewhere. Not sure where I've put it."

"Ross?" Nell threw back at him, concerned.

"Only joking," he laughed. "It's somewhere safe … I think."

"Nanny, may I go out to play? I'm bored, and…" Poppy's tremulous little voice asked from the foot of the stairs.

"Of course, but stay close to the house, mind," Nell replied quickly without taking her eyes from the yellow tongues licking the fireback.

"Can I go across to George's, please?" Poppy added, feeling she needed company other than with adults.

"Not really," Nell replied quickly. "I—"

"I'll take her," Ross offered. "I have to see Tom about some business anyway."

"All right, then," Nell agreed with a knowing smile, understanding full well what business he had to attend to at the Garside's.

A rattle on the door knocker startled her out of her reverie concerning her past life. She eased herself out of the chair as Mary bustled her way through the kitchen door, a steaming mug of tea to hand.

"Ross!" Nell spluttered, surprised to see her visitor. "What are you doing here?"

Mary's puzzled face said it all. Ross? Her son? Why should she question *his* reasons for coming home? It was only when she saw the upright form of Ross Senior – Ross Booth – that she understood and started to turn back towards the kitchen.

"Just the two ladies I wanted to see," he announced. "Please don't go Mary. I have a proposition I should like to put to you. Nell, I just couldn't keep away."

"Cup of tea, Mr Ross?" Mary asked.

"It's Ross, Mary, but no thank you," Ross Booth replied. "I've just had one. There are two reasons I have called. One for Mary, and one for Nell. Both not linked, other than that they are proposals."

"Oo!" Nell said with a smile. "Intriguing. Come and join us, Mary."

"It'll have to be quick Mr Ross, er, Ross," Mary replied. "I've several pies in the oven, and—"

"It won't take long," Ross Booth assured her. "A rather large bird has whispered in my ear that you would like to enter into the business world."

"Oh, I don't know about that," Mary stammered, flustered at being put on the spot. "All I want to do is to supply Gough's of Richmond with some of my baking."

"It's only baking that everyone in Richmond adores, and sells out there within minutes of being cooked," Nell explained with a reinforcing smile.

Mary's face took on a decidedly crimson embarrassed hue. Her mug rattled the table as she almost dropped it with a crack.

"Well, here's the thing," Ross Booth said. "Mr and Mrs Gough have decided that now's the best time for them to retire. So, I've bought the shop."

"Does that mean that I'm out of work there, then?" Mary asked unhappily, after a stunned silence.

"On the contrary, Mary – may I call you Mary? – it means that you have a job there for as long or short as you wish," he replied. "Wherever you would like to perform your baking miracles – there or here – it's all right by me."

"What if I want to maintain my place here, and do my baking for the shop here, part-time?" Mary asked, under no illusion about what might be feasible.

"I will, of course, provide transport for your wares from here to there," he added easily. "We just need to work out when you would bake and how much. Is it a deal, Mary?"

"What about payment, Ross?" Nell asked on Mary's behalf.

"I don't know," he replied, scratching his head. "Should we start with the cost of your materials and half of what each item sells for?"

"That sounds more than generous, Ross," Mary gasped. "It's more than I'm getting now. That will allow me to make bigger things than now, like full-sized apple pies, parkin, and drizzle cakes."

"Folks will be queuing halfway down the street!" Nell added with a grin.

"We'll leave the shop as it is for now, until we have established a routine, don't you think?" he suggested. "Then, if you'll let me know what needs changing to make things better, including newer and better equipment?"

"Is that all right, Mary?" Nell asked as Mary got up to return to her pies.

"Died and gone to heaven!" she uttered as she backed through the kitchen door.

"And your proposal for me?" Nell asked him as they sat together on the settee.

"It's just that, neither of is getting any younger," he replied simply. "So, my proposal is that I should like you to be my wife. Will you marry me, Nell, and allow us to pick up where we left off? I loved you then, and I have loved you throughout all those lonely years. I fully understand that you will need to think on it. Take your time and let me know when you have come to a decision?"

He stood up, leaned over to kiss her cheek, and was gone, leaving her in a stunned silence. She wasn't expecting that at all, and it left her in a serious quandary. She had always loved him, both as a gentleman, as a lover, and as the father to her son, wishing he had been there throughout her Ross's growing up.

What would be her answer? What should she do?

"This is where Poppy's attacker was cut by George's whack to the knee," Ross pointed out to the Townley brothers whose six dogs were already straining at the leash to follow the trail that had now registered in their nostrils.

Another thirty men stood behind them, ready to follow, two of them with Old English mastiffs ready for action should there be a need to bring the assailant down. These were unstoppable old war dogs that couldn't be fought off even by someone as powerful as the attacker appeared to be.

"The rest of us need to spread out behind the six bloodhounds and the two mastiffs," Ross went on. "All right. Let's away. The dogs are on the scent."

While the dogs made short work of shouldering their way through the clinging and tearing undergrowth, the humans found it hard going. Some had chopping blades, but others scraped, scratched and scoured their bare arms and hands. Periodically the hounds stopped to sniff around as if the scent had eluded them, to continue unabashed only moments later, after a wailing and baleful howl. Each dog moved along at its own pace in its own way, allowing the pursuing line to stretch out to cover a significant amount of ground.

It seemed like the search was about to bear fruit when, after an hour or so, a shout went up to alert the other pursuers that they were close. Both mastiffs were hurried to where a sighting hopefully had been made, ready to pounce should they be needed.

Within minutes the searchers had surrounded a small dense copse of mountain ash, dense undergrowth and virtually impenetrable bramble. A blanket of silence stifled all sound save the periodic howls of the hounds.

"What have we?" Joseph asked as he approached the vanguard of searchers.

"Don't know as yet, but there is definitely something large and hairy in there," Harry Townley replied, satisfied that his dogs had done what they were bred and noted for. "It's not an animal because that would have charged us by now. My guess is that we have cornered your attacker."

"What's to do now then?" Tom Garside asked, nonplussed by the stand-off.

"Probably, with the mastiffs at the other side of the copse ready for whatever is in there to come out, we start the bloods baying around this side in the hope the 'creature' will want to escape," Harry replied. "Can't think of anything else."

"Sounds like a plan," Ross said, rubbing his palms, eager to get on. "And a good one at that. Start 'em off, Harry."

A piercing whistle from the other side of the trees told Harry and all the other ambushers that the mastiffs were in place and ready. On Harry's nod, the hounds set up such a cacophony of howling that had not been heard before in this part of the North Riding. Not only did they yowl without break, they strained at their leashes and scratted the edges of the copse, eager to be in and at their prey.

Within a few minutes of the yowling, a large hairy, dirty

and dishevelled body crashed out of the trees and through the first line of pursuers. The only thing to halt his careering bulk was a hefty whack on his injured knee by Ross's wielded knotty-headed oak crook staff, and the two old English mastiffs locking their teeth around wrist and throat.

By the time the mastiffs were pulled away, the creature lay unconscious and still, in a gathering pool of blood.

"He's gone," Joseph said quietly as he tested for a pulse.

"Good riddance! Leave him to rot!" shouts from the gathering crowd echoed as they turned to return to their families, relieved that another threat had been lifted. Within minutes, Joseph, Ross and Tom were the only ones remaining.

"We can't leave his body here, even though we have no idea how many he has either violated or killed," Ross said. "He could even – dare I say it – be part of our family."

"How do you make that one out?" Joseph said sharply. "Where did you get that idea from?"

"From Mother," Ross replied, rounding on his brother. "She said that it is a possibility that he could have been the long-disappeared twin brother to Fatha Joss."

"How come *I* knew nothing of this?" Joseph insisted.

"You probably never asked," Ross replied with a mischievous grin. "Poppy said on more than one occasion that, even with the grizzled hair and beard, he bore a singularly striking resemblance to her Grandpa Joss. Out of the mouths of babes, eh?"

Joseph simply stood, astounded at what he neither knew nor had seen. With all this new evidence, why didn't *he* find it out for himself?

"We're not far away from Boulders Wood," Ross observed. "So, why don't you two stay here and I'll fetch a wagon to remove his body?"

Chapter 16

"Why did we never consider this before?" Joseph muttered as they sat in the front room with a stout mug of tea and a plateful of Mary's mince pies. They were a staple at Boulders Wood, and not cooked merely for Christmas – one of Ross and Joseph's favourites.

"Now that his face has been relieved of all that disgustingly matted hair, he is the image of Fatha Joss," Ross said with curled lip.

The body had been cleaned reasonably well so that people could see it laid out in the barn – the barn where Joss had met his end not long before, and in the same byre *he* had occupied just before the undertaker had taken him.

"It's him, Nanny!" Poppy's wailing and distraught voice burst upon the gathered throng, as she pushed the front door back on its protesting hinges. "He's come back for me!"

Nell rushed from her chair to catch the almost fainting child and drew her to her bosom to give her comfort and to calm her distress.

"It's not your Grandpa Joss, sweetheart," Nell soothed,

stroking her hair as she had done so many times with Annie in *her* short life. "He's not come back to haunt you. It's the other man you've seen many times about the place. It seems that he has been drawn here because he was grandpa's brother that disappeared from here many years ago; the brother that grandpa never spoke about. He—"

"Nell, Joseph, Ross," a familiar voice greeted them from the door. It was Joss's brother Fred, along with wife Victoria and new baby twins, Alice and Josephine, in a large perambulator. "What's this I hear about a long-lost brother?"

"Fred! Victoria!" Nell said as she moved to the door to greet them. "Come in. So good to see you. And the twins. How are they Victoria?"

"I was on my way to see you this evening, Uncle Fred," Ross replied. "We've had a bit of a to-do lately, and—"

"Did I hear that you have a body here?" Fred interrupted. "Joss's twin disappeared when I was ten. One minute here in the bosom of his family; the next ... gone, and he's not been heard of since. Until now, that is. Possibly."

"I'll take you out to the barn, Fred," Joseph said as he and Ross made their way to the door, followed by Uncle Fred.

"How are the twins getting on, Victoria?" Nell asked, still holding Poppy on her lap. Many's the time in her younger days she spent with her granddaughter on her lap. It brought back with a jolt also the times she did the same with her daughter, Annie. Only, Annie was much less manageable than Poppy; much less loving and lovable.

"They're hard work, Nell," Victoria gasped, settling into the soft settee with a heart-felt sigh. "It was all right in the early days until Fred started engineering in earnest. He has had to give up his farm engine fettling because it meant working eighteen hours a day. Then the young'uns became livelier and more demanding. Why did I want children, eh?"

They both laughed at the relaxing bliss they were enjoying – Victoria because the twins were sleeping soundly, and Nell because the inordinately brutalising demands on *her* time and life had subsided to next to nothing. Mary's timely tray of tea and titbits was very much appreciated by all.

"Tea and tasties? I don't mind if I do," Ross said with an anticipatory rubbing of hands and licking and smacking of lips.

"Well, Fred?" Victoria said with a slight, questioning tilt of the head.

"I *think* it's him," he replied slowly. "It's a long time since last I saw him, but he's t'image o'Joss, even tekkin' into consideration t'ravages wrought on 'is face by weather and rough livin'. Joshua McIntyre allus was more wayward than 'is twin, as far as I can recall. I often got a surreptitious clout across back o' mi 'ead from 'im in passing, and I often saw t'cruel side of his nature wi' 'ow he treated t'animals on t'farm. 'E wor allus at logger heads wi' mi dad, too. He often got a swipe from Dad because of his sometimes-vicious nature. It was said that there was summat of a bit of scandal wi' one o' t'lasses on t'farm before 'e disappeared. 'Good riddance!' mi dad allus used to say, but mi mam allus rued the day he took hissen off. Shall we be burying him in t'McIntyre family plot? I wouldn't fancy a pauper's grave for *my* brother, no matter how removed from t'family he'd been."

"Of course we will," Joseph said as he sat down with his mug. "Although it's likely, we have no evidence that he was the cause of Annie's demise, and, of course, he definitely tried to assault our Poppy, only to be dissuaded by a hefty crack from George Garside's club."

"Are you going to let the police know?" Fred asked.

"Tekkin' t'law into our own hands and all that."

"A difficult one, bearing in mind I did let them know what we were going to do," Joseph replied.

"What did they say?" Fred asked.

"Sergeant Fred Shaw said to let them know if we needed their input," he replied. "So, there's your answer, I suppose."

"A week on Wednesday," Ross said to his brother as they took an early breakfast before their day's work began.

"What is?" Joseph asked, a puzzled frown heralding his confusion at his brother's bald statement.

"You've not forgotten already, surely, that from tomorrow for the next week I have to protect you from all ills and misfortunes?" Ross replied with a chuckle.

Joseph's look of confusion told Ross that he had.

"Don't worry, Old Man, because I will look after you, and be thanked heartily by your SOON-TO-BE-WIFE, Lilly Victoria," Ross reminded him emphatically. "Tomorrow is the day we collect our wedding suits from Cuthbert's bespoke tailor in Richmond."

"Oh, *that* Wednesday," Joseph said, his eyes searching divine support from the heavens. "Wednesday 23rd June. Of course, *I* knew that."

"Have you discussed the ceremony with the clergy yet?" Ross continued.

"Twice, and we know perfectly well what the procedure is going to be," Joseph replied, pulling out his tongue. "Like I'd forget my own wedding day to the most beautiful woman on earth?"

"Have you remembered that we have to see Sergeant Shaw at our local clink this afternoon, to go through – again

– what happened with Uncle Joshua?" Joseph said once he had finished his eggs.

"Who on earth can that be at this ungodly hour?" Ross puzzled at a rattle on the front door.

"You'll only find out if you stir yourself to open it," his brother urged. "I'm off now to start my day's work."

"Hello, Ross," Joseph greeted his brother's father. "Come on in. Can't stop. Lots to do today."

"Father!" Ross said, shaking his hand warmly. "Good to see you. Mother's in the kitchen. See you later, perhaps?"

"Too right!" Ross Booth agreed as the door closed behind his son.

"Hello, Nell," he said, putting his arm around her as he was about to give her a kiss. "I received your note late yesterday. Urgent?"

"You could say that," she replied, smiling at the concerned look that had grown in his face. "Come and sit down with me on the settee.

"A couple of things, really," she went on, using the brass poker to stir the fire back to warming life. Although it was mid-June, it always felt chilly in the sitting room mid-morning. "Thank you for what you did for Mary. She is so happy with your suggestions and being able to work in a shop she knows won't close on her."

"I've spoken to lots of people in the area that use that shop, and they all say how wonderful her baking is," he replied. "Most bakery shop owners that I know would give their back teeth to have someone like her."

"And my second point is … yes," she went on without changing her look.

"Yes what?" he puzzled. "I don't understand."

"Yes, I will marry you," she explained. "Just one condition, though. We need to live here."

His mouth dropped open and his stunned look made her realise he wasn't expecting that at all.

"Well?" she insisted. "No answer?"

"Yes to both points!" he blurted out. "I didn't expect that!"

He put his arms around her, drew her unresisting body to his, and kissed her fully on the lips, enjoying every second of what he had missed for the past three decades.

"I bought this just in case," he said with a grin, giving her a small domed garnet-coloured box. "Please open it."

Inside, sitting in a silk cushion, was the most glorious five carat pink diamond in twenty-two carat gold setting that made her jaw drop, too.

"I think we have both dreamed about this moment for many years," he said quietly. "Now we need to enjoy it for all it's worth. Shall we set the date?"

"I think you've done a fabulous job, Albert," Lilly Victoria said to her cousin as she and Joseph looked around the outside of the yet-unfinished cottage that he had been doing up for them.

"Just one or two minor things to attend to and iron out, and a few surprises to fit in" he said. "You have the new-fangled flushing toilets, a fitted bath with running hot water, and Argand gas burner light fittings from the ceiling, and gas mantle fitments on the walls to install. You'll like *them*. New stuff throughout."

"Fantastic," Joseph gasped. "Now then, you will send me a proper bill when you've finished, won't you. Or you could just tell me how much I owe you, and I'll arrange to have the money for the next time we see you. If you feel like it and are not too busy otherwise, we have three other workers' cottages that need renewing and bringing up to standard. Don't know if you are interested."

"Too right we are!" Albert assured him. "Not much happening in the stone masonry business these days. Can we talk about it later?"

"Of course we can," Joseph replied, shaking hands as they took their leave.

"Only five days to go, my man, and everything is now in place," Lilly Victoria said, giving a shiver of excitement as she held tightly onto Joseph's arm and headed for Boulders Wood house.

"Can't wait to make you my wife, my lovely woman," Joseph said, drawing her closer.

"Is your mother in this morning?" Lilly Victoria asked.

"Went out earlier with Ross Booth, I think," he replied with a smile. "It's so good that she's finally found what we have. There was no love lost with Father, and with Ross's dad she has now found true happiness. I can't believe they are now engaged. She's waited thirty years or more for this."

"Good for them, I say," Lilly Victoria added. "As long as they are happy, that's all that matters. Isn't it? Looks like they're back. Isn't that Ross Booth's trap by the front door?"

"Mother! You're back," Joseph called, walking into the living room.

"Hello, Joseph," Ross Senior replied, with Ross Junior coming in hand-in-hand with Poppy. "Now that everyone is here, we have something to tell you."

"This morning, Ross Booth and I became Mr and Mrs Ross Booth," Nell announced proudly.

"Well," Ross Junior said, striding across to hug *both* his parents. "At last, a mother *and* father. Congratulation, and … thank you both."

Overcome by emotion at his parents' news, a tear began to well in his eye, and both he and Nell and her new proper husband were hugged by a smiling and rejoicing Poppy.

"We wanted to do it quietly so as not to distract from *your* wedding next week," Nell assured them quietly. "Life's too short to wait to do urgent things that have been put off for so long. Now we are as we should have been for the last thirty years or so."

"Well done Mother and our new father-figure, Ross," Joseph gushed as far as he was able to gush. "Now we can look forward to a happy and positive future together. When are you moving out, Mother?"

"It's a good job I know you, Brother, otherwise I'd think you were serious," Ross observed with a laugh.

"We plan to stay here for the time being," Nell replied. "At least, until we decide to retire from my lifetime of servitude. That will probably be some time after Ross's wedding with Martha."

"Mother!" Ross urged. "We've—"

"Not decided yet?" Nell suggested with a giggle. "Well, it's time you had. 'Life's too short' is what I've learned since Ross here and I parted company all those years ago, and never a day went by that I didn't miss him. Now…"

"We will be able to retire and do what *we* would like to do," Ross Senior added. "Once you are all settled and your lives are on track, we will take the ultimate decision to retire, but not *just* yet."

Chapter 17

"Is the carriage here yet?" Martha called to her other two sisters as they were finishing getting ready to support Lilly Victoria in her step into a new life with the man of her dreams.

"Not yet," Charity warned. "I should imagine you need to get a move on though. Fortunately, the sky is cloudless, and it's warm."

"How do I look?" Lilly Victoria asked.

"Absolutely gorgeous," Martha said. "Your orange blossom headdress looks divine and smells lovely."

"I wasn't too sure about the dress, but I hope Joseph likes it," Lilly Victoria added, a little apprehensively.

"It's tradition to have white satin with long sleeves and no shoulder showing," her sister assured her. "We have the same as you, and we like them. Queen Victoria could get away with off the shoulder and short sleeves – very daring in 1840 – but us ordinary folk must stick to modesty and tradition."

"Are you sure?" Lilly Victoria went on, more than a little unsure.

"Well, it's a bit late to be unsure, Sister, so you need to get used to it," Martha replied, positive she was right. "Besides, Joseph will love it."

"Time to be moving," Mother Lilly said, popping her head round the door. "Don't want to keep your new husband waiting. Carriage will be here anytime soon. Your bouquet of red roses is downstairs, and it looks beautiful. Don't forget to fix your veil and to look in the mirror before you leave. Your father is waiting by the front door. When you are ready?"

Lilly Victoria's sisters, Charity and Florence, giggled quietly as they followed her downstairs, while Martha helped her with her short train. Tom's waistcoated new suit looked well on him but he found difficulty adjusting to the new-fangled studded shirt collar and tie that his wife insisted he wear.

"Lilly Victoria!" her dad gasped. "Tha looks rayt grand. Carriage is here, so let's away to t'church."

"Why have you got a pair of my old shoes, Dad?" she asked.

"Tradition as 'as been 'anded down in my family to show that your father – and that would be me – will be handing over responsibility for you when I give these to your new husband – and that would be Joseph McIntyre," he replied seriously.

The close-topped two-seater emerald Brougham sparkled in the early afternoon sunshine, telling all that saw it that here rode a lovely young lady, off to marry her handsome beau, ready to spend the rest of her life in happiness and joy. The pair of Shires had been groomed to silky perfection, with white ribbons wafting gently in the warm breeze from their thick manes.

The rest of the family travelled to the church in a luxurious six seat covered Landau, also drawn by a pair of white Shires from the same stable.

The Landau was first to arrive at the church to allow the

family to take up their pews, with Lilly Victoria's sisters waiting to walk with her down the aisle as her bridesmaids. George, of course, would have preferred to be outside playing with Poppy, and although *she* loved her Uncle Joseph, she would prefer to have been running free.

Joseph stood in front of the altar, his best man by his side, nervously flicking an occasional glance towards the door, urging his soon-to-be bride to appear so they might become husband and wife quickly. Although he knew what was expected of him, he didn't like waiting unnecessarily for anything he knew would happen sometime soon.

Ross's nudge in the ribs turned him around. His mouth opened and his unblinking eyes widened to look at the most beautiful vision in white he had ever seen. It wasn't until she approached him to take up her place next to him that he started to breathe again.

"Lilly Victoria!" he managed to speak in a quietly hoarse whisper. "You look ... stunning."

She lifted her veil just as the minister started his order of service, and smiled at her man, never taking their eyes from each other until they had to sign the register.

A light wedding breakfast at the King's Head in Richmond was the perfect way to celebrate a wonderful day that Lilly Victoria and Joseph McIntyre would remember forever. The cake, of course, had been made by Mary, and was a splendid three-tiered affair, iced and decorated as only she knew how. The bottom two tiers were the only ones to be cut and consumed, with the top one being saved for the christening of their first-born.

"Well, Mrs McIntyre, are you looking forward to being

in our own home together?" Joseph said as they were making ready to leave the King's Head after all the speech-making and ribald jokes at his expense.

"Too right I am, Husband!" she replied with joy in both eyes and heart. "I haven't seen inside our cottage since it has been completely finished. What's it like?"

"Tha'll have to wait and see, Wife," he retorted with a mischievous grin. "If tha doesn't like it, we'll have to move to Whitby or Cleethorpes or somewhere else."

"Just one more thing to do before we leave," Lilly Victoria explained. Joseph's look of surprise brought a giggle from all of the Garside girls. Turning away from the gathered group of young unmarried ladies behind her, she tossed her rose bouquet over her shoulder backwards for one of them to catch. Whether by design or good luck, it fell into the hands of sister Martha to whoops of joy.

"And the meaning of this is?" Joseph asked, shaking his head.

"It means that the lady that catches the bouquet will be the next to marry, and that would be … Martha!" Lilly Victoria explained, looking across at brother-in-law Ross.

"What?" he replied with a sheepish grin.

They both laughed, making ready to leave their guests to finish off eating and drinking. On reaching the outside door, a further shower of confetti descended upon them as they made their way to the Brougham, followed by the other members of the family.

"I still can't believe tha's taken it upon thissen to marry *me*, an ordinary Yorkshire chap with no real extra qualities a husband ought to have," Joseph said quietly to his new wife as their new journey began. "You could have had the pick, and—"

"I *chose* the pick of the bunch, lovely man," she interrupted him. "I can't wait to start our exciting new life together."

He slid his arm around her and kissed her passionately as the carriage pulled away.

"Steady, Tiger," she said quietly. "All *that* comes later."

The Garside parental home seemed remarkably quiet as the bride and bridesmaids climbed the stairs to change into everyday clothing. The McIntyres arrived shortly after to help look through the heap of wedding presents, and to cut the remains of the wedding cake into slices to distribute among both groups of workers as a thank you for their support throughout.

"Hungry still?" Ross joked when Lilly Victoria passed him on the stairs carrying a pot plate with a slice of cake on it, followed by sisters one, two and three.

"Not really, Ross," she replied with a smile. "Just another custom."

"Custom? Eating a piece of cake … upstairs?" he said, puzzled at the reference. "I don't need to go upstairs to eat a piece of cake, particularly one of Mary's."

"She will throw it out of the window, and if the plate breaks on contact with the floor, she will enjoy a happy future with her husband," Martha replied with an indulgent smile.

"And if it doesn't break?" Ross asked.

"Her future would be grim," Martha explained again. "Simple superstition."

"And if I went outside and caught the cake?" Ross said mischievously.

"*Your* future would be grim instead," she replied.

They laughed together, becoming more comfortable in each other's company.

"Time to go home then Mrs McIntyre?" Joseph suggested to his wife after a wonderful day.

"Just one more custom to fulfil, Mr McIntyre," Lilly Victoria said.

"And that is?" Joseph asked, not knowing for the life of him what that might be.

"When we get to our new cottage, you have to carry me over the threshold," she advised him, knowing what his reaction might be.

"Can I suppose that is so you don't trip over the doorstep and give us bad luck or prevent you from stepping in with your left foot first or could it be an ancient custom where the bride was 'stolen' and carried off so you don't tread on our nice new threshold?" he offered, all complete guesses.

"All of those, my clever husband!" she gasped, clapping her hands quickly. "But, I don't know about the last one."

"Come on then," he urged. "It's been a long day and I'm tired."

"Not *too* tired, I hope?" she said with a mischievous twinkle in her eye and a smile hovering about her mouth.

The gentle swell and fall of her naked breasts captivated, entranced and aroused him. As he had got into bed, the sheets had moved slightly to reveal her smooth, slightly rounded belly invitingly close, the fine golden maiden hair blurring the edges of her firm thighs. He felt his loins stir, with the desire he felt for this lovely woman laying next to him in their marital bed, increasing gradually until he thought he might burst with love for her.

"You are allowed to *touch*, you know," she murmured, eyes still closed. "You *are* my husband, Joseph McIntyre."

"I know," he replied hoarsely. "But I've never seen a naked lady before, let alone slept with one. And here I am laying next to the most beautiful creature I've ever set eyes on in my life."

"Well?" she cajoled gently after a moment or two.

"Well," he replied, reaching out a nervous hand to touch her firm erect nipple, "I've never done, you know … *that* before."

"Neither have I," she replied more calmly than him.

"So, what do we do?" he asked again, nervously now it was obvious what was expected of him.

"We'll work something out," she said, a smile of happiness playing around her full sensual lips, as she reached out pull him on top of her. She felt him hard and big against her thighs as she opened her legs to guide him to their first love-making, their first union, their first climax of ecstasy which would cement their life together forever.

Chapter 18

"But shouldn't we do the same as Lilly Victoria and Joseph?" Ross said to Martha as they walked hand-in-hand by the River Swale a month after his brother's wedding day.

"I don't want that sort of social occasion, Ross," she replied quite firmly. "For a start, it's a huge drain on Ma and Pa's limited resources – there are two more after me, don't forget – and I'm not one for doing that sort of ostentatious stuff, as you know. I feel also that you are very similar to me in that respect."

"True," he agreed. "Then, what?"

"I should be more than happy to do what your mam and dad did just before the wedding," she added. "Just you and me and the registrar, with afternoon tea at Mary's Pantry in Richmond. Heaven."

"Done!" Ross said, drawing her close to his chest, a relieved look playing around his eyes. "Time?"

"Soon as possible, please," Martha said. "But we need to find somewhere to live first."

"How about if we speak to *my* ma and pa?" he offered as a possible solution.

She reached up to kiss him - this man she had been so fortunate to find that she wasn't going to let go. She had just as much right to enjoy as happy a life as her sister. She, too, wanted what her sister had, and she knew Ross would be the man to give it to her.

"What now then?" he asked after a few moments. "Where do we go from here?"

"Get somewhere to rent? Live as man and wife?" she urged. "I want to be with you, and so—"

"We have to be married before anything else," Ross interrupted her. "Marriage first; everything else comes later. We could live at Boulders Wood at a pinch until we find somewhere of our own. I have a few pounds saved…"

"I can't fault you for doing what you've done, Martha and Ross," Nell said with a smile. "After all, it's what we did, for exactly the same reasons. What will your mother say, Martha?"

"She'll be devasted because she can't get dressed up again," Martha replied matter of fact. "It seems like that's all she lives for these days."

"Only natural, don't you think?" Ross Senior said with a knowing smile.

"Not my cup of tea at all," Martha explained. "Our Lilly Victoria only went along with it to placate Mother, truth be known."

"And Joseph would have been happy doing what we four did without regret," Ross butted in. "He hinted as much a week or two before the event, and perhaps I shouldn't say this, but he and Tom came to an amicable agreement concerning the costs. Tom's cash flow had almost stopped flowing, and Lilly, his wife, had insisted that the family Garside should pay for it all. Joseph wouldn't hear of it, and that's why they kept it quiet from Lilly. I for one am ecstatic that we have done what *we* wanted to do, and I am convinced that Tom will be delighted for us, too."

"Well said, my lovely man!" Martha said quietly, reaching up on her toes to kiss him. "And you paid for our wedding in its entirety."

"Two and six isn't about to bankrupt us, my sweet lady," Ross added with a guffaw.

"How does this sound then, son and daughter-in-law?" Ross's father asked, over a cup of tea, after receiving a nod from his wife. "We won't be staying here for long."

"As in?" Ross asked, concerned that he didn't know what they had been planning.

"Retirement – no work – travelling – a life of leisure," his father explained. "Do any of these strike a note? Once we have taken that decision, we will be moving out of Boulders Wood to find somewhere that is not a ... farm."

"Sounds interesting," Martha added, ears pricking up. "Tell us more."

"We will maintain a foothold, a link to Boulders Wood to make sure the farm is never short of finance," Ross Booth went on. "In other words, we will still own it under the same terms as Joseph and your mother agreed after Joss's passing. But we *will* move to somewhere less intrusive and difficult to manage."

"The house will then be yours to live in until that day that you and Joseph will inherit," Nell said finally.

"Your most difficult thing now, Martha, is telling your mother that you are moving into your new, albeit temporary, home here," Ross's father said. "Congratulations on becoming Mr and Mrs Ross McIntyre."

"We have decided to change that name to ... Booth,"

Martha explained quietly. "Obviously Ross was never a McIntyre. And now has to claim his birthright that was his all along."

"I don't know what to say," Ross Senior gasped. "Are you sure you want to do this, my son?"

"Never surer, Dad," his son replied. "I've always wanted to belong, and I never belonged to the Old Man. I am sure Mum is ecstatic about changing her name to Booth as well. She never was a McIntyre either."

"Well, sweet lady, we had better hasten to tell your mam and dad the good and not-so-good news," Ross said as he drew his wife to him.

"And to pack my things ready to start my – our – new life together," she replied with a satisfied sigh and supporting smile. "I have been waiting for this for what seems like an age."

"But you can't be moving out!" Lilly Garside almost wailed at her daughter's news. "And … married? But we've not been—!"

"Accept this wonderful news, Lilly!" Tom insisted firmly, a new steely look in his eyes. "They are grown up! And now husband and wife. *We* are delightedly happy for you both."

"Thank you, Tom," Ross said, wringing his hand as Martha hugged and kissed her mother. "It means a lot to both of us. You're going to be rattling about in this place before long if your other girls move as quickly; not to mention the money you'll be saving. You'll be taking in paying guests before you can blink. Tara for now."

Tom burst out into a belly-shaking guffaw as he finally got to hug his daughter.

"Will you still be—?" Tom began.

"Working at Boulders Wood?" Ross interrupted with a

grin. "We've just got married, Tom, and are moving in there. We're not emigratin' to t'Antipodes. We've just got one of us back, and we're not off to send another out to replace him."

Martha's younger sisters were delighted to hear their news, both for her happiness and for the fact that Charity would now be able to move out of sharing a bedroom with her sister, Florence. At last, she would have a bedroom of her own. And George would have one fewer female in the house to contend with.

Their next, and last, visit was to his brother and Martha's sister's new cottage, to share their news. Although the brothers worked together on a daily basis, Ross and Martha hadn't been invited to visit yet, since *their* wedding, but that was perhaps understandable.

"Ross! Martha!" Joseph gushed. "Good to see you both. Come on in. Lilly Victoria!"

"Wonderful!" Ross said once they had been ushered into the front room. "This is so … twentieth century! I love all the modern lights and mantles and stuff that we have never even *seen* before."

"Sorry we haven't had you round before now," Lilly Victoria announced sheepishly, aware that they hadn't had time for any of their usual good-humoured sociability. "We've literally been run off our feet. That's what being married does for you."

"Yes, we know," Martha replied quickly.

"You know?" Joseph said, casting a puzzled look at them. "How—?"

"Because they're married," Lilly Victoria said with a giggle and a jiggle.

"How can you—?" Joseph added, even more confused.

"Because I worked it out," Lilly Victoria insisted. "Come on, Husband! Catch up!

"I thought you might follow on from your Mam and Dad, Ross," she continued after smiling at her husband's slowness. "Sensible thing, bearing in mind neither of you likes fuss or formality. Congratulations. Found anywhere to live? You could always stay here with us for a while."

"No disrespect to you, Lilly Victoria, when I say 'thanks but no thanks'," Ross answered, going on to tell them about his mam and dad's plans for the near future, and *their* taking over the living accommodation at Boulders Wood.

"Not taking over the running of the place, you understand," Ross added quickly. "That's not going to change, and neither are our positions in it."

"Any idea where Mum and Ross are going to live?" Joseph asked. "Anywhere close?"

"Don't know about that, but they did mention travelling and a life of leisure," Martha replied with a non-committal shrug.

"Could be anywhere then," Lilly Victoria agreed. "Tea and cakes, anyone? Perhaps not to Mary's standard, but we like them."

"Do you really mean that, Mr Ross?" Mary gasped. Saturday morning at Gough's bakery was beginning to fill with customers eager to buy Mary's glorious cakes and fancies and pies. A queue of around twenty or so gathered usually around mid-morning, emptying the shop by an hour later. This always obliged her – along with her staff of two other lady bakers that she had trained herself – to do a second or even a third baking on most days.

"Please, Mary, it's Ross. We've known each other what seems like an age," Ross replied. "I am entirely serious. Once we leave Boulders Wood, I have instructed my solicitor to make out the deeds of Gough's – building and everything in it – to you. It will be yours entirely. I also know that you would like to turn it into a Tea Room at some stage. So, here's the thing; I have set aside funds for you to do just that. How does *Mary's Pantry* sound?"

"I can't accept all that Mr ... er ... Ross!" Mary protested. "I would never be able to pay all *that* back. Besides—"

"Mary. Just stop for a second and hear me out. Please?" Ross butted in, ready to explain. "I made an obscene amount of money in Australia, from being almost a pauper. Right place, right time. I have *so* much money that I wouldn't know what to do with it, save leave it in the bank. What bankers do is to make even more money out of it – for themselves. It would please me no end to help you to achieve your dream. What I want to give to you to develop your business, I wouldn't even notice. No repayments. No strings. What do you say?"

"One day, perhaps, you will want to do your *Pantry* full time, and leave here," Nell added, sitting next to her sister-in-arms, with her mug of tea. "Ross and I will be moving out of Boulders Wood in the near future to retire, Mary, and you may not want to stay when we're gone. We intend to leave the youngsters to run and look after *their* farm, you see. Do you know of anyone that might be able to take over the kitchen at Boulders Wood when you decide to move on?"

"Well," Mary pondered, "my brother's eighteen-year-old daughter, Mary-Jane, would love to be able do what I do. I could train her for a couple of years. I wouldn't be able to pay her, but—"

"Leave that to us," Nell offered quickly. "It is still our house and farm, so we would make it worth her while to learn from the best."

"Missus, I couldn't—!" Mary gasped, cradling her face in both hands in shock.

"Mary, you can, and will!" Nell insisted. "Invite her up for afternoon tea next week and we'll put the proposition to her. Your brother and his wife ought to come along with her as she is underage, to see we are genuine and are about to offer her the job of a lifetime."

"I don't know what to say," Mary said quietly, overcome by their generosity.

"How about 'Would you like a cup of tea and one of my macaroons, Ross?'" Ross suggested, much to Nell and Mary's amusement.

"Right away, Sir," Mary said, still giggling as she disappeared into the back room. "Tea and one of my deluxe macaroons coming up."

In this part of Yorkshire, winters were not to be trifled with, nor to be enjoyed. Snow often blocked vital routes, making work and life for ordinary folk in general very difficult to cope with; that is, unless your life and livelihood depended upon it.

Even the sheep in the top field at Boulders Wood and Garside Holdings lived on a very keen edge, where they could be buried under ten feet of snow or frozen to death overnight.

Good roads were few and far between, with keeping them clear of snow after even moderate accumulations, falling to the families round about. It was reasonably easy for folk employed by the larger farms like Boulders Wood, to get into work because the majority lived in tied cottages within walking distance. Even so, getting there on foot, struggling at times through desperately deep drifts, was a difficult, time-consuming and dangerous affair.

During the winter of the year the two generations of Booth, father and son, took Nell and Martha to be their wives, incredibly heavy snowfalls made the roads between Swaledale and Yoredale all but impassable for several weeks. This made all markets and Tom Garside and Joseph McIntyre's market deliveries almost impossible. Almost, but *not quite* impossible.

Although walls of snow twelve to sixteen feet high barred the way over Buttertubs Pass, the dynamic duo battled doggedly through, often having to stay over in Leyburn or Bedale or Hawes or Aysgarth, before returning from their weekly market deliveries the following day. Iceberg-like chunks of frozen snow looked as if they had been scattered about by some untidy giants playing skittles.

"Can we continue with this sort of life, Joseph?" Tom Garside asked his partner at breakfast at the Green Dragon, by Hardraw Falls, near Hawes.

"We have no choice, Tom," Joseph replied, a shrug betraying his tiredness. "We are just on the edge of something big for both our families, and with Lilly Victoria now expecting, we need to carry on."

"Aye, an' that wor a great joy to us," Tom replied with more than a hint of emotion in his face. "Me, a granddad at last, eh?"

"Ee, an' me a dad, as well," Joseph said, a great sigh escaping his proud lungs. He couldn't have been happier. A bit less snow might have tipped the balance, though.

"Can't wait to sleep in mi own bed tonight," Tom sighed. "Does tha know 'ow many nights I've slept away from home in the nigh on fifty years Lilly an' me 'ave been wed?"

"Not off hand," Joseph chortled, eyebrows raised in amusement.

"Six," Tom replied seriously. "And they've all 'appened

within the last six weeks, while we've been doin' t'markets in this area."

"Has thy any idea how many nights I've spent away from Boulders Wood, in my *lifetime*?" Joseph put in, emphasising lifetime.

"I've no idea, but I expect tha's off to tell me," Tom guffawed loudly, drawing the attention of two well-dressed ageing ladies sitting at a window table opposite.

"Perhaps tha'll be very surprised that it's … none?" Joseph replied. "Never been away far enough so as I'd have to stay ower somewhere. Could never have afforded it either."

"What do you think about your Ross an' our Martha, then?" Tom asked once he'd finished his toast and tea. "Bit on a surprise, eh?"

"Not really," Joseph explained. "He's never been one for socialising; never had the time nor inclination. He always spent most of his time with our Annie until she…" he hesitated, his eyes filling and his lips becoming dry. "When Annie was no longer with us, he began spending his spare time with her daughter, Poppy."

"Then, he and Martha will be best suited, because she has always liked her own company and space," Tom added. "Bout time we were off then, owd chap?"

"Too right!" Joseph replied as he stood up. "Can't wait to see my Lilly Victoria again."

Chapter 19

The snows stayed well into March the following year, making most of the daily farming chores like milking, lambing, feeding livestock inside, very hard work, and tiresome in the extreme. Joseph and Lilly Victoria had been blessed, and more than a little surprised, by the arrival of baby Jessie … and her identical twin Joanie, finally making landfall after a significantly lengthy labour at home in their cottage. Lilly Victoria was exhausted by the event and was laid up to rest for several days.

Although still very hard-working, Joseph was as attentive to his girls as he had been throughout his courtship and marriage to his adored and adoring wife. Fortunately, during her resting days, Lilly Victoria had a string of supporting sisters and, of course, her mum, Lilly, to rely on. She made sure her new granddaughters were well looked after and doted upon throughout.

Lilly couldn't believe she had *two* grandchildren on the Tuesday of the week they were born, when she had had none the day before. *She* couldn't get enough of them, carrying Jessie up and down the drawing room, putting her down to pick up Joanie to do the same moments later.

Tom's feelings for his grandchildren ran as deep as his wife's, but he had never been an emotional man. The deepest emotion he ever came close to displaying was when Joey Smith, big lump of a clumsy lad, almost knocked Tom's pint of John Smith's over at the Farmers pub, after only one mouthful. Nothing else had ever come close after that, and he always kept his beer glass in his hand.

"Lilly, my sweet pea, is thy ever going to go back to butter churnin' in t'dairy?" he would ask his wife, a despairing frown adding gravitas to his simple request. "Or is thy off to cradle yon bairns until they are old enough to leave 'om?"

"It's a grandma's duty and prerogative to spend as much time with her blood little'uns, I'll have you know, Husband!" Lilly harrumphed with a look of annoyance letting him know he might be treading on thin ice. "Employ somebody else, if you must, until I find the time to re-enter t'dairy. Not really sure whether I want to."

"I'll remind thee once again, Wife, that ifn tha doesn't help out – significantly – in t'production of dairy produce, we may have to close down at least *that* part of our operations," Tom advised her sternly. "Because we are onny just breaking even before we break into the field big style, we can't afford either to employ any more labour or to lose one of our *team*. Bear in mind, before tha meks thi decision, that this is a joint business wi' our Lilly Victoria and Joseph. T'choice is thine, Lilly, but getting your arse out of that chair and giving back yon bairns to their parents is all it'll tek to keep both t'business, our family and *us* on an even keel. Get it? Now, I've got work to do."

That stunned Lilly as she watched her husband's back disappearing through the door. Left open-mouthed, she was surprised at what he had had to say, because he had never been so sharp before – mildly sarcastic perhaps, but never … pointed. Was there something he was trying to tell her in a different way from usual, that he had only hinted at before? The snick of the front door's latch drew her mind back into the here and now.

"You were miles away, Mother," Martha's melodic voice drew her in. "You going to stare into space *all* day? I'm off to the dairy. You going to join me, or are you baby drooling while *we* fulfil *all* our orders? Charity and Florence and I have been there an hour or more, and we could do with your help."

It had been touch and go drumming up support from local markets, businesses and to towns folk in general, and the fact that they were just about breaking even was down in no small measure to the amount of legwork put in by Joseph and Tom. They needed now to capitalise on that graft by producing as much milk, butter, cheese and beef as they could. Their workforce was just about as large as they could afford, and so it was a case of all hands to the pumps within the family.

This was a matter that had not gone unnoticed by Jenny Bott, the young whore who was still trying to keep a roof over head and food in her son's belly.

"I don't know about you, but Boulders Wood feels strangely quiet without my parents, even now into June," Ross said to Martha.

"Very true," Martha replied. "It is rather good to be on our own in our own home, and fortunately, Mary is still here."

"Aye," he agreed. "For how long though? She's onny here for two days a week to train her niece, and when that's gone, so will she be."

"Still, your parents aren't far away, and they do visit regularly," Martha added. "Richmond is only spitting distance. Don't forget, by the way, that it's Poppy's birthday next month, and we're almost halfway through this one. Any ideas on some sort of a surprise?"

"What sort of thing do you do for a twelve-year-old?" Ross replied, scratching his head, a nonplussed look adding an air of seriousness to the question. "I don't think the usual tea party with games will do for a youngster of her age. Do you?"

"I see what you mean," Martha said. "How would it be if we arranged afternoon tea for her with her close friends at Mary's Pantry? She does have some close friends, doesn't she?"

"One or two," Ross replied with a smile. "George for one – now she's very fond of him – Florence and Jonas. She sort of likes *him*, but Florence isn't too keen. Then she has a couple of friends from school – Alice and Annabel. Twin daughters of Harry Bull, out head carter and stockman. He's been with us since I was a lad."

"Check with your mam, eh?" Martha added. "She'll probably know if there are any more."

"If I know Mother, she'll have something organised anyway," he agreed. "Talk of the devil! I think I can hear her talking to Mary downstairs."

"Mother! Father!" he called with a grin, as he skipped downstairs with Martha just behind him. "Long time no see."

"Three days is not a long time, my son," his mother laughed as she hugged them both. "We just called to check with Mary if—"

"Her Pantry would be able to cater for several nearly-teenage youngsters one afternoon in, say, about a fortnight, by any chance?" Ross chortled.

"How on earth did you know that?" Nell gasped.

"Poppy's birthday party soon?" he laughed. "We were just running through the options as well, and Martha came up with the idea of a tea party at Mary's Pantry."

"Smart Alec!" Nell replied with a nod. "Florence, George, and her two friends Alice and Annabel – you know—"

"Harry Bull's twins," Ross added. "And Jonas?"

"Not sure about our Louisa and Ernest's lad," Nell said quietly. "He's a bit of a strange one. Arrogant and old for his years, yet he stood up to Maggie Jenkins' brother who was much bigger than him, to protect Poppy, and floored him with his fist."

"Yet, her best friend, Florence, can't stand him," Ross added. "That might cause aggravation at her special do, perhaps."

"We'll think on it," Nell said. "For now."

"We also have a special present for her," Ross Senior said after a moment or two's quiet.

"As in?" his son asked, not sure what sort of a 'surprise' Poppy might enjoy – or endure.

"We are taking her and her friends Florence, Annabel, Alice and George away for a week's holiday," Ross Booth replied.

"Holiday? What about school?" Ross asked, puzzled at why now – and where they would go. "And what about their parents? Do they—?"

"We've cleared it with school and all her friends' parents," Nell explained. "Poppy knows nothing about it."

"Where are you taking them?" Martha asked.

"We've booked seven days at the Grand Hotel in Scarborough," Ross Senior explained with a satisfied smile. "It's the new place to visit and stay, with lots to do that we think Poppy and her friends might enjoy."

"Amazing!" his son replied. "Lovely idea."

Poppy sat quietly between Nanny Nell and Grandpa Ross with her mouth and eyes wide in awe at what she had just been told.

"Tell me again, Nanny, please," she managed to utter finally. "We are going to do what for my birthday?"

"We will travel to Richmond by Landau carriage on your birthday," Ross Senior replied indulgently.

"Who will be going?" Poppy asked.

"You, Grandpa Ross, me, and your friends Florence, George, Alice and Annabel," Nell added, satisfied that her granddaughter was happy with the arrangements. "Will you be wanting Jonas to join us?"

"You haven't told me what we are to do in Richmond," Poppy asked, a frisson of excitement coursing through her body. "Jonas would irritate George and Florence no end, so…"

"That would be a no, then," Nanny Nell replied with a wry smile. "We will be having afternoon tea at Mary's Pantry. You know … our Mary?"

"And do they all know? I mean, when I didn't?" Poppy asked, eyes unblinking in a slightly puzzled face. She knew that her Unca Ross had always pulled surprises, but at least she knew almost straight away. Whereas Grandpa Ross … and her Nanny? They never gave even the *slightest* hint.

"Indeed, they do, and were sworn to secrecy a little while ago," Grandpa Ross added, an imaginary fist punching imaginary air in satisfaction. It hadn't been easy to keep such a secret as Poppy had asked time without number what had been planned for her birthday.

"It's not the only thing we have planned to celebrate your day," Grandpa Ross warned her, dropping another surprise in her lap.

"How do you mean, Grandpa Ross?" she asked, now completely nonplussed, palpable excitement beginning to flush her cheeks. "Am I getting a present to open as well?"

"Not *exactly*," Nanny Nell joined in, having received her husband's almost imperceptible nod to her raised eyebrows. "We have decided to take you on holiday, poppet."

"Holiday?" Poppy asked, not sure where all this was leading. "What does *that* mean? Never heard of that before."

"That's because Grandpa Joss didn't believe in them, and so we never had one," Nell replied, mentally cursing his name. "It means that we can stay somewhere exciting that's *not* home. You – we – are going to stay in Scarborough for a whole week, at the Grand Hotel."

"But I will miss all my friends if I'm away for a whole *week*," Poppy said, not too sure whether she would like that. "Where's Scarborough, Nanny Nell?"

"On the east coast," Nell explained," overlooking the sea, where there are sandy beaches and places to paddle in the North Sea. You won't miss your friends at all – because they're all coming with us."

That stopped Poppy in her tracks, eyes and mouth wide open in a look of bemused excitement. It took at least five minutes for all that to sink in before she began to squeal and jig around the room in unbridled joy.

"When are we going?" she said, her breathless excitement underlining the awe in her hoarse voice. "Can we go … next week, please?"

Chapter 20

"But why didn't you tell me?" Poppy gasped as she and her closest friend Florence sat on the two swings that Unca Ross had built at the front of the house. "Aren't I your closest of closest friends?"

"Of course you are," Florence replied. "We were all sworn to secrecy and we had to promise not even to talk about it among ourselves. You are happy, aren't you? I can't ever see me getting such a present from *my* grandpa."

"Grandpa Ross has lots of money," Poppy assured her almost dismissively. "So, we needn't be concerned about cost. Have you ever been to the Grand Hotel at Scarborough before?"

"No, but Mamma says that only rich people go there," Florence explained. "Can't wait to paddle in the sea and have an ice cream cornet and watch Punch and Judy."

"Punch and Judy?" Poppy asked. "Who are they?"

"Don't know but Dad says it's good to see," her friend replied. "He says to watch out for Mr Punch's funny squeaky voice, and to look for a sausage-eating crocodile with snapping jaws."

"I don't like sausages," Poppy said with a shudder as they went inside to have a cup of tea and one of Mary's niece's lovely scones. It was obvious who taught *her* how to bake. Sometimes with sultanas and sometimes with raisins and walnuts, Poppy could never tell the difference between raisins, currants and sultanas.

"Grandpa Ross?" Poppy said, sitting next to him at the huge oak dining table with her tea and scone.

"Yes, Lovely?" he answered. "Is that scone for me?"

"How will we travel to Scarborough by the Sea?" she said, ignoring his question but drawing the scone closer to her, just in case.

"Landau coach to York and then steam train to Scarborough," he replied. "All first class, of course."

"Steam train?" Florence said. "I think I've heard about them, but I've never seen one."

"Uncle Fred works building them, doesn't he?" Poppy butted in. "Is it in Middlesbrough he does that?"

"He does that!" Nell replied. "We're very proud of him, too, as we are with his wife Victoria and their twins."

"Have we met the twins yet?" Poppy asked. "Weren't they born sometime after Grandpa Joss … left us?"

"They'll be about two years old now, I think," Nell said. "Alice and Josephine."

"We haven't been to York before, have we?" Poppy asked, quietly excited by this big world of wonders that was just starting to open up before her.

"Until Grandpa Ross joined us, we hadn't been anywhere outside of this immediate area," Nell said, nodding sagely. "So, you see…"

"Richmond was as far as I had been," Poppy replied with a quietly rapid hand clap. "That was the first time I'd seen him and decided that he looked too much like Unca Ross not to be related. I had my suspicions."

"Suspicions?" Nell queried.

"It was obvious to me *then* that Unca Ross couldn't have been Grandpa Joss's son," Poppy said, dropping the bomb shell in her nanny's lap. "His resemblance to this new man I saw you chatting to near the marketplace was obvious. The fact that you fobbed me off with a stuttered explanation made me think even more. Two and two, eh, Nanny?"

Nell sat there in shocked silence, her mouth open but unable to work. Grandpa Ross smiled as he put his arm around his granddaughter's shoulders and drew her to him in admiration at her deductive powers.

"After all that time, we still thought our secret was safe, eh?" Grandpa Ross said. "There are always smart people that will work things out given half a chance."

"Were you my Mammy's father too, Grandpa Ross?" Poppy asked disarmingly pointedly, more in hope than anything else, as she turned towards him to look him in the eye.

"Unfortunately, no, Poppet," he replied, a wry smile telling her the truth. "I was in Australia by then. Knowing I would never be able to spend anymore secret, snatched moments with your nanny, and knowing I wouldn't be able to bear being so close yet so far away, I felt I had no choice but to leave. Australia seemed to be the obvious place. It was either there or the Americas, and I didn't fancy America at all."

A deep silence slunk into the room cutting out all sound save the cracking and hissing of new logs on the roaring fire. Poppy watched the intense yellow glow pushing the red tongues up the fire grate back into the chimney where they disappeared for lack of sustenance. Poppy snuggled next to Grandpa Ross on the settee, allowing her face to glow against his chest. Florence wished she was able to do that with *her* grandpa.

"I thought Australia would give me the new start that I needed to try to forget about a past life where I wasn't allowed to fulfil my heart-felt dreams," Grandpa Ross said. "Unfortunately, that wasn't to be."

"How do you mean?" Poppy asked, not quite understanding what he was saying.

"I couldn't forget what I had lost," he replied quietly, sadly. "Your nanny stayed in my thoughts. Not a day passed without she was drawn into my mind. Not a moment went by that she didn't remind me of our brief time together."

With a look of deep sadness in her eyes, Nell stole onto the settee at the other side of her man, drew his arm around her shoulders and kissed him, the loss of three decades drawing tears from her. She knew she had the right man now, but what trauma they both had had to endure to fulfil those long-held wishes.

"Annie was definitely Grandpa Joss's daughter," Nell assured her granddaughter.

"But, then, who is – was – *my* father?" Poppy asked quite simply, almost brutally.

They had always been able to side-step *that* particular question, but Nell knew that at some time she would be able to hide the truth no longer. That time had now thrust itself upon her.

"Unca Ross," Poppy said, rounding on her uncle at Sunday's breakfast the following day.

"Yes, my sweet pea, what can I do you for?" he replied, a fresh mug of tea in his hand.

"Would you look after my Toby for me please?" she asked.

"And why would I want to do that?" he said, playing her along. "Fed up with him already?"

"No, silly," she laughed. "You know we're going away on holiday directly after my birthday party, don't you?"

"I might do," he said slowly. "You know anything about this Martha?"

"What's that?" his wife said as she brought her toast and tea to the table. "Holiday, did you say, Poppy? Anywhere nice?"

"Well, would you look after Toby while I'm away on holiday in Scarborough, at the Grand Hotel?" Poppy began to explain patiently.

"Of course we will," Martha assured her. "It'll be our pleasure. Not seen him about much lately, but then that's probably because we are always at work."

"It's just that we'll be going places and doing … stuff that we won't be able to bring along a dog to share," Poppy went on unabashed, feeling she had to explain and justify. "I don't think other folks like dogs around when they want peace and quiet. I shall miss him, but I also want to enjoy my holiday with Nanny and Grandpa Booth; along with all my friends, of course."

"*All* your friends?" Ross asked, a wickedly naughty smile beginning to grow. "But I thought you only had Florence."

"Unca Ross!" she replied equally mischievously. She knew him of old; always poking fun to make her laugh. "George and Alice and Annabel are my friends, too, and they're coming."

"No Jonas?" Martha asked tentatively.

"No," Poppy replied simply and finally. No further discussion needed. Another cup of tea shouldered its way into the conversation. A cup of tea and a scone or cake or any other type of delicious baking was always more important that prolonging a pointless discussion about ... nothing in particular.

"Aren't you going to miss your schooling?" Martha asked, genuinely interested. In her day, boosting the family's finances was far more important than being taught the three Rs of reading,'riting, and 'rithmetic when they could already read, write and add up by the time they were five. Learning how to do useful things was much more important than 'book learning' to little purpose.

"I've just about finished going to school," Poppy replied casually. "Because I will be twelve soon, I don't need to go any more. Been a bit of a waste of time, really. We've not done anything I hadn't already done. If I hadn't been made to go, I could have done a whole lot of more interesting stuff."

"And that would have included?" Martha asked, intrigued by what might be going on in her mind.

"Going out and about much more with Unca Ross," Poppy replied, a disappointed scowl showing her annoyance at her aunt's lack of foresight and imagination. She liked Martha, but she wasn't her *real* aunt. She only *called* her aunt because she had married her real uncle. "Being able to spend time with my bestest friends Florence and George, instead of sitting with a lot of snotty noses that don't know anything, and who – quite frankly – smell."

Ross turned away to hide a huge grin that would have betrayed his humour at such a pointed observation. But then, *he* had never been to school either and so wouldn't have known about such things. He had always been made to bathe at least once a week so as not to ... smell. He couldn't help finding it funny, though.

"Two more weeks then sweet pea," Ross threw over his

shoulder as he and his wife reached the front door. "Will you bring me a stick of rock back from Scarborough?"

The door closed with a vague click as he chortled his way across the noisy path. Sunday it might have been, but jobs always needed attending to around a busy farm.

Although life in general excited Poppy, sharing it like she used to when she was much younger just wouldn't do. After all, she was almost twelve, and it would be too unseemly for such a genteel young girl to show her emotions to folks that occupied her world. She was becoming a beautiful young lady in both looks and character, reminding Ross and his mother that, in some ways, Annie seemed to have returned to charm them.

The differences between Poppy and *her* mother were marked, however. Annie, too, was smart but given to stubbornness when she wasn't able to get her own way. Poppy was clever, in that she never gave in to that wayward streak that had surfaced when she hit Maggie Jenkins, for example, with her doll, Tossy. No. She would keep her counsel and return to whatever the matter was at a later date when folks were least expecting it. It was *then* she got her way.

She did have moments still, when ghosts came back to haunt her – her grandpa's last actions and the means of his passing, for example. She would dearly have liked to share that episode with her dear friend and cousin Florence, but having given her word not to, she could hardly break that sacrosanct promise made to her nanny and her two uncles. That just wouldn't do.

"How did your grandpa really die?" Florence would ask. Poppy would reply quickly without fail – "A cat killed him."

They would both laugh and put the question away – until

the next time, when Florence would ask in another, different way.

Both girls had spent very little time in statutory schooling because of their age when the law was introduced, and what time they had spent in school served no useful purpose at all. They had both learned more than the school could offer *before* they had been forced to attend. Post-elementary schooling was not an option for them. What had they to look forward to?

"What shall you do when we reach sixteen?" Florence would ask her friend. "I mean, it's not as if there is anything that is meant for us, except for farm work and marriage."

"Well," Poppy would reply, "I have neither desire nor intention to follow either of those paths. Farm work is most definitely not for me, and if I do marry, it won't be because I have to."

"Then, how are you going to afford to live when your Uncle Ross and your Nanny and Grandpa Booth are no longer here?" Florence would ask in return.

"I have read a lot of books by good authors, and that is what I feel I can do," she would reply. Her answer was steadfast and had become the child of her deep imagination.

"I have hardly any books at home because Father can neither afford nor has the desire to buy them," Florence's answer fell from her mouth slowly and reluctantly. What child would ever wish to admit such a damning thing even to her closest friend?

"You can borrow mine for as long as you need them," Poppy said disarmingly. "I have read them over and over and feel like I need more to stimulate my mind further. I have a mind to try to emulate Misses Charlotte and Emily Bronte, George Eliot and Elizabeth Gaskell, who have shown what us women can do."

"Isn't George a man's name, though?" Florence asked, puzzled at Poppy's reference.

"It's Mary Ann Evans' pen name," Poppy explained. "Among others, she wrote *'Mill on the Floss'* and *'Middlemarch'*; both excellent novels about contemporary social times. I loved reading them."

"Pen name?" her friend asked, not understanding what she meant.

"Some women thought that they would be more successful if they adopted a man's name for their writing," Poppy went on. "Not sure whether that happened, though."

"I don't know any of those writers at all," Florence admitted. "I would surely love to. If I borrow one at a time—?"

"We'll take one or two to Scarborough with us, just for you and me," Poppy replied. "I'm sure Alice and Annabel – and of course, George – won't be at all interested. But you and I can read some and talk about them before we have to go to bed in the evening."

"Can't wait!" Florence squealed, rubbing her hands together enthusiastically. "Not long to go now. May I take *'Mill on the Floss'* home with me now?"

"Course you may," Poppy said, puffing out her chest in pride. "Saturday next is when we celebrate the twelfth anniversary of my birth, in Richmond, followed by our tour to York and Scarborough on the east coast. Don't forget to pack your nice clothes, and everything else you will need to spend a wonderful holiday."

"I won't," her friend answered quickly. "And don't you forget *'Middlemarshes'*."

"*'Middlemarch'*," Poppy replied with a giggle. "I won't."

"Stop! Stop!" Poppy cried out excitedly. "Stop the carriage. There's Alice and Annabel by their cottage wall with their mam and dad."

"That's a big suitcase!" George gasped. "Makes mine look like a handbag."

"How long Nanny and Grandpa?" Poppy asked almost too excited to settle. "How long before we reach Mary's Pantry in Richmond. She does know it's my birthday, doesn't she?"

"I should think everyone in earshot does now!" Nell replied with an indulgent smile. "It's now twelve o'clock and we are due to have afternoon tea at two. We've agreed the menu, so it should all be ready by the time we get there."

"Then are we going on to York?" Poppy asked, ever full of questions.

"There won't be time," Nell said. "So, we'll be staying at the King's Head Hotel there in Richmond overnight."

"We have a change of plan, too," Grandpa Ross chipped in. "As we believe there might be a steam train direct to Scarborough from Darlington – a matter of a few miles from Richmond – we'll be taking the Landau there early tomorrow morning to catch our train. I can promise an outstanding journey that I am sure you will all enjoy."

"Here we are," Nell announced, as the carriage drew to a halt outside a small tea house bakery, with Mary waiting in the doorway, clad in her usual working off-white pinny, and a glorious aroma of baking bread and cakes filled the doorway and drifted into the street.

"Missus. Mister," Mary said, addressing Nell and Ross in her usual way. Although Nell had tried to insist that she use their names, Mary found it difficult to change the habit of a lifetime in service.

"It's good to see why your shop is so popular, Mary," Ross

said, a look of admiration lighting his face as he looked around the shop and small tearoom. Glass display cases on the oak counter held all manner of large and smaller cakes, pastries, pasties, pies and breads. The tearoom was empty of customers because of a large, decorated table bearing a pristine white cotton cloth and seven settings for afternoon tea.

Poppy rushed over to hug Mary, knowing what a wonderful party she was about to share with her friends.

"Please sit down – your names are on your place settings – and we'll be along to serve you shortly," Mary announced. "Miss Poppy knows what to expect, but I am pretty sure her friends don't."

"Good heavens!" George gasped as foods of an unimaginable variety were brought to the table on tiered cake stands. "I've never seen anything like this before. Do we get to eat it *all*?"

"I surely hope so, Master George," Mary replied, to everyone's laughter, as she turned to leave. "Please help yourselves, and – many happy returns, Miss Poppy."

Chapter 21

"I can't believe what a wonderful day we spent yesterday," Florence said as she and Poppy started to stir in their fantastic hotel bedroom, ready to face this new exciting day. "I wish my grandpa would do such a thing for *me*."

"It doesn't matter, Florence," Poppy assured her as she stretched and yawned. "This wasn't just for me, my bestest of friends. Yesterday, and the rest of the week has been for all of us. I am lucky that my Grandpa Ross came back from Australia with more money than he knew what to do with. So, if he wants to spend some of it on me, you will always be included."

"Thank you, my dearest friend, Poppy McIntyre," Florence replied, not quite sure what to say. "I've never been to Scarborough, and, in fact, I've never seen the sea before – ever."

"Me neither," Poppy agreed, clapping her hands quickly and soundlessly. "But I think, too, that Nanny and Grandpa have some other things up their sleeve that we have no inkling about. I can't wait to see what will come with each day. Time to get ready and dressed for breakfast. I don't know about you, but I'm starving."

"That went rather well, don't you think?" Nell said to her husband as he shaved in preparation for the day ahead. "The last time I saw Poppy speechless was when her pup Toby came into her life."

"It was great fun, wasn't it?" Ross replied, chuckling at what he remembered. "Five little faces trying to appear grown up, with a look of awe in their eyes. Priceless. And Mary's spread was, well, out of this world. Did you see the queue out of the door and down the street when we left?"

"What time shall we get to Scarborough, Grandpa Ross?" Poppy asked once they had finished breakfast. "Will it be in time for dinner?"

"I don't think so," he replied. "These contraptions – these steam trains – are very slow and are not allowed to travel very fast. We have since heard that it will be York then Scarborough after all. So, I should think it will be mid-afternoon before we get to York, and then early evening to Scarborough."

"Will we be eating at some time?" George asked, rather alarmed that he might not be fed for the rest of the day. "Only—"

"Don't worry, George," Nell butted in with a giggle. "I've asked Mary to do us a picnic basket – a very *large* picnic basket – that we can dive into on the train before we reach York. You won't starve. We'll collect it this morning on our way to the railway station in Darlington."

The last comment brought a huge sigh and a grin from

the lad, as he settled back in his chair, his eyes firmly on the remaining pieces of buttered toast that were begging to be consumed.

Much of the journey from Darlington to York was undertaken in whispered awe as they sped in their comfortable carriage which had glass windows in the roof to let in more light to augment the oil lamps fastened to the walls. They passed through breath-taking countryside, dark tunnels and over gargantuan viaducts in their quest for their journey's end.

Their starting point had been the wonderfully newly constructed stone railway station at Darlington, with its glistening steel tracks that seemed to have been forged out of silver that rested on new oak sleepers.

York Railway Station, by comparison, had been built and opened just four years earlier, and its size and splendour took away the breath and startled the eyes with its scale and graceful lines. This was a place to stun the senses and allow the spectator to marvel at the skill and cleverness of his fellow man.

"We have just twenty minutes to find our platform and to board our steed that will take us to our week's holiday in Scarborough," Grandpa Ross urged his charges. "This place is so vast we won't be able to find *that* without studying the timetable at the edge of the platform. Come on fellow explorers! Let's get moving."

Platform four was easy to find, as was the gleaming monster of a chariot that was about to bear them away in their luxurious first-class carriage, through a very different part of the North's beautiful countryside to the North Sea and their really grand hotel.

Once seated, they all heaved a huge sigh of tired relief as

the train pulled away from the platform.

"Now, George," Nell said once all the intrepid explorers had rested a while, as the inhabitants of the beautiful villages of Haxby and Strensall waved at their passing, "do you feel like a little sustenance?"

"Yes please, Nanny!" Poppy replied eagerly.

"Me too!" Florence and Alice and Annabel echoed.

"George?" Nell asked again.

"Yes please, Mrs Booth. That would be lovely," George replied politely.

The picnic basket opened to 'oos' and 'ahs'. They couldn't believe the delicacies and exciting-looking food that was wrapped in beautiful white cotton napkins, and loaded in white card boxes, ready for them to satisfy their eyes and fill their bellies.

The three-and-a-half-hour journey to Scarborough flashed by in what seemed like a trice, along with villages with exotic names like Flaxton, Kirkham Abbey, Huttons Ambo, and on through the glorious countryside of the Howardian Hills. At times the train slowed to meander with the picturesque River Derwent for around four miles or so, giving them a scenically pleasant experience.

Crossing the Derwent Viaduct and stopping at many of the villages and towns en route like Malton and Seamer, their senses were almost overwhelmed. They had never seen such a diversity of sights and heard so many sounds, from the clickety-clack and screech of the train's unforgiving wheels over the tracks, to the rush and gabble of people on the stations they passed through and stopped at.

The slow, stately slide into Scarborough was … different.

The town was much larger than anything they had seen so far. Stone and brick buildings silenced their chatter and held their awe-stricken gaze to allow the screech of seagulls and the unmistakeably salty tang of the sea to creep in.

"What's that noise?" Poppy asked, grimacing as she held her cupped hands to her ears, trying to blot out the incessant sound of herring and black-backed gulls. "I can't even hear what my friends are saying!"

"Sea gulls!" Nell replied loudly. "They are supposed to spend most of their time at sea catching … fish."

"But they spend more and more of their time inland because they are lazy," Ross nodded. "They find their food around humans, stealing what they have and scavenging rather than earning what they eat by honest endeavour. So, if you have anything to eat while outside, make sure they can't see or smell you, because they will take it from you. In your case, George, I don't think they would even dare to try, particularly after how you handled that ruffian that tried to kidnap Poppy."

They all laughed yet were glad that George was *their* friend. Better to have somebody like him on your side, they all agreed.

"Are we going for a paddle in the East Sea, Nanny?" Poppy asked eagerly.

"North Sea," Nell corrected. "It's called the North Sea."

"But why is that?" Poppy queried again, confused by the terminology. "It's to the east of our country, isn't it?"

"Indeed, it is," Ross replied. "But it's called the *North* Sea, probably because it is one of the most northerly stretches of water in the world."

"You see," Nell went on, answering Poppy's question, "we have to get to the hotel, find our rooms, have a wash and unpack before dinner, and then after, it will be bedtime. Grandpa Ross has a special surprise for tomorrow."

"Dinner?" George puzzled. "Didn't we have that in the train? Lovely it was too."

"Most rich people in places like this, call the evening meal 'dinner', and the early afternoon feast, 'lunch'," Ross explained. "I know that we call them different names in Yorkshire."

"Lunch is dinner," Florence ventured, "and dinner is tea."

They all chuckled at this strange language, though they weren't sure why.

By the time they had walked the two or three streets from the new station to the Grand Hotel, it had reached five o'clock in the afternoon. They all felt reasonably tired and in need of a wash and a snooze. Their rooms were close together on the fourth floor and were sumptuous like they had never experienced before. Even Nell was flabbergasted at what she saw. Situated in such a way that they all had views across the bay and out to sea, which is how Ross had wanted it.

Annabel gasped as the door closed behind her and her sister, Alice, and she stood in front of the arched window.

"North Sea?" Alice asked. "Is that what they call the North Sea?"

A rapid knocking at the door startled them. The other three friends burst in, excited in the extreme at where they were, and at the unknown things they were about to experience. A week in a new and expensive hotel such as this made their homes feel a little ... ordinary.

"Are your rooms all right for you?" Grandpa Ross asked with an encouraging smile at dinner. "And are we all going to have a grand time?"

"Saw what you did there, Mr Booth!" George grinned. "Funny."

"We have no need to be formal, George," Grandpa Ross said. "Call me Grandpa Ross if you wish. Sounds much better."

"Funny?" Poppy butted in. "What's funny about having a grand time?"

"Where are we, Poppy?" George asked his friend patiently.

"Why, you know where we are!" Poppy harrumphed indignantly. "We're in the … Grand … Hotel. I see what you mean."

Her face started to turn a shade pinker that it was before in embarrassment, which, fortunately, didn't last long.

"What have you got planned for us for tomorrow, Grandpa Ross?" she continued unabashed. "Paddle in the sea, perhaps?"

"We'll have to see," he said, again with a twinkle, emphasising his last word.

"You did it again!" George giggled, trying not to make too much noise as there were other guests in the dining room.

This time, they all chortled, taking up George's lead. The dinner had been grand in the extreme, consisting as it did of all sorts of unordinary foods that even eclipsed what they had on offer from Mary's Pantry the day before. In fact, there was so much wonderful food that even George was stuffed to the gills at the end of it all.

"Tomorrow is Monday, 1st August 1881, and an extraordinary event will take place just around the corner from here," Ross explained quite seriously. "For us to be part of that event will be something rather special."

"Special?" Florence asked, wanting to know more. "In what way? Even more special than riding on those puffing metal train things?"

"Well … we'll have to wait and see after breakfast tomorrow," he replied tantalisingly.

"Ah!"

"Oh!"
"Arr!"
"No!"
"Please?"

The favoured five gasped, uttered, growled, grumbled all at the same time, disappointedly.

"And now," Nell said, "time to retire to get a healthy dollop of sleep ready to … have a fantastic time in the morning."

Without demur, they all left the table and made their way to their rooms, very full and satisfied from dinner.

"I didn't expect *that*," she said when they all had disappeared into respective rooms. "I would have expected Poppy at least to have complained."

"Tiredness is a welcome thing for both weary youngsters and their supporting adults," Ross said with a relieved smile. "I should imagine they'll all be into bed quickly, ready for a busy day tomorrow."

"At last!" Poppy sighed as she snecked their bedroom door behind them, throwing herself onto her bed. "I enjoyed today, but it's nice to have a bit of peace and quiet, don't you think? Time to be able to relax and to just … think."

"Agreed," Florence replied with a serious look on her face. "Time to be at peace with one's thoughts."

Looking through one or two booklets on the dressing table that had been left for guests by the management, Poppy stopped in her tracks, noticing a note that said, 'Room Service'.

"I wonder if that means us?" she said quietly, showing the words to her friend. "I'll ask Grandpa Ross tomorrow, and perhaps tomorrow evening after dinner we might be able to have a cup of tea and a piece of … cake?"

Florence clapped her hands silently, and grinned. That obviously resonated with her.

"Have you had chance to read '*Mill on the Floss*' yet, Florence?" Poppy asked after a few moments with her eyes closed. "I mean, it would be good to see what you think about it."

"Read it all before we came on holiday," Florence replied with a satisfied smile. "What did *you* think about Maggie and her brother Tom? I *liked* Maggie. She behaved exactly as I would have expected her to behave from the first words about her when she was little. She certainly knew her own mind."

"I liked her as well," Poppy agreed. "Though I wasn't too sure about her brother. Brothers are supposed to stick by their sisters, aren't they? No matter what they do."

"There were lots of words I didn't understand, and it did ramble on a bit," Florence went on. "Sad ending as well."

"But they died in the River Floss floods together, trying to help other people," Poppy sighed. "I cried when that happened. Have you brought it with you?"

"Why wouldn't I?" her friend assured her. "Why?"

"Would you mind reading the last page of Chapter 5 of the seventh book?" Poppy asked, a ring of quiet excitement edging her voice. "You know, the one that tells us about … their …"

"End?" Florence added. "Of course I will."

They both settled back on their pillowed headboard as Florence read the last few paragraphs, enunciating George Eliot's words quietly but with feeling.

All the while she read, tears coursed down both faces, and lips quivered with emotion.

Chapter 22

"And the largest in the world," Grandpa Ross added after breakfast, as they left the hotel.

"This hotel? Largest in the world?" George gasped. "Unbelievable!"

"As we go around the corner, you'll be able to see that it has also four towers, each one to represent one of the seasons," he went on. "It also has twelve floors – one for each month of the year – fifty-two chimneys for the weeks in a year, and three hundred and sixty-five rooms to represent the number of days in a non-leap year. Oh, and if you could see the building from the air, you would see that it is built in the shape of the letter 'V'. Any ideas?"

"The initial of the Queen's name – Victoria?" Alice answered,

"Well done, Alice," Grandpa Ross replied with a grin. "Exactly."

"Who decided on the numbers thing, Grandpa?" Poppy asked, her questions becoming more and more detailed. "Who built it and who decided on the 'V' shape and—?"

"Woa! One at a time please," Ross urged, throwing his

hands up, almost in surrender. "It was designed by a gentleman called Cuthbert Brodrick, and I don't know, but I would imagine that as the designer and architect, he would have thought up the numbers thing and dedication to Her Majesty."

"And—" Poppy started again.

"When?" he said, pre-empting her question.

"How—?" *she* replied, somewhat perplexed.

"Ha har!" he laughed tantalisingly. "It was opened just two years before you were born, Poppy, which was when, then?"

"Opened in 1867, taking four years to complete," she said with a self-satisfied smile and nod of the head.

"How did you work *that* one out?" George gasped.

"We saw a plaque on the wall," Florence explained. "By the front door."

"Started in 1863, and finished four years later in 1867," Poppy added. "Two years before I was born in 1869. I think I know what we are about to do today."

"Come on then, tell us, please!" her friends urged, crowding around her as they asked, eagerly, desperately wanting to know.

"Well," Poppy confided, looking both ways as if making sure she wasn't being overheard, as she had seen her Unca Ross do many times as she was growing up. "I am sure we will be heading for the sands at some stage, but the question is ... how do we get there, perched on a cliff top as *we* are?"

"I bet you are only guessing," George said, butting into her intrigue.

"So, how do we get from here to ... there?" Poppy mused almost to herself. "I bet Grandpa thinks he has got one over on Poppy McIntyre."

"What is it to be, then, young lady?" Grandpa Ross asked, a slightly mischievous look in his eye. "How are we to be spirited from this cliff face to the sands some hundred or so feet below? Are we to sprout wings and glide to dampen our toes in the North Sea, then?"

"Oh, Grandpa Ross!" Poppy complained at his pretence. "Please?"

"All right," he replied with a chuckle as the whole group gathered around him. "Up this street here – Nicholas Street – and turn right at the top and right again. Then you'll see what we are about to embark upon."

A steady stroll took them to where Grandpa Ross had said, to find—.

"A railway station?" Poppy puzzled. "But how can a railway train run up and— gracious! That's a long way down."

"But we *can* see the beach and … the North Sea! Hooray!" George cheered, drawing gleeful smiles and giggles from the girls.

"It's not a railway engine," Ross explained. "It's called a Central Tramway that is designed to transport you from here to down there and … back. As you can see, there are two tramcars. One goes down as the other goes up, and so on. All run by steam. "It is Monday 1st August 1881, and today … it is opening. We are booked on it to go down after all the important dignitaries have ridden up and down. Beach here we come!"

"That *was* scary!" Annabel muttered to her sister as they squeezed out of the tramcar and spilled on to the sea front with the summer sun glinting on the water before their incredulous eyes, and drifting sand crunching under their feet.

How inviting did that stretch of water look! Although they had never seen sand and sea before, to a child they felt a sudden, almost primeval urge to take off shoes and stockings and to … paddle, just like many other children were doing. Raising their eyes from the water's edge, they caught sight of strange, wheeled contraptions, like moving sheds, being hauled into the sea by huge Shire horses.

"Look, Grandpa Ross!" Poppy gasped, pointing desperately at the horses. "Why are they pulling those … those … small houses into the North Sea? Won't the people inside get their feet wet?"

"They are called Bathing Cabins," Ross explained with a smile. "They are used so that people can get changed in private without being seen and can bathe in private away from everyone else."

"Bathe?" George asked, puzzled. "What does that mean? Do they use soap and a scrubbing brush in the North Sea? Won't it leave a scum on the surface?"

"Bathing, my dear George, means to paddle and splash and to swim in the sea," Ross explained.

"The only time I bathe is on a Sunday, with soap and water and a loofa in a tin bath in front of the fire," George replied. "Whether I need to or not."

His hosts laughed and the girls giggled at the picture George had painted, as they turned to walk along the promenade.

Because usually well-to-do people took their holidays in the summer in this chic resort, the clothes they encountered were opulent and expensive. Women's bodies were generally fully covered, with dresses almost to the ground.

"What's that funny noise I can hear coming from that big, tall box-like thing on the beach?" Poppy asked. "That large striped box surrounded by laughing and shouting children?"

'That's the way to do it!' a cracked, squeaky voice interrupted her question, followed by a slap-slapping sound.

"That, my dear granddaughter, is a Punch and Judy show," Nell explained. "You sit in a circle around the striped booth you can see, and watch the performance."

"Performance of what?" Florence asked.

"You'll have to go over, sit down and wait for the next performance," Nell replied. "Once the performance has finished, a gaily dressed person will weave its way through the audience with a bowl."

"What for?" George asked, puzzled at all these strange customs and performances.

"You drop a farthing – or if you're feeling very generous – a penny into the bowl to show your appreciation for the performance," Ross interrupted. "I am sure you will enjoy it. Want to watch? Florence? Annabel and Alice? George and Poppy?"

"Yes please!" they all chorused excitedly, stamping feet and clapping hands quickly in front of them.

"Let's go then!" Ross urged. "It's a lifetime since I last watched Punch and Judy."

"What was your favourite part of today?" Poppy asked her friend Florence as they sat on their beds after a wonderful dinner with food they'd never seen let alone tasted.

"It has to be … the wooden crocodile snapping next to Mr Punch, and eating the string of sausages," Florence laughed, clapping quietly as she giggled. "Yours?"

"Paddling at the edge of the sea, feeling wet sand between my toes and watching those bathing machines," Poppy replied enthusiastically. "I would love to feel all that water around me."

"I should like to know what people might … do … in the water before I would allow myself to be immersed," Florence said, a distasteful grimace distorting her face. She had seen what some people did outside at home, so why wouldn't they do the same when they couldn't be seen? "There are lots of things I would *like* to do, but bathing in human waste is definitely *not* one of them."

Poppy giggled at the thought but didn't reply.

"I also loved the scary ride down and up the tramway in those little steam-driven carriages," Florence added. "I could do that all day long."

"I wonder what's on offer tomorrow?" Poppy said, breeching the silence that had enveloped them several minutes before.

"I bet it will be sitting on one of those floppy stripy – what do you call them? – deck chairs either on the sands or on the promenade," Florence offered. "Now, *that* I should like."

"I think it will be a walk around town and a cup of tea in one of those tea houses we saw today," Poppy said.

"Alice! Alice!" Annabel urged in a forced whisper once they had gone back to their room. "You're not asleep, are you?"

"Mmm," Alice groaned, eyes tightly fastened against the light thrown out by the oil lamp perched on the little table under the window. "Mmm. Not really. Just resting my … eyes…"

Then, silence again.

"Wake up, Alice, or I'll come and … shake you and pour cold water on your face!" Annabel warned her sister. "I'm not sleepy and I want to talk."

"For goodness' sake, Sister!" Alice grumbled. "I'm tired and I want to sleep. Get into bed and leave me alone or go and talk to George. He's next door."

"I can't do that!" Annabel harrumphed. "He's a … boy, and I'm …not. I only wanted to find out what you thought about today. That's all."

"Oh, if that's all," Alice replied. "It was good. Now, good night, and go to sleep."

Turning over away from her sister's tutting and sighing body, Alice closed her eyes and immediately fell into a deep slumber, from which her sister could not rouse her. Annabel got into bed, closed *her* eyes, and fell into a shallow, fitful nap from which her overly excited and over-active brain insisted on keeping her awake.

"Successful today?" Ross asked Nell over a glass of Napoleon brandy when the youngsters had gone to their rooms. "It seemed to go all right."

"All right?" Nell replied. "It wasn't all right. It was amazingly successful. You had only to look at their faces. They've never seen such sights nor done such amazingly awe-inspiring things before, because of circumstance. What you are doing for them is … wonderful."

"We, my sweet lady," Ross answered quickly. "What *we* are doing with them. I couldn't have done all this without your love and support."

"You old romantic, you!" she gushed, putting her arms around him. "I feel like—"

"So do I my lovely wife," he added quickly, putting his brandy down. "So do I."

Although their week of excitement at Scarborough's amazing seaside resort was fantastically impressive for them all, Poppy, Florence, Annabel, Alice and George were glad to be on the train back to York and beyond.

Sitting back comfortably in their first-class carriage after a sumptuous breakfast at the Grand Hotel, George's eye rested on an enormous hamper Nanny Nell had organised for their journey. They enjoyed the countryside as it swished by them, recognising some of the villages and towns en route that they hurried leisurely through from their inward journey. Some of them, too, rushed by in a relative blur.

"The steamer visit along the North Sea coast to Whitby and Saltburn was amazing," Annabel said with probably the most excited and animated look in her face that they all had seen.

"And the tiny coastal villages along the way like Robin Hood's Bay, Whitby, Sandsend, Runswick and Staithes," her sister added quickly.

"I didn't know Robin Hood lived this far north," George puzzled. "Wasn't it Shirewood Forest he lived in?"

"Sherwood Forest," Ross corrected with a laugh. "We're not even sure he was a real person."

"I liked the steamer trips downwards to Filey, Flamborough and Bridlington," Florence announced. "Although the others *were* lovely, it was exciting sailing into the harbour at Bridlington, with all the fishing boats, and women cutting and gutting all those fish."

"There are stories – dare I say it – about smuggling?" Grandpa Ross whispered, leaning forward while looking around as if to check no-one else was about to hear.

"Smuggling?" George whispered back, eyes wide, as he too leaned forward as if to share a private hearing that nobody else would be party to. Nell smiled quietly at the look of intrigue on the lad's face.

"They were desperate men who wanted to make a fast pile of money through illegal means," Ross began to explain, an almost inaudible croak creeping out of his mouth. "They would sneak goods into the country that were either against the law or that smugglers didn't want to pay excise duty on. If they were caught, they could be put into prison for several years, or even hanged."

"What on earth did people want to smuggle?" Poppy asked. "Isn't that wrong?"

"Indeed, it is," Ross agreed. "Some things that were brought into the country for sale were made extremely expensive by the taxes levied by the government. If there were no taxes, some of the things like tea, wine, spirits, and even lace, would be much cheaper to buy. The taxes we have to pay even now go into the government's bank.

"Do you remember those tiny cottages when we walked up those steep steps from the harbour in Robin Hood's Bay?" he went on after a brief pause. "Well, they were so close together that smugglers could walk through from one house to another to another, making it almost impossible for them to be caught and punished."

Nell sat quietly in her corner seat, her knitting to hand, watching those quiet little faces in awe of the tales her husband was spinning for them. What a wonderful experience they were having, doing things most children of their age would never do.

"Did you know," Ross continued, "that the wonderful fish we ate for dinner at the Grand Hotel on a couple of occasions was caught off the East Coast in the North Sea, only that same morning, and landed and gutted in Scarborough's harbour? That's how important all these fishermen are."

"I saw quite a few ladies knitting outside their cottages, Nanny, in Robin Hood's Bay," Poppy said. "What were they knitting? Scarves and socks?"

"Probably 'ganzies'," Nell replied, knowing there would be

the inevitable questions about them.

"Ganzies?" George asked in emphatic disbelief. "What's that?"

"They are jumpers or pullovers knitted in different colours for the fishermen to wear at sea to keep them warm," Nell explained.

"They also serve another purpose that is not as pleasant as being kept warm," Ross added.

"What do you mean?" Annabel asked, not really understanding where this question was about to take her.

"As you can no doubt guess, fishing in a very stormy and rough sea can be extremely dangerous," Ross began. "Sometimes boats – even big ones – are almost swamped by huge waves. Inevitably, men are washed overboard and ... drowned. Bodies do become washed up on beaches further up or down the coast. If that does happen, when the body is found, the 'ganzy' will tell which port that seaman came from."

"How come?" Florence asked sceptically. "Is his name knitted into the garment?"

"Each port has its own pattern of ganzy," Nell explained. "So, the missing sailor fisherman can be identified."

"Well, *I'm* not going to be a fisherman!" George declared, to a peal of laughter from all present. "I'd rather be a ... a ... farmer!"

Chapter 23

"Nanny?" Poppy said, taking her head out of her new book of the hour.

"Yes, my poppet?" Nell replied pausing her knitting for a while. She loved sitting in the front room of her new house with her husband and her knitting in Richmond. So close to amenities and so far away from farms, animals and … smells, with little cooking and baking to satisfy hulking workers umpteen times each day. Mary had been her hard-working friend for more years than she cared to remember, and now, she too had started a new life. "What is it?"

"Where does Mary live now?" Poppy asked as she flicked another page of her latest novel.

"She lives in Richmond," Nell replied. "Why?"

"Not seen her for some time," Poppy answered after a moment or two.

"Apart from her Pantry in Richmond, she has also found herself a new … husband," Nell said. "Geoffrey is a lovely man with a very caring nature – much like Mary herself."

Quietness crept about them once again while Poppy stared

into the beyond, to the clickety-clack of her nanny's knitting needles.

"Nanny?" she asked again, looking directly at Nell.

"Yes, my lovely," Nell responded immediately as if she was expecting the next question.

"How old was my mother when she died?" Poppy started. "Is it true that she died because of me?"

Nell was stunned. What sort of a question was that, and how was she supposed to answer it honestly? She put down her knitting needles and, patting the settee next to her, she beckoned her granddaughter to sit by her.

"Your mamma was sixteen, the age *you* are now," Nell started her explanation. "Unfortunately, there were ... complications when you were born and ... she didn't live to see you. But it was no fault of yours, because you didn't ask to be born and so couldn't be held responsible."

"I know I have never had a father to see and ... hold, like Florence and Annabel and Alice have, and ... George has," Poppy went on as she was wont to do. "Yet, I must have had a father, otherwise I would be like Jesus from Mary's immaculate contraption. Do you know who my father is? I remember asking before, but I don't remember ever having had an answer."

"Immaculate *conception*," Nell laughed, sliding her arm round her granddaughter's shoulders and drawing her closer. "The truthful answer is ... we ... don't ... know. She sneaked out one early winter's late afternoon when we were all busy. Your Uncle Joseph found her next morning a little way from the byre, battered and bruised and unconscious."

"But why did she go out on her own at such an inhospitable time?" Poppy asked, seriously puzzled at her mamma's dangerous action. "I don't understand."

"She was always … wayward, was your mamma, I'm afraid," Nell tried to explain. "I don't know where she got it from, but there it was. We didn't find out she was expecting until months later. We don't know but we believe she sneaked out to meet some … boy."

Poppy was dumbfounded at this unexpected revelation of her possible origin, her possible father. Who was he? Was he still around? Would she ever meet him? Would she, Poppy, ever do such a thing; ever disobey her nanny in such a way whom she loved to the ends of the earth? She didn't *think* she would, but wasn't there more in life than vacillating between the busy smells of an open farm and the quietly sedentary ways of her grandparents?

Florence was her very close friend in whom she could always confide, but they didn't live close enough to each other to be able to walk to spend time together more than once or twice a week. They always had to rely on adult menfolk to transport them, and *they* weren't available all that often because of adult work interfering.

The time they did spend in each other's company was quality, occasionally enhanced by their good friend George, who lived close by to Poppy. He was growing up to be a fine, handsome lad of the same age – a fact not missed by both girls. He was gentle, kind and considerate of their feelings and ways as females growing up in a male dominated world. However, *he* would never abuse their friendship nor consider himself to be any better or more important than them. He could always be trusted, too, to look after them both in any circumstance. This was one of the reasons why they liked his company on some of their lone outings into the close countryside.

They ribbed him occasionally about his ways and his bluff, no-nonsense exterior, but they wouldn't have changed him for the world. He took everything they had to offer in his quite considerable stride. Secretly, he worshipped them both, calling them to himself 'my girls', although he would never have dreamed of letting them know how he felt. He was simply ... happy in their company.

"Do you think we'll ever find out, Nanny?" Poppy asked again, loth to let go of the subject. "About my ... father, I mean."

"Unless somebody comes to us?" Nell replied. "I don't think so. Even then, we wouldn't be able to prove either way."

Poppy fell into a deep thoughtful silence, not knowing what to say or how she might solve this insoluble problem. Perhaps she would never know her father. Perhaps she was destined to be an orphan forever. She loved her Nanny Nell and Grandpa Ross dearly, but having no mother and father had dropped a whole bundle of sadness into her young lap that she could have done without.

Early autumn at Boulders Wood was a delightful time of year. The weather was still warm if a little damp, and the subtle colour changes to the forest's canopy were more obvious each day. This was the time of year that Poppy and her cousin and dearest friend, Florence, loved the most. Strolls among the forest's eaves were their favourite, especially when they were accompanied by their close friend, George. They often considered themselves to be a latter-day group of musketeers, protecting the lands from heathen marauders.

Although their lands afforded them a high degree of physical safety, it always felt safer when George was with them. He would never let them put themselves in harm's way, and he always directed them to the physically safe parts of the forest.

"Do you like George?" Florence would ask nonchalantly during their walks alone, when he was doing something on the farm for his dad.

"He's all right, really, I suppose," Poppy would reply, almost reluctantly. "You?"

"I suppose he does have his good side and his uses," Florence seemed to reply almost with an air of reluctance, not wanting to admit to anything serious.

In their heart of hearts they both knew their feelings ran deeper, much deeper than they both wanted to admit, and they both *knew* instinctively how the other felt. Only sixteen, neither was old enough to proclaim real and true feelings for a boy they had been around since early childhood, and who they were aware felt equally for *them.*

A deep dense mass of wickedly sharp and clawing brambles, with their tantalisingly bountiful luscious black, ripe berries, barred their way and obliged them to detour significantly from their chosen path. Unbeknown to them, this path had been trodden sixteen years earlier by another sixteen-year-old in the dark in terror.

"Well, I never did!" a startlingly familiar voice crept upon them, making them jump in sharp surprise. "Two young ladies on their own without some hulk to protect them from this wicked world. How is your fat buffoon of a so-called friend? George isn't it? Not here to protect you?"

The two girls spun round, surprised looks on their faces, not expecting to meet Jonas of all people.

"Not pleased to see me, dearest Poppy and your not-so-delightful ... friend ... Florence?" Jonas went on, a sardonic sneer disfiguring his face, as the insults flowed from his ugly mouth.

"Jonas?" Poppy gasped. "What are you doing here? We haven't seen you for ... years."

"I think the last time was just before you took your *friends* on your wonderful jaunt to lovely … Scarborough … wasn't it?" he went on, a slightly threatening tone entering his foppishly insulting remarks. "Only, you didn't take *all* your friends, did you?"

"We didn't have room for *everyone*," Poppy harrumphed.

"Then, why wasn't I included in your mean little group?" he added sharply with a snarl.

"I think it's obvious, don't you?" Florence burst in. "Your unpleasant and unnecessarily sharp, nay, rude comments are uncalled for and would not have been made by a gentleman which, undoubtedly, sir, you are not!"

"Woaho!" he retorted gleefully. "So, the little mouse *does* have a voice and—"

"Which she is not afraid to use with slithery worms like you!" Florence interrupted.

Her last comment brought about a sharp change in his attitude. His eyes narrowed and his deprecatory sneer became more threatening, as he took steps towards her.

Florence backed away, alarmed at what he might do, when he lunged at her grasping her arm and dragging her frail but resisting body towards him.

"Don't *you* worry, my little waif," he spat at Poppy. "I won't forget you, because you are next!"

Taking off his coat and loosening his trouser belt, he backed Florence against a tree. Flailing ineffectually against him with fear in her eyes, understanding what he was about to do, she turned to try to escape, but to no avail.

"Now I'll show you—" he said but was stopped in mid-sentence by a large fist exploding against the side of his head. He staggered, uncomprehending eyes not functioning as they should have, when another fist crunched into his face, splitting his lips and smashing into his nose with blood and tissue exploding in its wake. *That* blow dropped him unconscious in a heap by the tree he was going to use in his assault on Florence.

"There you go, sap. Just what I've been wanting to do for ever such a long time," Florence's saviour snarled as he lifted Jonas's unconscious body partly off the floor before delivering a final crunching blow to the jaw and stamping on his groin. "You don't pick on *my* girls and not live to regret it!"

It was George.

"George!" Both girls gasped, flinging their arms around him as tears streamed down shocked faces.

"Steady, my lovelies," he urged, not wanting to disappear under a windmill of flailing limbs. "Why didn't you tell me you were on your way up here?"

"We thought you were busy on the farm," Florence said through heart-felt sobs, "and—"

"We didn't want to disturb you," Poppy added with a desperate sigh. "You saved us from—"

"It was clear to me what the coward was aiming to do," George said. "He had obviously been planning his dastardly action for some time. It was fortunate this time that I could work out where you might be. If I had known what he had in mind, I would have sorted him out long before this. He won't recover from *that* in a hurry."

"But won't he come back?" Florence asked, afraid of the future, knowing what Jonas was like.

"Let him try," George snarled again. "The fop will lose more than a few teeth and his dignity."

"So, what will happen to Jonas now, Nanny?" Poppy asked her

grandmother. "He was definitely intent on raping both of us."

"How do you know that?" Nell asked, not sure what to believe.

"I could see it in his eyes and how he loosened his trousers!" Poppy insisted, not understanding why she was almost taking his side. "He would have done it as well, if George hadn't come to our rescue. We owe our safety to *him*. Shouldn't we report it to the police or something?"

"Not sure how they would view it," Nell replied reluctantly.

"Nanny!" Poppy protested. "But he attacked us!"

"Don't forget that he's family," Nell said, defensively again.

"Oh no he's not!" Poppy shouted. "He's not part of my family after what *he* tried to do. And I thought you were *my* nanny!"

Stamping her feet in annoyance and frustration, Poppy stomped out of the room in anger.

"Well, that could have been handled better," Grandpa Ross said with a disappointed shake of the head. "Are you sure that that was the right decision, seeing Poppy's reaction?"

"No! … Yes!" she replied hesitantly. "*I don't know!*"

"I'm telling you now that he won't give in," Ross warned. "I've seen too many young men like this Jonas chap not to know where it might lead. He belongs to *your* side of the family – niece's son? – and you should at least speak to his mother about it. Hey, it really is none of my business, but I wouldn't allow him to go unchecked if he were part of *my* family. It could lead to serious repercussions for the ones you love if something isn't done about it – and quickly."

Louisa sat quietly on the settee as Nell described Jonas's actions to his mother. Once Nell had finished, her niece sat in stunned silence, a disbelieving look on her face.

"I have no idea what this is all about," Louisa sobbed once the telling had finished. "That can't be my boy! He wouldn't dream of harming Poppy, because he thought too much about her."

"That's not what he said to Poppy and Florence," Nell told her. "Both of the girls and their best friend George told what he said and was about to do to the girls just before George intervened to save them. He had to stop Jonas physically."

"I don't know about that, because I haven't seen him for days," Louisa said quietly with a worried and haunted look playing in her eyes. "He hasn't been home, and his bed hasn't been slept in."

"The girls wanted to involve the police, but I persuaded them to hold on for a while at least," Nell offered, trying to soothe and calm her distraught niece.

"I've tried to ignore it, and to decide it was just a phase, but there has been a change in him since he was about thirteen," Louisa went on once she had control of her emotions. "It's been gradual over the last three years or so, but it's been there. I've gotten to a stage, really, where he has become something of a stranger to us. His dad has had to confront and chastise him on many an occasion, and so we put it down to adolescence, but the worries have been there for us for a while. And now … this…"

She burst into shoulder-heaving sobs, to think that her bright boy was turning into a … thug. Even so, as his mother, she was desperately worried where he might be, He was her son after all.

"Nell!" Tom Garside's wife called as she reached the front door.

It was Boulders Wood and Nell was paying her son Ross and his wife Martha a visit. "Nell!"

"I'm here, Lilly. Come yourself in," Nell replied. "You look flustered. What can I do for you?"

"I can get no sense out of him at all, but something's happened with our George," Lilly said, blunt as ever. "He's even hurt his hand, but he won't tell me why or how."

"I don't know," Nell assured her, although Lilly could tell straight away that she was being economical with the truth.

"Nell," Lilly replied slowly with the raise of the eyebrows and inclination of her head, knowing full well that she would tell her – eventually.

"Tea, Lilly?" Nell asked, trying to divert her attention from her urgent question.

"Nell?" Lilly chided her friend and erstwhile neighbour gently. "George?"

"He's a hero, Lilly," Nell said after a few moments of hesitation. "He saved his two friends, Poppy and Florence, from being attacked in the worst sort of way – by Poppy's cousin, Jonas. That's how important he is to our family. We can't thank him enough, and he will always be welcome in our households."

Lilly was stunned, not really understanding how, why, he would want to do a thing like that. She had always been selfish with other people, putting family first and never rising to some-one else's need. George was much more like his father than her, and this brought it home to her – at last.

"Well, I never!" Lilly said finally. "Our George did all that? Are you sure it was *our* George? I mean—"

"He is a gentleman and a knight in shining armour, Lilly," Nell urged. "I can't believe you don't know your own son! We've known what he is like for some considerable time. Don't you remember when he saved our Poppy from that ragamuffin on the way home from school all those years ago? We, at least, owe him such a lot."

"Your nose is broken, and you have lost several teeth," the young woman said to the young man she was tending. "How on earth did you manage to get those injuries? Fall over after too much to drink, or walk into a door, or walk into a … fist?"

"It was the latter, my dear," the foppish young man replied, eye socket swollen and badly bruised as well, and blood spattered across his white shirt and light-coloured jacket. "From some dashed coward, the blighter, that attacked me from behind."

"Did he steal your wallet?" she asked. "Have you any money to pay for my services?"

"He did not!" the young man insisted with a grimace and a significant wince of pain. "I do believe it must have been a 'crime passionel' – a crime of passion I will not forget. I cannot forget that dashed ugly face, and I *will* see him again. And maybe the next time he won't see *me* coming either."

"You can stay here with my son and me," she went on. "But we will need money to buy the usual things that will allow us to live. Agreed?"

"Of course, my dear, of course," he replied, a knowing smile spreading.

He would not forget the disservice that had been done to his features, and he *would* return the favour, in his own good time.

Frank English
Author

Born in 1946 in the West Riding of Yorkshire's coal fields around Wakefield, he attended grammar school, where he enjoyed sport rather more than academic work. After three years at teacher training college in Leeds, he became a teacher in 1967. He spent a lot of time during his teaching career entertaining children of all ages, a large part of which was through telling stories, and encouraging them to escape into a world of imagination and wonder. Some of his most disturbed youngsters he found to be very talented poets, for example. He has always had a wicked sense of humour, which has blossomed only during the time he has spent with his wife, Denise. This sense of humour also allowed many youngsters to survive often difficult and brutalising home environments.

In 2006, he retired after forty years working in schools with young people who had significantly disrupted lives because of behaviour disorders and poor social adjustment, generally brought about through circumstances beyond their control. At the same time as moving from leafy lane suburban middle-class school teaching in Leeds to residential schooling for emotional and behavioural disturbance in the early 1990s, changed family circumstance provided the spur to achieve ambitions. Supported by his wife, Denise, he achieved a Master's degree in his mid-forties and a PhD at the age of fifty-six, because he had always wanted to do so.

Now enjoying glorious retirement, he spends as much time as life will allow writing, reading and travelling.

Other books for adults he has written:

Jack the Lad	Published 2016
Jack	Published 2016
Hit the Road Jack	Published 2017
Welcome Back Jack	Published 2017
All Right Jack?	Published 2019
Carry On Jack	Published 2020

Children's books he has written to date:

Magic Parcel: The Awakening	Published June 2010
Magic Parcel: The Gathering Storm	Published March 2011
Magic Parcel: A New Dawn	Published August 2012
18 Mulberry Road	Published September 2011
25 Primrose Walk	Published January 2013
Autumn Adventures	Published September 2013
Winter Tales	Published September 2014
Towards Spring	Published September 2016
Juniper's Tale	Published August 2018
Honey	Published January 2019
The Story of Lemuel Pecker	Published April 2019
Josephine's Journey	Published June 2019
Holly's Prize	Published April 2020
Garnett's Grand Getaway	Published May 2020
Sara's Astonishing Story	Published June 2020
The Boys in Black	Published August 2020
The Magic Whistle and the Tiny Bag of Wishes	Published October 2020
Half Moon Farm	Published March 2021

Milton Keynes UK
Ingram Content Group UK Ltd.
UKHW020442010524
442011UK00001B/12

9 781914 083174